THINK OF HORSES

A NOVEL

Mary Clearman Blew

University of Nebraska Press · Lincoln

The University of Nebraska Press is part of a land-
grant institution with campuses and programs
on the past, present, and future homelands of
the Pawnee, Ponca, Otoe-Missouria, Omaha,
Dakota, Lakota, Kaw, Cheyenne, and Arapaho
Peoples, as well as those of the relocated Ho-
Chunk, Sac and Fox, and Iowa Peoples.

Library of Congress Cataloging-in-Publication Data
Names: Blew, Mary Clearman, 1939– author.
Title: Think of horses: a novel /
Mary Clearman Blew.
Description: Lincoln: University
of Nebraska Press, [2022]
Identifiers: LCCN 2022007203
ISBN 9781496229656 (paperback)
ISBN 9781496232700 (epub)
ISBN 9781496232717 (pdf)
Subjects: BISAC: FICTION /
Literary | FICTION / Women
Classification: LCC PS3552.L46 T55
2022 | DDC 813/.54—dc23
LC record available at
https://lccn.loc.gov/2022007203

Set in Whitman by Laura Buis.

FOR MYAH

who lent her name and her
beautiful athleticism to this novel

AND FOR CALI AND LUKAH

who brought their love

Think of Horses

From Tam's laptop journal:

Rob was born by caesarian section. Does this matter? I have wondered for thirty-three years. I am fifty now. A moment of simple subtraction, and you are free to imagine the frightened seventeen-year-old, she with the big dreams everyone shook their heads over, she who was pain-wracked and exhausted and panic-stricken after nearly twenty hours of labor, being wheeled into surgery in the knowledge that, for her, all big dreams were over.

Do you think you could summarize the years that followed? The subsidized apartment, the food stamps? The howling, colicky baby? The recalcitrant young father, refusing to pay child support although the county authorities pursued him until he moved out of state? The seventeen-year-old watching her life flatlining ahead of her, turning to boxed wine and bottom-shelf bourbon and worse, until the county authorities intervened and took away the boy?

But no. That's not what happened. The wildcard in the dreary narrative is the seventeen-year-old. Do you recall that she had big dreams? Picture her, then, nursing her baby by the kitchen table, while she scribbles sentence after sentence on a lined pad. When she moves the baby from one breast to the other, she also moves the ballpoint from one hand to the other. She's learning to be ambidextrous.

So. Tam Bowen. She's sitting on a board floor, blue-jeaned and barefoot, hugging her knees and watching through a dirty window as the long June twilight of Montana's northern latitude begins to fade. Soon it will be fully dark, and she'll have to feel her way out to her car for her suitcase and her whiskey, but still she tracks the dimming light, turns her father's gold wedding ring that she wears on her left thumb, and lets her thoughts drift out of focus.

Yes, she's fifty years old and feels older, but during the past year she has let her hair grow out from the close crop she wore most of her life, and now her hair falls over her shoulders, pale gold and heavy, with only a few white strands (maybe some Scandihoovian, as the old folks called it, in her lineage, maybe on her vanished mother's side). She's still in good shape and slim, although she may feel a bit stiff when she finally rises from the floor to deal with the dregs of her life.

Log walls around her. A tongue-and-groove ceiling above her and a big river-rock fireplace opposite the window, like ghosts of themselves, ghosts of what she remembers from when she was the horsebreaker's daughter and lived with him in this mountain cabin. Why has she returned? She's going to reevaluate her current work, she had told her agent.

It had been midafternoon when Tam turned off the oiled highway and followed the graveled road that led southwest into Montana's Snowy Mountains. A cloudless sky arced over one of those summer days that seemed so fleeting in the backcountry. Nine months of winter and three months of damn late fall, Tam's father used to say about the Snowies, where snowfall began early and lay late and deep. Where, he told newcomers, if summer came on a Sunday, they usually had a picnic. It took Tam years to understand that her father's cursing of Montana weather was an expression of pride: *It takes a tough bastard like me to live in God's country!*

Tam had driven slowly, feeling gravel under her wheels for the first time in thirty years, gravel that rattled behind her and raised a complaint of dust as she drove higher into the foothills. Had she missed her turn? No, not yet, although pines frowned down on both sides of the road and turned it into a tunnel that sunlight did not penetrate. When she braked for a cattle guard, she startled as two white-faced calves raised their heads from the underbrush, stared walleyed at the intruder, and crashed off through the brush as wild as deer.

She crossed the county bridge over Sun Creek—was this her turn? The two-track dirt road looked right and wrong at the same time. Surely the Bowen road was never so narrow, so overgrown with grass and underbrush. But yes, this had to be it. Tam made the sharp turn, rattled over another cattle guard, and pulled over on a narrow verge in the shade of the pines, protected from road dust by a clump of hawthorns. Rolled down the window, leaned back with her eyes closed, and tried to feel what she'd hoped to feel.

The air smelled of pine needles and grass ripening in the sun. Hawthorn leaves whispered in a breath of air too subtle to stir the grass. Somewhere from the other side of the cattle guard, a cow bawled twice, three times. The creek, rapid here at the top of the pass, roared under the bridge, but the familiar sounds and scents were made foreign by Tam's overlay of memory.

She followed the imprint of the map in her mind: the graveled road as it angled north beyond the bridge and down the other side of Sun Creek Pass toward Fort Maginnis, the county seat. The dirt road, the Bowen road, which she would continue to follow, would climb higher into the mountains as the creek spilled alongside it for another two miles to its source in a spring and the end of the road at the cabin. But she wouldn't follow that road yet. She would give herself these few minutes. After all, she had all summer.

At the sound of hoofbeats, her eyes shot open, and she rose in the seat to see two kids on horseback, a girl and a boy, clattering over the bridge at full tilt. The girl's face was turned away, looking back at the boy, but Tam caught a glimpse of her red shirt and flying dark hair and heard her shout of laughter. The boy was perhaps fifteen or sixteen, and briefly Tam saw his face, drenched with laughter and deep-tanned until it was darker than the blond hair that hung from under his battered hat. Neither noticed Tam's car behind the hawthorns as they thundered past her in a cloud of dust and bouncing gravel. They were around the bend in seconds, leaving a fading trail of clatter and laughter and settling dust.

The silence in their wake was framed only by the roar of the current and the faraway anger of wind in the ridge pines.

Tam's father would have belted her if she'd galloped a horse on a graveled road and risked its hooves and legs. And this girl had been riding a horse of quality, a black with thoroughbred lines, that somebody should have been worrying about.

But yes, she'd been just about that girl's age when she rode a horse for the last time. For that moment, as the kids raced past her, she had been Tam in the innocent days, riding mountain trails on a cold-mouthed little buckskin mare her father had traded for and hadn't yet resold. Now she allowed herself to drift while a breeze played with a strand of her hair. The rhythm of riding bareback. The warm working muscles between her legs. The illusion of the horse becoming an extension of herself. Itch of horsehair, itch of sweat. Stop it, damn it, Tam! You'll never ride horseback again.

She touched the gold ring on her thumb, turned the key in her Focus, and pulled back onto the two-track road. She was tired from driving all day but now had only a couple of miles as she eased along the rutted tracks and across a third cattle guard. Here the pines crowded each other and grew spindly as they reached for sunlight. Underbrush choked both sides of the tracks, closing over the road and scratching the sides of her car, and Tam shuddered with a claustrophobia she'd never felt as a girl. No evidence here of life, where cattle trails once had cut back and forth through the underbrush and timber. Even in June, Montana's rainy month, the grass was beginning to cure, and dust seeped into the car. Too dry, unseasonably dry, for the mountains.

Tam slowed for the last curve with the old fear of wildfire festering at the back of her mind. Then she was past the giant pine that still grew on the crest, and she was looking down across the meadow and the cabin that once had been home to the horse-breaker and his daughter.

It was more a rambling log house, two-storied, than a cabin. Tam's grandfather had come to Murray County, Montana, with a little money, or so the story went, and had the house built. It would have taken money. Many old mountain houses sagged upon drunken stacks of sandstone slabs, but the Bowen cabin's logs sat on a poured concrete foundation. The logs needed to be resealed, but they were still sound, Bunce had written in his tortured scrawl, although the old back porch was gone. It had started to rot thirty years ago.

Bunce, her father's old friend, had written that he'd replaced the shingles with a dark green metal roof, which looked alien to Tam, seeing it now for the first time. It jarred against the silvered logs and left the massive river rock chimney looming over the cabin like a lonely sentinel from another time.

Except for the roof, Tam could have imagined she would step from her car and be fifteen again and dreaming of Allen Heckman on the next ranch. Or ten years old and dreaming of the great world and her eventual escape from the mountains. But no. She got out of the Focus, stiff from driving and wearing a worn-out flannel shirt and jeans, an old woman who had considered buying a few new clothes for a last summer in the Montana backcountry and decided it was pointless. She picked her way through the stretch of grass and wild roses that led to the front door, caught the heel of her sandal on a weed, and told herself at least she should buy sturdier shoes if she planned to last out the summer.

The front door had been a heavy slab that stuck. In her father's time everyone left it stuck shut and came and went through the back door off the kitchen. But someone, she supposed Bunce, had changed the hinges and painted the slab a dark green to match the roof. It swung open without a creak.

Then she noticed the new lock. As much out of place in a mountain cabin as Tam was.

The lock gleamed against the dark-green paint, ready to repel the efforts of any stray junkies or carousing teenagers who made it this far out of town. Frowning, Tam walked into the hallway and let the door close behind her.

On the inside of the door was a bolt and chain.

Tam stared at the bolt, perplexed. Had the mountains changed as much as she had? She walked farther into the big main room, her sandals echoing her intrusion with every step she took on the bare fir floorboards that had helped to hold the cabin together through the years.

Coatings of dust, dust in coils in the corner. Spiderwebs hanging in shrouds from the ceiling.

The back door, repaired and locked and bolted.

But none of the repairs she had requested. None of the books and few pieces of furniture she'd had shipped from Portland to Fort Maginnis and that Bunce had promised to truck out to the cabin.

She walked across the room to the north window to look across what once was a small lawn and now was a miniature wild meadow of knee-high grass and thistles. An overgrown hedge of diamond willows overlooked the ravine carved by the creek below the cabin. Hidden by the willows would be the pool formed by the spring that fed the creek. On the opposite slope, aspen groves rose and merged with miles of pine-covered hills that faded into the remote blue peaks of the mountains.

Her father's woman—what had her name been, Marjorie?—liked to stand at this window at night, watching the beacon from the airfield at Fort Maginnis to the northwest and the answering light from the fire tower in the national forest reserve to the northeast. In those days Tam's father, Hube Bowen, was gone a lot, off on his horse-swapping, and Marjorie hadn't lasted long in the silence. What became of her, Tam had no idea. Perhaps she'd fled the big loneliness. Tam had had her own reasons for fleeing the Sun Creek country, and yet here she was, with her knees shaking until she sat down on the floor and hugged them.

In the northern latitude in mid-June, the light takes a long time to give way to the night. Tam, unmoving on the dusty floor, her head resting on her knees, cannot hear the gathering wind outside the solid cabin logs, but through the window she sees it heave and ripple like a tidal wave tormenting the tops of the darkening ridge pines.

Headlights, pale in the not-quite-dark, sweep past her window and stop. Disappear.

Bunce?

Footsteps on the doorstep. A tap on the door.

People in the mountains, as Tam remembers them, don't knock on doors. They drive up and stop and wait for whoever is home to look out and see them. Once someone opens the door and recognizes a neighbor's outfit is plenty of time to turn off the ignition and get out and say howdy.

After dark, maybe, somebody would knock.

Another knock, more insistent this time, and still Tam sits in a disconnect of time and place, unable to move as the door opens to someone carrying a Coleman lantern that briefly blinds her until she makes out a man's silhouette and realizes he must be over six feet tall because his hair nearly touches the top of the doorframe.

He takes a tentative step or two into the room and hangs the lantern on a hook from the ceiling. Has there always been a hook hanging by a chain from the ceiling? Tam can't remember.

"Are you Mrs. Bowen?"

The sound of his voice brings her back to herself. Now that the lantern shines from overhead and not in her face, her vision clears, and she sees the man is young, surely not many years over thirty, with brushed brown hair and hazel eyes in a face of straight lines. Level brows. Vertical lines framing his mouth. A shadow of beard. A withheld grief in his face, and Tam with her own grief doesn't want to know more, doesn't want to know this man.

But how ridiculous she must look, an old woman sitting on the floor with her head on her knees.

"I'm Tam Bowen," she says and puts a hand to a knee to rise to her feet.

"I brought your freight out from Fort Maginnis in the back of my truck. Bunce. He's been—"

"Not sick?" Tam bursts. She has been counting on seeing Bunce, who remembers Hube, and now, seeing the gravity on the young man's face, she has an awful surmise. The lack of repairs, the uninhabitable cabin. Bunce, after all, will be nearly eighty, the age of Tam's father if he had lived, and Tam has asked so much of him.

"No. Bunce was shot."

Shot! When?

She doesn't ask the obvious—shot *dead?*—because she sees the answer written on the young man's face, and she looks away because she doesn't want to know what Bunce was to him or he to Bunce. That Bunce is gone, really gone—a breath lost in the wind. *Can't be*—but she knows she has to hear what happened to him.

"A couple weeks ago. And I didn't know anything about you until Suze called a friend of mine this morning because the freight office had called her and said your shipment hadn't been picked up."

Suze. Bunce's wife. Suze called the young man's friend, who called the young man. A message too convoluted to make sense.

"Suze told my friend you asked Bunce to get the place ready, and she was going to come over and clean for you. I'm sorry. You must have had a shock to see it like this."

Tam nods.

"Do you—want me to unload any of it for you? Or maybe take it back to the freight office to ship back to Portland?"

Bunce. The kindest man in the world, the last man she had felt she could trust. Gone. But this man has asked her a question. She has to answer. Find words. "No. I'm not going back. If you're good enough to unload for me, I'll stay here."

"*Here?* In the cabin? You can't do that."

"Yes, I can."

He stares at her. "The power hasn't been turned on, the water hasn't been turned on, there's no phone!"

"I have my cell."

"You won't get a signal here. You'd better go back to Fort Maginnis and get a room and decide what to do in the morning."

Tam doesn't bother to answer. She turns to look out the darkened window, as though there is anything to see in the gathering dusk, while silence stretches between her and the young man.

"All right," he says and shrugs. "I can at least set up your bed and mattress for you. And if anything happens—my brother and I live on the old Heckman place. The road around the spring is still drivable, if you need us. Oh, and Bunce and I fixed your doors. Here are your keys. Lock up behind me."

Tam nods, knows she should say more. Pull herself together, show courtesy. "Thanks for your help. What's your name?"

"James," he says and doesn't elaborate.

2

From Tam's laptop journal:

I am a mother whose son has cursed her and wished her dead, and I am reminded of the old conundrum from a Philosophy 101 class: Posit a father whose son hates him so bitterly that he will do the opposite of his father in all his actions. Is the father morally obligated to commit evil acts so that his son, bent on doing the exact opposite, may be virtuous?

Is dying the last thing a mother whose son wishes her dead can do for that son?

His letter has been the last straw.

Early morning dawn slants through the east window and wakens Tam. Disoriented, she sits up in her own bed, tangled in her sheets and blanket. What time is it? She retrieves her wristwatch from the floor beside her bed as strengthening sunlight illuminates filthy walls and cobwebs. It's 6:00 a.m.

No wonder she feels groggy. Last night she had watched the taillights of James's truck out of sight on the still-drivable road around the spring, and then she groped her way out to the Focus and fetched her suitcase and her flashlight and her bottle of bourbon. She'd looked into the tiny bathroom Hube had plumbed into a closet off the kitchen when Tam started high school, and when she found a rusty sink and shower and a toilet half-full of something dark and desiccated, she averted her eyes and shut the door hastily.

She had dug out sheets to spread on the bed James had set up for her, and she tore off the tape on one of her boxes of books and pulled out something at random to read, anything to keep herself from thinking of Bunce, whom she'd last seen when? At Hube's funeral, must have been, fifteen years ago. She poured three fingers of premium bourbon into a Styrofoam cup and propped herself up in bed and tried to interest herself in her book, which turned out to be *The Complete Works of John Keats*, much of which she didn't have to read to remember.

Now more than ever seems it rich to die.

In the morning she could drive back to Fort Maginnis and buy some deli and maybe an ice chest, find a liquor store to buy more bourbon, and see about getting the water and electricity turned back on in the cabin. Arrange to have a landline strung. Oh hell, she'd think about all that in the morning. She had sipped warm bourbon, longed for ice, and read a few pages of *Lamia*, which she'd never known well, and then she stifled any thought of Bunce and laid down the book on its face on the floor, turned off her flashlight to conserve its batteries, pulled sheet and blanket over her, and slept.

Now, torn from sleep by the first light, she feels groggy. Had she, or had she not, gotten up in the night to refill her cup of bourbon? She'll have to check the level in the bottle. As light sharpens the outline of distant mountains and the ridge pines resume their color, perhaps she can go back to sleep. But no. She has to pee, and she struggles to sit up and thinks another purchase in Fort Maginnis will have to be a chamber pot. Or she can use the disgusting toilet that probably, certainly, won't flush—*no*.

She slips out of bed and runs, naked, to the meadow behind the cabin, leaving the kitchen door open behind her. Runs past the remains of the collapsed outhouse, shelters behind a clump of chokecherries, squats, and lets flow with a surprise like a tap on her shoulder from a former self: she still knows to face downhill when she pees. She shivers, not just from chill dawn air, and feels goose bumps rise on her bare arms and shoulders. Her puddle reeks and steams before it soaks into the dry soil, and she rises and tears off a handful of grass to wipe herself.

Then she's fully awake because a burst of—what, *semiautomatic rifle fire?* no, can't be, but firecrackers maybe—has rattled the dawn and set crows lifting from their nests and flapping skyward and somebody's dog barking in the distance.

No. It wasn't firecrackers. Tam knows rifle fire when she hears it, and this had been a burst of twenty or thirty rounds in rapid succession.

Tam sprints to the cabin, closing and locking the kitchen door behind her. She is reaching for the robe she dug out of her suitcase last night and feeling thankful she hadn't ignored James's advice and failed to lock her doors when a loud knock sounds. She hesitates, shrugging into her robe and knotting the cord.

"Who is it?"

"James. Are you all right?"

"Yes."

"Will you let me in? I've got my brother with me."

Tam runs from the bedroom in time to see the doorknob twist. And with the twist, another round of automatic gunfire bursting into the morning. Was it closer this time? Acting on instinct— surely the sad helpful man she met last night is not dangerous— Tam turns the lock and opens the door on two dark figures, the taller carrying a rifle, the shorter carrying an unlighted lantern.

James reaches behind him, pulls the door shut, and locks it again. The light is strong enough now that Tam can make out his features, and she is struck again by the unrevealing brows and level eyes and mouth but sees nothing but the sadness she noted last night. What makes her think he is not dangerous? Shouldn't she be frightened?

But his brother is just a tawny-haired kid in blue jeans and inside-out sweatshirt who reminds Tam of someone she can't quite place as the boy looks around the room for somewhere to sit. Finally, he upends one of the boxes of books she has not unpacked and sprawls on it, looking bored, with the lantern on the floor beside him.

"What's happening?" Tam asks.

James has been watching the windows. He drags his attention back to Tam. "I didn't want you to think there's a war breaking out. And it's usually nothing."

"*Usually?*"

A pause while James seems to consider his answer. "My friend, a guy called Zenith, lives down the gulch on that little ranch that used to belong to the McIntoshes. Maybe you remember the McIntoshes? Zenith likes his firearms. Likes to make some noise to start his mornings. Some of the neighbors complained to the county sheriff, and what they learned was that if Zenith wants to fire off a few rounds with his AK-47 at dawn, it's not illegal."

Tam is trying to process all this information. The McIntoshes, gone. Somebody by the name of Zenith celebrating the dawn with an AK-47. She starts to ask James how many of the old neighbors still live in the Sun Creek country, and then she wonders how long James, himself, has lived here and how much of the past he may know. Too young to know much, surely. She looks from him to his brother and recognizes in the strengthening light the boy she saw riding full tilt with a girl across the Sun Creek bridge. The tawny shoulder-length hair, the sun-darkened face.

James is saying something. "Come home with Calvin and me. Have coffee and a decent breakfast and somewhere to talk—what you want to do about this place, what Suze is saying—at least be comfortable."

He glances down at the rifle he still carries, glances from the rifle to Tam's bare feet, and averts his eyes.

Breakfast. By this hour Tam's father would have fired the wood-stove in the kitchen and started fresh coffee and fried bread in a skillet. Maybe some bacon. Tam has a thermos of coffee in her car, probably lukewarm by now. The bourbon last night had been her dinner, and Hube is long departed from this filthy room, where the sunlight of a strange new day silvers the cobwebs that shine in the ceiling.

What the hell. She's got to eat. "All right," she says. "That's kind of you."

James nods. "We'll wait outside while you get dressed. Come on, Calvin. Don't forget your lantern."

Clean underthings from her suitcase. The flannel shirt and blue jeans she had worn during her two-day drive from Portland will still do. She pulls on her clothes, buttons and zips. Unclips her hair and brushes it out, still unused to its soft fall across her shoulders. Warren's fingers touching her cropped hair—*Wish you'd let your hair grow!* Damn Warren.

She drops her baggie of toothbrush and toothpaste into a pocket. When had she last brushed her teeth? Her mouth tastes foul. She'll have to hope James has running water and a sink he'll let her use. He and his brother look clean, and their clothes look clean, which suggests they have bathroom and laundry amenities.

Full morning sunlight hits her in the face as she opens the door and sees the two brothers, James and Calvin, as silhouettes with their backs turned while they scan her meadow. As her vision clears, she has to smile at their resemblance, the boy a smaller replica of the man. Then they're turning as she flicks the lock on the door.

"Got your keys?" James asks Tam, and Calvin gives an exaggerated sigh.

"Yes."

Tam counts the ways the morning seems serene. The wind just starting to move through the ridge pines, a hawk soaring on a thermal draft. Nothing to show that Bunce is dead or that someone called Zenith likes to greet the dawn with rounds from his AK-47 or even that Tam herself is back in the mountains. Nothing except James with his rifle and his eyes scanning the perimeters.

"We'll drive you." and Tam sees a dark-blue pickup truck, a newish model with an extended cab, parked behind her road-dusty car. James opens the passenger door—"Get in the back, Calvin"—and Calvin scowls at him but obeys.

James hovers at her shoulder to see if she needs help up to the high seat, but Tam is limber, if she is fifty years old, and she's always resisted assistance. She reaches for the over-door handle and swings up easily to the seat, and James shrugs and walks around to his side of the truck.

The still-drivable track, as James has called it, crosses Tam's meadow and rises to skirt an outcropping of sandstone boulders that overhang the spring. Someone—perhaps Tam's grandfather, with his legendary money—had dammed the natural basin around the spring with rough-cut sandstone blocks to form a good-sized pool that draws wildlife and neighboring ranch children, who have to be scolded away from it. Tam notes the ample water level of the pool, even in this dry season, and the rushing spillway that feeds Sun Creek. At least the spring is still strong.

Then the spring is behind them as the track leads down an incline and through spindling pines for perhaps a mile before the ruts climb again and emerge on higher ground that spreads into a meadow where the two-story Heckman house, unpainted and weathered to gray—James's house now, she has to remind herself—greets Tam with an indifference that makes her wince.

Beyond the house stretch barns and sheds and corrals, all weathered to gray and shrunken, from what Tam remembers. But she is most struck by absence. James's ranch yard is no longer a ranch yard. No longer contains a junk pile. No battered trucks, each older than the last, pulled up by the house. No tractor by the barn, no mowing machine or dump rake or manure spreader parked where it was last used. No old auto chassis by the fence where the children used to play, where she and Allen Heckman met to do whatever they called it in those days. Making out. Feeling each other up. Damn Allen Heckman. Damn him right along with Warren Wetzel.

James barely has braked the truck when Calvin bails from the rear seat, dropping his lantern and making a run for the corrals.

"Are you coming back for breakfast?" James calls after him, gets no answer, and shakes his head. Carrying his rifle in one hand and rescuing the lantern with his other hand, he guides Tam ahead and sets down the lantern to take a key from his pocket and unlock the front door.

More locks and keys.

James disappears into the kitchen, while Tam finds herself in what once was the Heckmans' cluttered front room and now is sparsely furnished with white walls, a dark polished floor, a pair of leather armchairs beside a woodstove, and, surprisingly, a whole wall of bookshelves. The books draw Tam to scan titles. She can't help herself—she always scans the titles of other people's books. On James's shelves she finds a number of popular histories and biographies, along with a whole shelf of what appear to be the college textbooks of someone who majored in history. No poetry or fiction—no, she's wrong there. On a lower shelf, stuck among a collection of what must be current reading, Tam recognizes a book in a lurid dust jacket with a photo of a bare-chested young man with a full-body tattoo, a beard, and glinting eyes.

James comes out of the kitchen carrying two steaming mugs. He catches Tam examining his books, but he makes no comment and offers her a mug. The fragrance of the coffee is intoxicating, but Tam, who recently has wiped herself with a handful of grass, has a more pressing need.

"Is there a bathroom?"

"Oh—sure. Back of the kitchen."

Tam finds a door into a bathroom fitted with what must be the original pedestal sink, a tub with its own clawed feet, and a scarred toilet with, of course, its lid up. But a clean toilet! Such amenities exist. And soap and hot water.

Tam soaps and rinses her hands at the sink and dries them on the towel hanging from a hook on the door. Then, in the hallway outside the bathroom, she notices a framed photo, an enlarged snapshot, and pauses to examine it. A middle-aged man and a much younger woman pose in front of shrubbery with a glimpse of an opulent Victorian-style house with a surrounding verandah. The somber-eyed young man standing to one side is James. The little blond boy laughing up at the couple is perhaps five years old. Calvin?

You're snooping, Tam.

Well, why not? How much James hasn't told her. His last name. Any details about his background and Calvin's. The reason why he has set up a home for himself and his brother on the old Heckman ranch in the middle of Montana and apparently made friends with Bunce and Suze.

Bunce. The last time she saw him, tears had run down his face and coursed his wrinkles at the loss of his old friend Hube. Now the realization of Bunce's death, the possibility of—*murder?*—robs her of her breath.

To steady herself, she wills herself to think of strange people moving to the middle of nowhere for strange reasons. Somebody called Zenith, for example, or—she recalls the Unabomber, years ago, who built himself a plywood shack in Montana mountains wilder than Tam's but no more remote and who minded his own business as far as his neighbors knew. He might wave at a passing car as he pedaled toward the post office with a package for mailing strapped to his bike. The fifty or so people living in cabins scattered around the Unabomber's neck of the woods had no idea what his packages contained and were astonished when a battalion of FBI agents descended on the neighborhood.

Tam doesn't suppose James is building bombs in his cellar, but what is he doing in the Sun Creek country?

Tells herself she doesn't need to know. Tells her curiosity what it can do with itself.

When she returns to the living room, James is sitting in one of the leather armchairs by the woodstove, drinking coffee and scanning what he can see through his front window of the track and the meadow. He waves Tam to the other chair. Another mug of coffee waits for her on the woodstove, which apparently does duty as a side table during the summer.

"Damn kid anyway. I put off breakfast hoping he'd come home, but no. He's running wild."

"How old is he?"

"Fifteen."

"He looks older."

"He thinks he's older."

A silence, a country silence characterized by what it does not contain. No rumble of passing traffic. No television talking to itself in another room. No cell phone set to vibrate, bouncing on a desk. No faint click of a computer keyboard.

No, not quite a complete silence. Tam realizes she is hearing music from an invisible speaker with its volume tuned so low that it seems faraway, no more than a whisper of guitar chords and an indistinct tenor lamenting his troubles.

Why does this country silence contain, besides faint country music, a tension between Tam and the man in the opposite armchair?

"Tell me about Bunce," says Tam.

For a moment she thinks James will not answer. His gaze remains fixed on the track and the meadow outside the window, but his hand tightens on the handle of his coffee mug.

"He used to talk about you. And your work. When I saw your book in a bookstore in Missoula, I bought it. Curious, I guess."

Another pause. "I found him. He was slumped over in his truck about halfway between your place and his. He'd rolled the window down, as though he'd stopped to talk to somebody. I had to"—he was forcing his words now—"had to leave him there, alone, so I could get to a landline, call the sheriff. His house was the closest, and I didn't think about—about Suze, she was there, alone, and I had to tell her."

"But *who?*" asks Tam after another long pause.

"Nobody knows. The sheriff came out and looked around, but it just looked like somebody stepped out of the pines and flagged

Bunce down. Nothing missing, and he had his tools with him. Suze told the sheriff he'd gone to start repairing the"—he pauses, glances at Tam—"the Bowen cabin. And no tracks—well, there wouldn't be—the ground is dried hard. If there was a shell casing, the bastard picked it up. No motive anybody can think of. Who'd want to hurt Bunce?"

Who indeed. Tam has pried what she can out of James. She must talk with Suze, preferably before this day is over. What else?

"Suze is living in town with her sister," says James. "But if you're really staying in the cabin, I'll turn your water on for you, and if you call the electric company in Fort Maginnis, and you can call from here, they'll turn your lights back on. Telephone, I don't know. It'll probably take longer. You never had a landline run out to the cabin, did you?"

"No."

James seems to have taken a new interest in his hands. Studies them, flexes his fingers. "I don't read much fiction. Like I said, I was curious. But—"

It dawns on Tam that he is trying to tell her he didn't much like her novel. An unwelcome memory of Rob at fifteen, hurtling a line from one of her novels back at her: *Oh! Jared! I want to watch you come! And the vein in Jared's cock throbs and the fluid pulses out, and she bends her head to lick it from him.*

"It's all right," Tam says to James. "You don't have to like it. I don't like it much either."

He glances at her, looks away. "And you still haven't had any breakfast. The hell with waiting for Calvin. He wants to chase after Vay Evenson, he can go hungry. Come back to the kitchen with me, and I'll hot up your coffee and rustle you something to eat."

But then a clatter of horses' hooves, flashes of riders past the window, and now James is on his feet, he's making for the back of the house, where there sounds a frantic knocking, and Tam follows.

3

From Tam's laptop journal:

*Rob, overheard on the phone: Dad! Goddamn! That fucking book
she wrote, and its cover with that bare-assed woman on those red-and-
gold sheets so you can't walk down the hall without seeing that book
under somebody's arm and a snicker on his face, because he knows
my mother wrote it. Yes, and there's old Hairy Balls standing in front
of his locker with her book! He grins at me and opens the book and
reads a couple of sentences to his asshole buddy.*

Dad! How'm I supposed to live with a mother like her?

"Okay, okay!"

James shoots the bolt on the kitchen door and opens it to Calvin
and the dark-haired girl Tam had seen riding with him the day
before. Out at the fence, she sees the girl's black thoroughbred
and Calvin's chunky brown gelding tied to a rail, shining with
sweat and breathing hard.

"You won't guess what we saw!" bursts Calvin, and then he sees
Tam and drops his eyes. Tam, struck all over again by the boy's
ridiculous resemblance to his older brother—what is it about a
smaller replica that is comic?—takes what she hopes is an unob-
trusive step back to spare his embarrassment.

Calvin's friend, the dark-haired girl, shows no such restraint.
Bubbling with excitement, she takes up the story. "Jamie, Jamie!
Some guys have moved into the Simmons place! We watched
them! They were having target practice!"

James, who has set a skillet on the stove, turns and stares at
her. "Bunce Simmons's place? Moved in? You sure?"

"Oh! Yes!" The girl's eyes glow with her pleasure at having exciting news to deliver. "They've got a black SUV parked in the yard by the house."

"It's a Chevy Tahoe," Calvin puts in.

"Whatever, one of those big ones. An older guy and a younger one. And they'd set up a target in the yard, with the shape of a man painted on it, and they were practicing with pistols, and they're pretty good!"

"Maybe somebody Suze knows." James shakes his head and turns back to his cooking. Tam, sensitive to the rigid line of his back and shoulders, his dismissal of the girl, deduces that he doesn't much like Vay. Or—Tam surprises herself with a sting of irritation at the other possibility—he's attracted to his brother's girlfriend and doesn't want to show it.

After all, why wouldn't James be attracted to Vay? Now that she's in the same room with the girl, Tam sees she's indeed beautiful, with her long luxuriant hair and her big dark eyes and dark fringe of lashes. Even in jeans and a Montana State sweatshirt with the sleeves cut off, she's a will-o'-the-wisp who will look striking in a saddle. Probably a year or two older than Calvin but still so young.

"You had any breakfast, Vay?" James says without turning from the stove. He has a griddle going now, along with bacon in his skillet, and he's beating a batter with hands that are long fingered and limber, with clean clipped nails. Tam remembers Hube's hardened hands, with fingernails like horns.

"Nobody cooks at my house!" cries Vay. "Are you inviting me, Jamie? I'm starving!"

James jerks his head at Calvin, who sticks out his lower lip but goes to lay plates and forks and knives on the table, while James pours his batter on the griddle and studies the results while he stands by with a turner. Tam cannot remember watching a man cooking since she used to watch Hube, and she wants to smile at James's concentration on his task as he flips his flapjacks and turns his bacon and lifts it out to drain while he breaks eggs into the skillet.

"Jamie! The sweetheart of the rodeo!" Vay suddenly screams what Tam at first takes to be an endearment. Then she sees that Vay has snatched up a CD case from the counter to display its photo of a cowboy with a white hat and a pretty face. Tam remembers faint guitar chords. This must be the cowboy with the sad sweet tenor.

"Ooh, Jamie! Isn't he just too sweet?" Vay coos, and James's shoulders stiffen over his cooking. Tam sees Calvin's face, wrung with—what? Anger? Or is he hurt that the young girl, *his* girl, is making fun of his brother's taste in music?

Currents are running deeper here than Tam can follow. Reminds herself she doesn't need to follow these currents.

"Knock it off," James tells the kids. "Sit down and eat."

Everyone finds a chair at the haphazardly laid oak table by the kitchen window, and Tam suddenly is famished. She waits to see if this group says a blessing over a meal, but no, Calvin has put away his hurt, or whatever troubled him, and he is heaping his plate and teasing Vay with the syrup bottle, while James shakes his head at them and pours more coffee for Tam and himself.

"You're planning to drive to Fort Maginnis today to see Suze?" he says under the cover of Vay's squeals. Calvin is pretending to dip a lock of her hair in syrup.

"Yes. Does her sister still live on Water Street?"

James nods, but whatever else he might have said is lost in the commotion. Vay unwisely has ducked to avoid Calvin, and a lock of her hair really does end up in a puddle of syrup. She shrieks and Calvin laughs and reaches for a dishcloth.

"God," says James.

Tam is seeing a lopsided family around the table. James as the too-young father of two teenagers, with inexplicable electricity between him and his brother's girlfriend. But Tam has nothing to solve here and nothing she'll need to work into an erotic novel.

She'll never write another novel, and she's only a guest here, invited out of kindness and soon to depart.

Fort Maginnis in the late morning is a dusty town with a core of worn native sandstone buildings studded with a glitz of coffee bars and galleries and a sprawl of new housing that spreads across the bluff above town. *Lotta new people moving in*, Bunce had written. *I hear they're retired from someplace else.*

Tam had kept up that correspondence with Bunce for years. She wrote him regularly, sensing that it pleased him to open his mailbox and find an envelope addressed to him in her handwriting. Not that she ever had much news or news that would interest him. Bunce, on the other hand, in his infrequent letters, always included detailed reports on the weather in Murray County, the condition of the grazing, and—in recent years—the intrusion into the Sun Creek country of never-before-seen elk and bears from higher in the mountains. Like people, wildlife on the move to find someplace better.

Always a Christmas card from Bunce, always a birthday card. With Bunce gone, she'll never receive another birthday card.

She turns on Water Street, which follows Sun Creek through town, and parks at the curb in front of Suze's sister Em's house, a 1920s bungalow with a glassed-in front porch and a sidewalk that leads Tam around the house to the back door, where she's observed by an elderly neighbor watering his lawn, who shoots her a look over the spray of water from his hose.

Tam knocks, waits for several minutes listening to the unhurried chuckle of the creek behind a hedge of golden willows, then knocks again. Hears shuffling footsteps as unhurried as the creek current.

The door opens on Em—well, Tam guesses it's Em, whom she hasn't seen for many years. This gnarled woman, who has shrunken into herself like a potato forgotten on a windowsill, wears a cotton housedress and bedroom slippers and peers out at Tam through clouded spectacles.

"I'm Tam Bowen. My father and I were neighbors to Bunce and Suze—"

Still the old woman shows no sign of recognition or even that she has heard Tam, and Tam tries another tack.

"You're Suze Simmons's sister, aren't you? I just heard about Bunce's death. Can I talk to Suze?"

This time her words seem to register because the woman moves aside to let Tam through the door and trots ahead of her into a kitchen, where rolls of dust have accumulated like gray growths across a pool of grease on a stovetop and more grease on counters. A petrified orange has been left on the drainboard of the sink.

Suze sits by a window in a rocking chair. And not that Tam's seen Suze for years either, but at least she *knew* Suze once. Suze, who baked cookies for Tam, the motherless neighbor girl. Let out the hems of Tam's school dresses as she grew. Explained to her about her times of the month and the need for pads when the time came.

Now, shrunken and gray like her sister, Suze looks up at Tam in bewilderment.

"—don't think I know you—" It's little more than a whisper.

"Suze, I'm Tam Bowen! Hube Bowen's daughter. Don't you remember? We lived just above the spring. We used to ride over and visit with you and Bunce when I was a little girl."

If the eyes are windows to the soul—a line from a poem, Tam thinks—this old woman has lost hers in an empty unblinking stare. Of course, Suze must be nearly eighty. Tam resolves never to come to this state. Never.

But currents still must be connecting in Suze's head because she whispers, "Hube Bowen—yes, he had a little girl. Her mother run off and left her when she was just a baby. Tammy Lou, that was the little girl's name. A pretty little thing with such a pretty name."

Tam winces. She's always hated the name on her birth certificate. None of her current acquaintances knows her as Tammy Lou. Probably Allen Heckman has forgotten it. Rob has never known it. She signs checks as Tam Bowen, has signed book contracts as Tam Bowen.

Something must have cleared for Suze, for her expression is troubled. "Are you Tammy Lou? You don't look like her. She was so pretty, but she was no good, you know. Just as bad as her mother. She had to leave town."

Tam decides not to untangle Suze's syntax—*who had to leave town? Tam or her mother?*—and picks up a thread of the conversation. "Yes, I'm Tam. I'm home for—well, for the summer. Staying in our old cabin. But I was so sorry to hear about Bunce."

"Bunce." Suze draws out the name as though it is something she has mislaid and only now remembered. "That's right. Bunce had a letter from her. Said there'd be a Bowen on the old place again. He was all thrilled about it, after he'd been a-writin' all those birthday cards to her."

A framed black-and-white snapshot of a young Bunce and a young Suze stands on a small table beside the chair where the old Suze huddles. The young Bunce in pearl-snapped shirt and stockman's pants and boots, with his hat pushed to the back of his head as he grins down at Suze, Bunce's familiar grin, while Suze in a print dress and laced shoes has folded her arms and stares unsmiling at the camera. Behind them is the unpainted siding of their house. Their porch and screen door. Lilac bushes to either side.

"Someone is living in your house, Suze."

Suze surprises Tam with a smile that bares her remaining teeth as she searches for the name. Comes up with it. "It's Allen Heckman. Do you remember Allen, Tammy Lou? And he's got his boy with him. A course he wanted to live on his own ranch, but his dad sold out to—" This time the name eludes her—"it was years back and those folks are gone. A couple of them Bohunks are living there now. So Allen came and talked to me about my place for him and his boy."

Details. Outside the dirty window, a row of pink hollyhocks rear their heads and seem to peer inside. But Tam's head reels with Allen's name. And Rob's. They are her neighbors now, living in the Simmons house.

"—that Bohunk living on the Heckman place now, James something or other, one a them terrible foreign names he's got. And he's a terrible man. He killed Bunce, you know."

Tam stops listening. Too much, too much. First James's news about Bunce, now Allen and Rob. She tells herself it can't be coincidence. There's a reason Allen and Rob—*Rob*—have set themselves up on the Simmons ranch, and is that reason her? But how—who would have told them her summer plans? She had been carefully vague with everyone she knew in Portland.

Bunce? Why should she believe she had been his only correspondent?

Allen and Rob, target shooting.

Suze gives Tam a sudden suspicious look. "You say you're Tammy Lou? You sure don't look like her. Tammy Lou was a pretty little thing, but she was no good. She tried to trick Allen, and now she's been trying to trick Bunce."

Em has trotted to the kitchen stove to lift the lid off something she's been simmering, and Tam, dragging herself back from wild surmising, realizes it must be close to noon and lunchtime for the old women—dinnertime, they'll call it—and of course they'll invite her to eat with them. It's the country way. Her stomach lurches at the thought. She absolutely cannot bear the idea of sitting down for a meal, not in this kitchen of gunky surfaces and rimes of grease and stink of ancient females. And not with the thought of Allen and Rob peering through streaks of filth and the pink faces of hollyhocks at the window.

She manages her excuses, which neither old woman seems to hear. "So good to see you, Suze—so sorry to hear about Bunce—

must run, I've got errands—I'll come again." As an afterthought, she adds, "Nice to see you, too, Em," and gets no answer.

Once out the back door, Tam breathes deeply in the scent of creek water and overgrown grass and takes a moment to steady herself. Her errands—she'd thought of buying a few groceries and cleaning supplies, more bourbon, maybe today's local paper—now seem huge tasks. And it's pointless to speculate, but maybe, like Tam, Allen had kept up a correspondence with Bunce over the years. Maybe Bunce mentioned Tam as a piece of news, along with the new retirees moving into Fort Maginnis and the bear he'd seen in the cow pasture and the weather. What difference does it make how Allen has managed to keep track of her or why?

The creek chuckles its slow way to the river; the sun shines down. Tam tells herself to get a grip. What does she have to fear from Allen or Rob? All their presence in the Sun Creek country alters is her pleasure in the summer she has gifted herself.

"They ain't as stove up as they look. Or as empty upstairs as they act."

Tam glances up. It's the neighbor with his hose. Wispy white hair, belly bulging under his coveralls.

"I do my best to keep an eye on them. You related to 'em?"

"No. Just—friends from years ago. But thanks for"—for what?— "for asking."

She is back in her car before she remembers Suze's words— *James something or other, and he's a terrible man. He killed Bunce.*

If Bunce had never mentioned Allen in his letters to Tam, he'd never mentioned James either. And yet James had spoken of Bunce as a friend who had bragged to him about Tam and her novels.

He's a terrible man. A *Bohunk,* a local corruption of *Bohemian* and the carryall term for all the incomprehensibly chattering immigrants from Scandinavia or Central Europe who had tried to find a better life by filing for homesteads in Murray County.

4

The Murray County courthouse and grounds take up a whole city block on Fort Maginnis's South Main Street. Weeping willows droop their fronds down to tended lawns on either side of marble steps that lead up to the golden brick and pale marble of the courthouse facade.

For Tam Bowen, already disturbed by her visit with Suze, the courthouse and lawns and willows look familiar and yet strangely diminished, as though a testimony to the frightened teenaged girl who last stood at the foot of those steps.

Well. She's no longer that girl. She no longer needs Hube at her right hand and Mrs. Eckles at her left, although their ghosts climb the steps with her and reach with their invisible hands to open the door for her.

Same granite-floored foyer, same hush in the air. Hube's ghost raises his eyes in silent respect and removes his black Stetson.

To Tam's left, a closed door used to open on the office of the county superintendent of schools, maybe still does, although from Bunce's letters she knows the rural schools mostly have closed, one more sign of passing time in Murray County. To her right, a door has opened to show a clerk studying a computer screen behind a counter and a sign that reads DRIVERS LICENSES in bold capital letters. No one is waiting for a driver's license today. Tam walks past that door and climbs the next flight of marble stairs.

At the landing, with a bank of windows and a corridor that leads past the doors to the courtroom and the judge's chambers, Tam pauses. Stain-streaked marbled floors, dark wood paneling that has faded where light from the windows has fallen, faint odor of dust and ancient crumbling paper. The courthouse is an anachronism Tam once researched for one of her novels. The big ideas people in Murray County had a century ago, when rain fell and the Enlarged Homestead Act lured emigrants from all over the world—Bohunks—to stake their claims on free land in Montana and make their fortunes. Rain fell, crops grew, and two railroad lines were built through Fort Maginnis, the better to carry more settlers to stake their dryland claims and freight out their wheat and barley. Believing that prosperity knew no limits, the prominent men of their day raised the funds to build this opulent courthouse as well as banks and dry goods stores and groceries and lumberyards.

Then the rains stopped falling. Crops shriveled. Banks foreclosed on worthless homesteads and closed their own doors. Just as it had doubled, tripled, quadrupled, the population of Murray County shrank, and Fort Maginnis's Main Street grew dusty. Men like Hube Bowen and Bunce Simmons cinched their belts and doubled down and shook their heads over the folly of newcomers who trusted the weather.

What do the newcomers of this new century trust in? James, for example? Tam shakes her head, thinking of her homestead novel, which skipped over the dust storms and disappointments to delineate the desires of the heart. Settler's daughter falls in love with passing cowboy. Has terrific sex with him before he rides on. Will the cowboy return for the settler's daughter before her pregnancy shows and shames her?

Tam tells herself to keep her focus on what she came to the courthouse to do. Ahead is another sign: MURRAY COUNTY SHERIFF'S DEPARTMENT. Tam enters the open door where a woman sits at a desk and glances up from a desktop computer. In her red shirt and slacks she is a dash of color in an otherwise dull office with dark wainscoting and dark frames around the tall windows. This is Murray County space, all right, and except for the phone and the computer, it won't have changed since the courthouse was built.

"Help you?"

"Could I speak with the sheriff?"

"Um—" The woman glances at the wall clock above her desk. "I think he might have some time. Can I tell him who—"

"I'm Tam Bowen."

The woman gives Tam a sudden sharp look, but she picks up her phone, taps a number, and speaks Tam's name in a low voice. "Yeah," she says to Tam after a pause and points to a door behind her. "You can go right in."

SEIDEL on the sign beside the door, which Tam opens to find a grayish blond man in a dark-blue uniform, fiftyish, with his feet in cowboy boots propped comfortably on top of his desk. He lays down the file he has been reading as his mouth drops open.

"Tam! It's really you!"

Tam stares for a moment before she recognizes him. "Libarriby Sibidibel!"

The sheriff winces but laughs as the years peel back for Tam. It had been a junior high school thing, somebody's older sister introducing seventh graders to a jargon she called Ibo Jibo, in which the syllable *ib* was inserted after consonants in words to result in a chatter that sounded incomprehensible to outsiders, which was the whole point. Then somebody got the idea of translating each other's names into Ibo Jibo. Hence, Libarriby Sibidibel for Larry Seidel, which for some reason had stuck to him. For a while even the teachers were calling him Libarriby Sibidibel. Larry hadn't been crazy about the name. Tam wonders why she remembers it.

"Damn! Why does everybody remember Libarriby Sibidibel? Why don't they remember Tibam Bibowiben? Or maybe somebody does."

"I doubt it."

"But hell, it's good to see you, Tam. You've been a long time gone, girl, and you're looking good too." Larry swings his feet off his desk and stands, looks Tam up and down, and smiles the big smile she remembers. "Not in a hurry, are you? Hey! Nona! Can we have some coffee in here?"

Tam takes the chair under the windows that Larry offers, where she feels the afternoon sun warm on her back and hears the small ordinary sounds of the courthouse. A phone ringing somewhere, footsteps in the corridor growing more distant, a voice half-heard. Also muted sounds from the street. Passing traffic. Somewhere a dog barking, unalarmed. Maybe the dog just wants to hear himself bark. Small-town ordinary. Small-town safe.

She sips the coffee poured by Nona and thinks Larry looks small-town ordinary himself. Thinning hair and a lined face dashed with freckles that remind her of the football tight end, the skinny high school basketball star, who could jump like a kangaroo rat. Now he's grown a little paunch that strains his dark-blue uniform shirt and the belt of his pants. Still smiling the big smile but uneasy. He's probably guessing what has brought Tam to his office.

"So Tam! And now you're famous! The only famous one from our class! My wife's a big fan of yours! I think she's got all your books. Maybe you remember her, she was Barb Monroe, a couple years behind us in school. She'd love to meet you."

The sheriff pauses. Swallows coffee, makes a face, and sets his cup down.

"So what brings you back, Tam?"

"I wanted to see Bunce." Which is the truth, as far as she can speak it.

"It was a hell of a thing, Tam."

"Can you tell me what happened?"

He shrugs. "What I can tell you, Tam? It looked like Bunce had pulled his pickup over and rolled the window down, maybe to talk to somebody. Took a bullet in his face."

With his eyes on Tam's face, Larry softens his words. "It had to be quick. His pickup was still running when a neighbor found him and called us. We looked around, of course, even had a couple homicide consultants down from Great Falls, but nothing. The ground was too hard for tracks, hadn't rained in I dunno when—"

It was no more than what James had told her.

"Take a look at this."

From a case mounted on a wall, Larry draws down a map. Tam studies it for a moment before she realizes it is an aerial photograph, many times enlarged.

"Here's the county road up from Fort Maginnis—" Larry traces it with a finger. "And here's the Sun Creek bridge. Here's your road branching northeast, away from the bridge. You can just make it out through the timber. And here's your cabin."

It takes Tam a moment to understand she is seeing what a hawk gliding on a thermal current might see. The roof and chimney of her cabin, the foreshortened walls. The photograph must be a recent one because the cabin's roof is a metallic green.

Larry is guiding her through a flattened Sun Creek country as seen by the hawk. "Here's the boulders around the spring. The timber hides the road where it drops down and loops around the spring, but here it is again, climbing up to the old Heckman ranch."

He glances at Tam, and she sees he remembers the old stories. Tam Bowen and the scandal with Allen Heckman.

"The man who lives there now, with his brother, he's the one that found Bunce. James Warceski. Now you can follow the road as it widens after Warceski's ranch buildings and bears west and follows the ridge above the old McIntosh ranch—another fella lives there now, calls himself Zenith—and continues past Bunce Simmons's ranch just before it dips down to meet the county road again."

And above the road, the trail along the ridge, which is hidden in the pines but lives on a map in Tam's head. The trail where she and Hube once rode horseback to visit Bunce and Suze.

"A man named Evenson lives over here, on the west side of Sun Creek and the county road." Larry taps a finger on what clearly is an extensive set of buildings. "Just on the edge of what Bunce and Hube used to call the Sun Creek country, which is a whole different country now."

"Money?"

Larry snorts. "The pack of them are loaded, and none of them seem to have any work to do. Unless you count what James Warceski does as work."

"Which is what?"

"He told me, but damned if I could figure out what he was talking about. Some kinda online financing. He's got more computers and gadgets upstairs in the old Heckman house than they probably got in all of Fort Maginnis. Must run 'em off fiber optics. Thing is, Tam—you can see, just looking at this map. It's backwoods out there. You got half a dozen families scattered over fifteen miles or so, and to get to them, you have to know those roads and how to drive on them. You shoulda seen those homicide guys from Great Falls struggle and get lost and curse."

"So it wasn't a tourist who just happened along and decided to kill Bunce."

"No, and not a homicidal maniac either, which is what some folks keep harping about. And which is why you're all of a sudden seeing doors and windows closed and locked like you never saw before."

"Suze told me James—what is his name?—killed Bunce."

"James Warceski. She tells that to anybody who'll listen. I s'pose because Warceski found him."

A pause. "Oh hell, Tam. It's an open case, and we're working on it. Well—keeping it open, at least. Sometimes rotten stuff just happens. Hard as I know it is for you to back off from anything—remember when we used to call you the boy-girl? Because you all the time tried to lead when we had ballroom dancing in gym class? And that super-short haircut—I have to tell you, Tam, you look a whole lot prettier with your hair grown out."

The boy-girl is not a name Tam wants to remember either. Memories battle for position. High school girls giggling together in the corridor—*I about fainted, I thought it was a boy in the next stall, but it was her with that haircut!* Or Warren—*Why don't you let your hair grow, honey?* Damn Warren. Damn, damn. Maybe she'll shave her head. Meanwhile, she's staring at Larry's map until he says in a lighter voice, "You'll come in and have dinner with Barb and me one night, won't you, Tam? Barb will want you to sign your books for her."

Tam nods. She can think of nothing else to ask Larry.

By evening Tam has a bad crick in her back. Libarriby Sibidibel's friendliness must have restored her after her visit with Suze because she left the sheriff's office and went shopping in Fort Maginnis, had her power turned on, and returned to the cabin with food and bourbon and a scrub bucket and rubber gloves and a stiff brush and plenty of bleach. Somewhere between the town and the bridge over Sun Creek, she promised herself she didn't have to alter her slow walk toward the end of summer, no matter what mysteries or threats loomed.

She doesn't have to live with spiderwebs either. Or a filthy toilet. She has swept down the walls, scrubbed the floors, swept out the fireplace, and washed and polished the windows until they sparkle with late sunlight. Worn a mask and tackled the bathroom, tried an anti-rust solution on the toilet. Now she strips off her gloves and rubs her back and looks around a room bare of everything but a stack of boxes. In this moment of quiet, Tam can believe in the space of her mountain summer to meditate and sit in judgment on herself.

But meditation is not to be, at least not this evening, because there's a knock at her front door.

Tam hesitates. She hadn't heard a motor, but of course the log walls shut out sound. Maybe it's someone on foot? She wishes

Bunce and James had installed a peephole in the door, and then she wishes she hadn't thought of Bunce or James.

"Who is it?"

"It's me. Zenith. Your neighbor."

Zenith.

Tam thinks of distant gunfire at dawn and shrugs. She opens the door on a tall white-bearded individual with a bobblehead of white hair like a gone-to-seed dandelion. A man perhaps in his seventies who carries not an AK-47 but a dish covered in foil, which he thrusts at Tam as he beams down at her. A red-speckled dog hovers at his heels, sniffing at the foil-wrapped dish and wagging hopefully.

"I live down the gulch from you! Makes us good as next-door neighbors in these here parts! So I thought to bring a welcome to you. Here 'tis!"

Tam looks from Zenith to the covered dish and finds her voice. "Thank you—um, Zenith. I'm not really settled yet, but won't you come in?"

Zenith beams even more warmly and gives Tam a little bow and stumps after her, while she shakes her head at his plaid shirt and new Levi's held up with suspenders and tucked into lace-up boots. He's a caricature of an old ranch man, but he would be picked out at any county fair or bull sale as an outsider. A not-one-of-us, in spite of his "these here parts" artificially countrified talk. It occurs to Tam that the not-one-of-us folks now outnumber *us*, whoever *we* still are, in these parts, as Zenith calls the Sun Creek country.

"Sit and wait, Spotty," he tells his dog, who rolls reproachful eyes but curls up by the fireplace and tucks his nose under his tail.

"Maybe set your dish down on one of these boxes of books?"

Inwardly, she's interrogating her own judgment. She instinctively had trusted James, after all, but then Suze: *He's a terrible man.* Still, whoever—*whatever*—this man is, with his smile and his hot dish, he may not be what he pretends, but she doesn't think he's a killer. "This is very kind of you, Zenith. And I'm Tam Bowen."

He's taking the foil off his dish, which contains something dark with a rich fragrance, a stew, Tam thinks.

"It smells wonderful," she says. "My dishes are still packed, and my back hurts from scrubbing floors. But have a seat there—" She indicates one of the futons she'd had shipped from Portland. "Would you care to have a drink with me while your dish keeps warm?"

His eyes light up, and she adds, "If you can stand to drink good bourbon from a Styrofoam cup, that is?"

Which is how it happens that an observer outside Tam's lighted windows, an owl perhaps, pausing on its hunt, or a teenager on the prowl for trouble—could it be Calvin?—might see Tam and Zenith, each seated on a box of books as they raise their Styrofoam cups to toast each other.

Calvin Warceski pauses just outside the oblong of light that Tam's newly restored electric power casts through her uncurtained window. The deepening twilight transforms the fringe of weeds and underbrush into shadows but not so deep that a sudden movement of Calvin's might not alert the man or the woman he watches. Zenith and Mrs. Bowen. How have they become acquainted, what animates their unheard conversation, their laughter even, as they raise their Styrofoam cups?

Calvin feels as though he's watching a scene in a film with the sound turned off. He has to imagine the dialogue between an actor with a dandelion puff of white hair and an actress with pale gold hair that shines when the light falls on it. The actress reminds him of someone, but he can't pin down the memory. Well, yes, he can. Someone he once knew whose hair fell to her shoulders and shone, whose head tilted when she laughed. He finds himself drawn to the actress, he feels protective of her, and when the old dandelion-head actor touches her hand, Calvin's involuntary flinch is enough for the actors to interrupt their scene and look out of their frame toward his watching post, and he shrinks back into the underbrush with his heart pounding.

He scolds himself for being a damned fool. Thinks what it would be like to be caught looking into other people's windows at night. Thinks what James would say and do. But gradually his heartbeat steadies, and he melts deeper into the underbrush until he finds the ridge trail. He has other windows to inspect tonight.

5

Tam again is wakened as the first daylight breaks through her uncurtained windows along with a distant burst of automatic rifle fire from down the gulch. She yawns and stretches, smiling as she recalls her evening with Zenith. When he told her goodbye and stumped off into the dark, replete with beef stew and drunk on good bourbon, she had crossed her fingers for him and his patient dog Spotty, but the gunfire tells her that he made it safely home.

"Just makes me feel good," he explained when she asked him about his noisy way of saluting the dawn. "It's a fine thing to make yourself feel good first thing in the morning."

For all his pretentious folksiness, Zenith has depths that Tam senses. For one thing, he's remarkably well-spoken when he isn't pretending to be the backcountry hick in boots and suspenders. She'd noticed him checking out her book titles as he helped her unpack them and stack their shipping crates for temporary shelves. She'd like to scan the titles on Zenith's shelves as she had scanned James's.

James. He must be about thirty-three, the age Rob is now. Is that why her thoughts keep circling back to him?

For a self-described hermit, Zenith knows a lot about his neighbors, as Tam learned last night, and he's not at all averse to gossiping. Even as she suspected any scraps he could ferret out about her would be distributed along his route through the Sun Creek country—and what narrative would Zenith piece out of her scraps?—Tam found herself fascinated enough by his tales to pour him more bourbon to keep them flowing.

Ed Evenson, who has more money than anyone else, led the attempt to force Zenith to stop saluting the dawn with AK-47 fire. And that daughter of Ed's! Her mother lives in California. Some kinda custody battle going on between her and Ed. The girl's a pretty little thing but a spoiled brat. Does Tam know her name?

"Vay?"

"Nevaeh. That's *heaven* spelled backward. Who'd name a child Nevaeh?"

It was not a name Tam had heard before, and she shook her head.

Bunce and Suze? Salt of the earth. A shame what happened to Bunce, and nobody had an idea who pulled the trigger. Well, Zenith had his opinions, which he would keep to himself, but his opinion of that new outfit Suze rented out to? Or maybe sold out to? When to Zenith they smelled like a pair a them damned survivalists? Also, Zenith didn't believe Suze's head was clear enough to remember exactly what she'd agreed to. It was a damned shame about Suze.

"And that sister of hers is just as bad, if not worse. I try to drop by every time I go down to Fort Maginnis to see how they're doing. Somebody ought to step in, but there's no other family that I could find out. Just a neighbor to keep an eye out. Don't like to see those two fellers taking advantage of her. They ran me off when I tried to talk to them."

Finally, Zenith got around to James and Calvin Warceski, whom Tam had been biting her lip to keep from asking about.

"James. He's a man with a big problem on his hands, but he buys good whiskey, and he and I got to talking one night. His folks were killed in a car crash, ten-twelve years ago, and he's been trying to raise his little brother. Brought the brother out to the Sun Creek country to keep him out of trouble, and what happened but he found more trouble."

Now, in morning sunlight, Tam's thoughts return to James. His kindness. Hauling a stranger's freight out from Fort Maginnis, reassuring her about Zenith and his firearms, turning her water back on for her. Cooking breakfast for her. She wishes she'd pressed Zenith harder about the two fellers, as he called them, on the Simmons ranch. Two fellers he thought were holed-up survivalists. Who were Allen and Rob Heckman.

In the unfamiliar confines of his daughter's classroom, under a calendar for October 1985, Hube Bowen loses his temper. "The boy-girl!"

He has nothing to gain, maybe a lot to lose, by raising his voice to his daughter's English teacher, but a red haze colors the classroom clutter and even the face of the woman behind her desk. His head throbs, and his fists twist his Stetson nearly in half while he itches to bash through something, maybe the goddamn blackboards that haven't yet been erased of dependent and independent clauses. But at least he can contain his physical urges, if not his voice.

"That's what they're calling her? My Tam? When she can, by God, out-boy the whole pack of them! I'd like to see any one of them hotshot football players handle a green horse like she does! Or a lariat! Or mend a bob wire fence or stack hay bales or—"

Mrs. Eckles makes calming motions with her hands. "Mr. Bowen, please, can't you see that what you've just described Tam doing, what she knows how to do—"

Hube paces back and forth across her classroom, in front of the empty student desks. From listing Tam's daily chores, he recounts older grievances. "And what the hell did Marjorie or Suze Simmons, damn her, expect me to do? Left on my own with a baby girl? I did what I knew how to do, I raised her the way I was raised."

"Please! Mr. Bowen! *Hube!* Let's please talk this through calmly. How old was Tam when her mother left?"

At least that stops Hube's outburst. He stops pacing to think back. "She was two—maybe two and a half—I don't think she

41

remembers her mother at all. I took care of her, did everything she needed done for her." His face softens, then hardens again. "And that goddamn Suze Simmons telling me I didn't know she was a girl."

"You taught Tam well."

"I taught her what I know."

"You taught her to believe she can complete any task that's set before her. And now she's sitting for the Patrick Adams scholarship, a full ride through the University of Montana."

"Yeah. And I'm damned proud of her. I always knew she was bright as day."

Mrs. Eckles smiles at Hube, and Hube feels better than he has in days.

"Ma'am, have you got a name, I mean besides Eckles?" he asks and surprises himself by the huskiness in his own voice.

"It's Helen."

With the cabin clean, her bed freshly made up in the room that once was Hube's, and her books unpacked and shelved, Tam can't think of another pressing chore, so she takes the Keats paperback and, locking the front door behind her even though she feels foolish doing it, follows the track toward the spring. The sun warms her hair, and she tosses it back over her shoulders. The air in the meadow barely stirs, although the muted roar of wind surfing the ridge pines never stills. As if through transparent layers of the many times she has walked along this track, she sees the grasses of summer bending with seed heads, the aspen grove spreading out its shoots, the arc of blue above her with its elusive white puffs of clouds that seem not to move but drift like time itself beyond the trees.

Her own mind drifts. Allen. Rob. How many years since she's seen either of them? Last May 3 was Rob's thirty-third birthday—she supposes he has grown, filled out. Would she even recognize the scrawny fifteen-year-old if she passed him in the street?

Would Rob recognize Tam, with her hair grown out, after eighteen years?

A therapist she'd visited sporadically in Portland had suggested that she write Rob a letter. What would you say to him, the therapist had asked, and Tam had shaken her head. What was there to say to a son who wished she were dead?

Rob's hate-filled letter to her . . .

When she comes to the sandstone outcropping where the track bends above the spring, Tam sits on a warm boulder and looks down through dancing sunspots at the pool and its spill into the creek. Peels back a layer of memory to see children playing in the water. Peels back another to see herself and Allen Heckman nude and knee-deep in the water.

Had it happened, herself and Allen skinny-dipping in the pool? Seems un-Allen-like when she considers it. Un-Tam-like, for that matter. Maybe what she's seeing is her own wishful thinking. The way Tam and Allen should have been. Their innocence.

Then she blinks to see through the sunspots, because yes, there really are two figures beside the pool, and she hears their fervent voices, although their words are indistinct. To lessen the dazzle, Tam stands from her boulder, shades her eyes, and steps into the shade of aspens.

It's Calvin and Vay, and they aren't nude but fully dressed, as though for riding, in shirts and boots and blue jeans. Vay interrupts her sobbing to spew an angry stream of words, while Calvin appears to be trying to soothe her, trying to take her in his arms. She flings away from him angrily and runs along the pool and out of sight in the trees, and he throws up both hands before running after her.

A lovers' quarrel? They are the right age, after all, for dramatic world-coming-to-an-end confrontations. And here is Tam, an elderly voyeur, observing them unseen. Embarrassed for herself, Tam returns to sit on her boulder just as Vay bursts over the crest of the track with Calvin right behind her.

At the sight of Tam, Vay skids to a halt and stares. Calvin nearly rams into her in his haste but manages to stop himself in time.

"Mrs. Bowen," he says, blushing.

"Calvin," Tam says. "And Vay."

Vay, with her hair tangled and her face swollen and tear streaked. Calvin, looking from her to Tam.

"Is there anything I can help you with?" Tam offers, not expecting an answer but hoping to give the kids a moment of grace they can use to withdraw from her inspection.

But no.

"It's terrible!" sobs Vay. "I can't bear it!"

"Her dad's going to sell her horse," says Calvin.

A bird complains from far away; a lazy air current shakes the aspen leaves and dapples the grass with sunlight and shadow. "The black thoroughbred?" Tam ventures.

Vay nods, a child's nod that catches at Tam. Where have the grown-ups gone from the Sun Creek country?

"The mare won't let Vay ride her," explains Calvin, his voice also on the verge of a wobble, although he's trying hard to be the man. "Vay's dad says, No point in feeding a horse that can't be ridden."

Just what Hube would have said. But Tam thinks of a moment a week ago on a verge where she had parked her car and smelled grass and pine needles and listened to the thousand voices of the creek and heard the sounds of hoofbeats on the county road. The girl on the expensive black thoroughbred, the boy on the crossbred brown gelding, tearing along too fast on gravel.

"But I've seen you ride her!"

Calvin hesitates. "Along the road? When we were racing each other over the Sun Creek bridge?"

"But that was the day I got her!" bursts Vay. "The breeder delivered her, and she was so beautiful when she backed out of the trailer and looked around at us, and she seemed so gentle! And Calvin showed me how to bridle and saddle her, and I just loved her! And she came with a lot of names, and I just picked the one I liked best. Fancy!"

With the name Vay breaks down again, tries to go on and can't. "But—but—"

"What happened," Calvin explains, "it'd been a great day. Vay was so happy, and she and Fancy outraced me and Buddy, and—anyway, the next day we were riding home and talking—James, natch, always knows best, says we probably weren't paying attention—and something flew up in front of us, and both horses spooked, and Vay fell off."

Tam could tell the rest of the story herself. The frightened girl, taking a spill she hadn't expected, bruised and scraped at the very least. The frightened young mare, finding herself on unfamiliar terrain, quivering and snorting.

"I caught Fancy," says Calvin, "but she didn't like me much, and she wouldn't let Vay near her. I had to take Vay up behind me on Buddy and lead Fancy home."

Tam sighs. "Where did you learn to ride, Vay?"

"At a stables. And Dad says—says I have to ride her or else—and I *can't* ride her. I can't even get *near* her."

"Does your dad ride?"

"Oh, no. He doesn't even *like* horses."

Somewhere in time Hube is shaking his head. Tam wonders again about the grown-ups of the Sun Creek country. "Would you like me to take a look at her?" she hears herself say.

6

Tam at fifteen is small but strong, and she's been breaking horses with Hube since she was eight. This three-year-old mare is a line-backed buckskin with wide frightened eyes that roll and show their whites. She cringes when the saddle hits her back. Snorting, she sidesteps, but Tam has caught the cinch, and she buckles and tightens it under the mare's belly. She leads her a few steps, shakes the saddle to make it rattle again, and then leads the mare across the corral where Hube waits on his big roan gelding, Sandy.

Now she hands the mare's halter rope up to Hube, who takes a couple of dallies with it around his saddle horn and watches as Tam lays the bridle reins across the buckskin mare's neck, finds the stirrup with the toe of her left boot, grips the saddle horn with both her hands, and swings astride in one quick motion.

Panicking at the unfamiliar weight on her back, the mare crashes into Hube's gelding, but Sandy stands his ground with a mere laying back of his ears. He's used to snubbing green horses. Hube nudges him with his spurs, and Sandy moves out and circles the corral, drawing the mare with him. She's already halterbroken, having been tied every day for a week to the post in the middle of the corral and learning she can't fight the post and win. Learning, too, that she can't fight the rope if she wants to be led to the water tank twice a day. No, she can't fight the rope, but she doesn't have to like it, and she trembles in fear and revulsion with every step she takes in tandem with Sandy.

Three laps around the corral in the strengthening heat of the sun, the odor of dust and dry pulverized manure rising under the horses' hooves, and Hube cocks an eyebrow at Tam—"Let's do it."

Hube leans from his saddle to unlatch the corral gate and swing it outward as sunlight glints on the gold ring he always wears. He touches Sandy with spurs again and leads Tam and the mare with him to the dirt road that runs past the cabin and soon will fork toward Bunce and Suze Simmons's place. The mare dances against Sandy, gulping the air and tantalized by so much open space ahead, so much promise of freedom from ropes and leather straps and the sweaty stench of humans. But no. She stands no chance.

With plenty of trails to meander around the Sun Creek country, checking on the horizon for any signs of smoke, always fearing the scent of fire in the air they breathe, checking on the grazing in the upper pastures, watching for signs of whitetail deer—fresh venison!—it makes a ride of about an hour. When they reach Bunce's, Hube lets out a *Whoop!* which brings Suze to the door, squinting against the sun. He and Tam tie the horses to the hitching post to drowse in the shade of a diamond willow, and they are welcomed into Suze's kitchen, where Hube drinks coffee and smokes cigarettes at the gateleg oak table and visits with Bunce for maybe an hour, while shy, silent Tam watches the men and Suze hovers with the coffeepot.

Then another hour's ride back home. Plenty of riding for a first saddling. The mare will come home to the corral with a wet saddle blanket. Ride her for a week of wet saddle blankets, and she'll get used to plodding alongside Sandy, and she'll be responding to the bit in her tender mouth. Tam can bridle and mount her without the halter and snub rope under her bridle, and Tam and Hube will ride several turns around the corral with the mare keeping step with Sandy as though she's still snubbed.

Then—like cutting an umbilical cord, Tam will think years later as she ponders the layers of the simile—it'll be time to open the corral gate and ride out on the road.

But on this June morning, the air is cool and sweet. Grasses bow on both sides of the road as Hube and Tam ride past. Stir of air ruffles Hube's dark hair, the same air that lifts Tam's hair, which was blonde-white when she was younger and now has deepened almost to the gold-buckskin color of the mare she rides. Her eyes, once blue, have clouded to gray. *You favor your mother way more than you do Hube,* Suze Simmons has told her, and Tam understands without asking that favoring her mother is a bad sign.

Hube never says much when they ride together, no point in telling Tam what she already knows, like don't let your mind drift when you're riding a green horse for the first time. Hube's mind never drifts, as far as Tam can tell. Stetsoned, narrow eyed, steel shouldered, he's got a three days' growth of dark beard, which in the unimaginable future Tam will learn is such a fashion statement that special three-day-growth razors are offered on the market so men can maintain the look.

But all that irony waits years ahead, and in the now, handsome Hube has been letting himself go. After Marjorie moved out, he stopped bothering to shave or clean his teeth or drive all the way to Fort Maginnis to get regular haircuts, and now his dark hair curls around his ears and down his neck.

In the eyes of Tam, who cannot remember her mother, Hube just looks like Hube, and she has always ridden beside him. And yes, she does let her mind drift a bit in the pleasure of riding a green mare through the mountain morning. The turpentine scent of the pines, toast scent of grass seeds beginning to ripen, even the stink of sweating horses or the rich plop of dung into the track as Sandy lifts his tail without breaking his stride, sensations all too familiar for Tam to notice, although the time will come when she will dredge deep and deeper into memory to recover them for the sake of the novel she's writing. For now it's the easy rocking in the saddle, the balancing with her boots in the stirrups, the feel of the mare's muscles working between her legs and under her buttocks, that lures away her thoughts to a boy whose face she has memorized and longs to touch.

A whirring out of the underbrush, a dark something flopping at the side of the road, and the mare startles, hits her snub rope hard, and tries to rear in her panic, and even Sandy wakens from his doze and shies violently sideways, dragging the mare with him. Hube reins in Sandy, growling at him in what Tam will remember one day as alpha male baritone. In the moment Tam's hands are full of her own reins, and she's crooning and calming the frightened mare until the little buckskin stands trembling and blowing rollers through her nose at what, Tam now sees, is—or was, gone now—a timber grouse faking a broken wing and drawing attention from what must be her nest in the hawthorn brush.

"*Hrrmp*," says Hube and gives spur to Sandy, drawing Tam and the mare with him. He's told Tam that horses will spook at the damnedest things. No need to tell her again.

Tam at fifteen has been giving thought to the way Hube has raised her. She feels awkward in the stiff clothes she has to wear to high school in Fort Maginnis; she doesn't know how to do the things the other girls can do—bake and sew in the home economics room, practice dance steps and cartwheels in the gym—or what they talk about when they gather and giggle. What Tam can do sounds outlandish to the other girls. When she gets home and changes into her boots and dirty Levi's, she can rope and halterbreak a colt, saddle a horse and round up the rough string, fire a rifle and bring down a whitetail doe, skin and dress out the doe, hang her carcass, and butcher it as Hube has taught her.

Maybe if she'd been raised by a mother, she would be different. Recently, it has occurred to her that Hube's raising of her was the cause of Marjorie's leaving.

Hube! You ain't gonna put that little girl on that bronc! No! You're gonna get her killed, and I can't stand to watch!

Hell, she's eight years old—she's good for it. She's real good at sticking on a horse.

Bunce's wife, Suze, lately has been showing some of the same disapproval. *Raised you to be a boy, he did. I s'pose it was all he knew how to do. Wasn't right, though.*

Suze is beginning to irritate Tam, although Tam doesn't know exactly why. Suze is still cookie-baking Suze, maybe rounder faced with deeper lines that fan around her eyes and draw furrows down her cheeks, always with her apron tied over her housedress and her short white socks under her laced-up shoes. It's something about the goddamn apron (*goddamn* not a word Tam would ever utter in front of Suze or Bunce or Hube) that rubs Tam the wrong way. Suze, in her apron as she hovers over the men with her coffeepot, Suze making sure their plates are full, wiping her hands on her apron and keeping out of their way, speaking only when spoken to.

Although: Suze has plenty to say to Tam when the menfolk are out of earshot. *Raised you to be a boy! What good is that gonna do you when you grow up and want to get married?*

Although: Suze is plenty capable out-of-doors when she wants to be. She can swing an axe and split kindling as well as Bunce, and Tam has seen her snatch Bunce's .22 rifle from its rack over the door, run outside and draw a bead on the hawk circling over her chicken yard, and bring it down on the wing.

From Tam's laptop journal:

Did I wish I'd been born a boy? Well, yes. In ranch country, even in the 1980s, boys were valued more highly than girls.

A more difficult question. Did I believe I was a boy born in a girl's body? In those days no one I knew, much less myself, had heard of transgenderism, much less gender fluidity. Now I ask myself whether, if I had grown up in different economic circumstances and a different climate of social awareness, I would have had counseling, hormone therapy, even surgery, urged upon me.

But long before I could begin to grapple with such questions, there came the Allen complication.

Tam secretly has loved Allen Heckman since they were children and rode the school bus to Fort Maginnis together. Not that they ever sat near each other. Tam, who lived at the end of the bus route, got on the bus first, and she always chose a rear seat. When the bus stopped at the Heckman gate and the driver jacked open the door, she watched Allen climb the steps and sit midway down the aisle, where he and the other boys punched each other and told secret jokes all the way to town. Allen never looked in Tam's direction.

Sixth grade, seventh grade, and by eighth grade Tam knows every wisp of Allen's blond hair that trails over the tender spot at the nape of his neck. She knows which shirts are his favorites, and she longs to trace his neck and shoulders with her fingertips, to run her fingers down and—oh, daring thought—touch the buttons on his shirt. Touch his belt buckle. She can distinguish the sound of Allen's footsteps from any other boy's when he walks to the pencil sharpener or leaves the classroom to use the bathroom, and thinking about what he's doing in the bathroom makes her squirm in her seat and bury her face in her book. When it's his turn to pass out art supplies, she keeps her eyes cast down. She knows she would die, just die, if anyone guessed what she's fantasizing.

In high school it's even worse because suddenly everyone seems to be keeping secrets Tam can only guess at. The other girls still gather in clutches and giggle, and now they toss glances over their shoulders to see who might be listening or which boy might be paying attention to them. Girls are permitted to wear slacks or jeans to school now—*was always dresses in my day*, Suze sniffs—but the other girls wear blue jeans with sparkles set into the fabric and designer names embroidered on their butts, and they bleach their hair blonde-white and curl it, and all dun-haired Tam can do is walk woodenly from class to class in the school clothes Hube bought her from the J.C. Penney's catalog, keeping her eyes on where she's walking but darting glances when she dares at Allen, several lengths ahead of her and oblivious on his way to class with his books slung under his arm.

Mostly, the kids who ride school buses are ignored by the town kids and most of the teachers, but the town girls flock around Allen, with his good looks and his surprising knowledge of arcane interests that Tam overhears—*Did you watch* Mork and Mindy *last night? Did you watch* The Dukes of Hazzard? *How about that new Bee Gees album?*

Who are these folks? Mork and Mindy? The Dukes of Hazzard? Tam, excluded, watches from the corners and turns to her fantasies to keep her company until she can escape to the school bus and the Sun Creek country.

By the time she's fifteen, the summer Hube sets her astride the linebacked buckskin mare for a first saddling, Tam is running her favorite fantasy over and over in her head like strips of a movie that has no beginning or end. In the fantasy she's riding horseback, maybe the very buckskin mare she's really riding—no, wait! Maybe she's riding another, classier horse, a tall black thoroughbred, when she meets Allen on the trail! Allen's also on horseback, and he glances over his shoulder as he rides past Tam.

Over and over Tam replays that imagined moment. The expression on Allen's face. The way his eyes widen, as though he's seeing not the crop-haired neighboring ranch girl but *her*, Tam, for the first time. The catch in his breath.

Truth is, though, Tam never sees Allen from one end of the summer to the next. He's off doing—what? He's playing baseball, she learns from Hube's conversations with Bunce, and he's playing tennis. Tennis! Hube and Bunce disapprove. In their view a ranch boy belongs on the ranch during the summer, working for his father. If old Heckman keeps spoiling that boy, he'll have nobody to blame but himself when the kid runs wild.

I hear Heckman bought a car for that kid of his to drive, says Bunce. Hube shakes his head.

That fall Allen no longer rides the school bus. He drives himself to school. Tam has to wait for the high school corridors to fill again to get an occasional glimpse of Allen's blond head as they pass on their way to classes. Sometimes, waiting for the school bus, she sees his red car flash past the high school. Sometimes he's giving a few lucky girls a ride. Sometimes she hears a shrill of laughter through an open car window.

Tam's fantasies grow darker. She pines away; she grows ever more pale and thin until Allen weeps at her funeral: *I always loved her. I didn't know she cared.*

But even Tam knows she's being maudlin, which is a new word she's picked off a page in a book. For all her love of make-believe, Tam contains a core inherited from no-nonsense Hube. If Allen can love her only as her head imagines him, her head can give her somewhere else to pour her feelings because one thing Tam always has been good at, besides sticking like a burr to the backs of her father's broncs and keeping their saddle blankets wet, is reading and remembering what she reads—and liking what she reads. Her classmates groan when Mrs. Eckles assigns *Romeo and Juliet*, but Tam has already been to Montague and Capulet country.

The fall that Tam begins her senior year, Mrs. Eckles asks her to stay after class, but Tam is edgy, hoping as usual to get a glimpse of Allen as he dumps his books in his locker and heads for the exits or as he flashes past the school bus stop in his red car. She hardly takes in what Mrs. Eckles is telling her. That Mrs. Eckles is nominating Tam to sit for the Adams scholarship.

7

Vay's mare stands, saddled and bridled, her reins dragging on corral dirt. Her eyes show faint lines of white, her ears flick back and forth, her breath rattles as Tam approaches her.

"Stand still, you damned hellbitch."

"Watch out, she'll bite!" shrills Vay from the corral fence, and the mare takes a step backward and tosses her head, making her bridle chains jingle and the reins sweep the corral dirt.

"You keep quiet," Tam snaps at Vay over her shoulder while not taking her eyes off the mare. "Whoa, damn you."

Tam watches the mare for a long minute without making a move toward her, and the mare watches Tam.

"Whoa. Whoa."

The mare's ears flicker. It doesn't matter that she's never been taught what *whoa* means, because what she's picking up on is Tam's best approximation of Hube's alpha male baritone, and what she's sensing is the dominant human ordering her into submission. Curious, really. She weighs perhaps twelve or thirteen times what Tam weighs, and—fight or flight—she easily could outrun Tam, jump over the corral fence or at least try to crash through its ancient posts and poles, or she could bare her teeth and charge with striking hooves, as a feral horse might.

But. With domestication comes submission. Tam takes another slow deliberate step, growling *Whoa, Whoa*, and the mare wants to retreat, but her rump is pressed against the corral poles, she can't back up any farther, and her only option is to dive to one side of Tam or the other. Her eyes move back and forth, measuring her chances, but it's too late, Tam has caught her bridle reins.

Desperate, the mare bares her teeth for Tam's arm with a snake-like lunge of her head and neck, but Tam simultaneously jerks the bridle reins, digging the bit into the mare's tender mouth, and meets her lunge with a side-hand blow to her nostrils.

"What do you think you are? Goddamn it, Hellbitch, behave yourself."

Quivering, the mare shrinks back, but she can't withstand the bite of the bit, and Tam has looped the reins around her neck and found the stirrup with the toe of her sneaker and gripped the saddle horn with both hands, and she swings astride. The mare side-steps under Tam's weight and rolls her eyes to try to see her, but Tam, wishing she was wearing boots with spurs instead of sneakers, wishing she didn't look ridiculous in jeans and a blue T-shirt, drives both heels into the mare's sides until the mare takes a tentative step and then another and another into obedience. Somewhere in the dim spaces of time, Hube's ghost watches and nods.

Tam reins the mare in a tight circle, then in a widening circle, then thumps her with sneaker heels to bring her to a trot twice around the corral before reining her to a halt. She blows Hube a kiss in the direction his ghost is fading and looks up to see that James has joined Calvin and Vay to lean on his arms on the top corral pole and watch the show, and she feels a jolt at his unexpected presence.

"Wow," says Calvin, after a long pause, through which a ripple of air current rustles the cottonwood leaves that overhang the house and gathers force to answer the roar of the ridge pines along the horizon.

"Can I ride Fancy now?" calls Vay.

Tam nudges the mare with her heels and rides up to them—clueless Vay, Calvin with his mouth hanging open, and James emerging from whatever distant place he keeps himself and looking almost as amazed as his brother does. Tam stifles another spark, which the tension between her knees tells her the mare also has felt, and warns herself to keep her attention where it belongs.

"Vay," she says. "Here's how it is. As long as you're afraid of her, you won't be able to ride her. If you're going to ride her, you have to show her who's boss."

She pauses, thinks about the words she's just spoken.

"How'd you learn to do that?" says Calvin. With his rumpled hair and wide eyes, he looks so young, so new hatched and innocent of the lines in his brother's face.

"My dad taught me."

"Could I learn to do it? Learn to talk to a horse like that? And ride her?"

"Probably. If you want to do it badly enough."

Tam dismounts, and Vay scrambles through the corral poles but stops in her tracks when the mare lays back her ears and blows rollers through her nose.

"Oh, Fancy!"

"Hellbitch! Behave yourself." Tam catches the bridle reins before the mare can back away. "Vay, she knows you're spooked of her, and that's spooking her. Tell you what. I'll give her a long ride this afternoon and wear her out, and then you can ride her around the corral and see if you can't get the feel of each other. And we'll take it like that for a few days."

"We don't *have* a few days! Dad's taking me to Los Angeles tomorrow, and when we get back next week, I have to be able to ride her!"

She thrusts out her lip, but Tam shrugs.

Vay stalls a moment, but what can she do? "Oh, all right," she mutters and flounces back to slip through the corral poles, where she catches Calvin by the hand and drags at him. Calvin pulls back.

"Will you teach me?" he asks Tam.

James watches, expressionless, with his arms crossed on the top corral rail and his chin resting on his arms. And Calvin, eager eyed. Fifteen years old.

Rob at fifteen, Rob at five years old, Rob as a newborn, folded into her arms. Rob had no interest in horses—but when had he been given the opportunity? When he learned to toddle in the upstairs apartment in Missoula during Tam's university years, when he learned to skateboard on Portland sidewalks after the advances for her books grew substantial enough that she could afford the bungalow? When his grandfather Hube was a stranger to him, whom he met three or four times in his life?

So you went back to Warren after all, Rob had written on a page crumpled and smoothed again. Stains blurring the ink. *The only thing that would give me peace would be to know that you're dead.*

Tam forces her thoughts back to the sun-warmed corral. The mare between her legs. The two children waiting for her answer. James with his arms crossed on the top corral pole.

What would be required of her to teach horsemanship to Calvin? Getting him a colt no more than green broken, maybe just halter broken. Setting Calvin astride and snubbing for him in the corral, maybe with herself riding reliable old Buddy. After a few days, opening the corral gate. Riding for long wet saddle blanket hours on mountain trails. Somewhere Hube is nodding. *Best thing I ever did was teach you to ride.* When had Hube said that?

No. Recalls her plans for this final summer. Turns to tell Calvin no.

Calvin's young face. Rob's young face.

"Maybe I can," she says, and Calvin's face lights up before Vay drags him away.

Hot sun beating down on the corral, wind roaring through the distant pines. Tam with her gaze fixed on the middle distance, although she feels James's eyes on her as the mare begins to drowse at her shoulder. The moment stretching until James speaks.

"Bunce used to talk about your dad."

Their eyes meet.

"They were good friends," she says and looks away.

"Bunce said he was the best hand with a horse he ever knew."

Tam shrugs. "He was a breaker of horses. It was what he did."

"Breaker of horses," James repeats, and Tam realizes the words resonate for him in ways she doesn't understand. Before she can reply, he's gone back to his distant place to ruminate on untold matters. At Tam's shoulder the mare rouses, nudges Tam with her nose until Tam turns absently and fondles her.

James returns from his thoughts. "Those damned kids are off who knows where for how long. Come up to the house, and I'll make you lunch, Tam. There's nothing I'm working on that can't wait. I'll ride with you this afternoon if you can stand my bad company."

Handsome Hube has taken some pains with himself on this late afternoon in January 1986. A shave, clean fingernails, a pair of Levi's new enough not to have faded in the wash. He wants to make a good impression for Tam's sake, but damn if he isn't the one having trouble keeping his mind on what he's doing, which is driving on ice down the county road toward Fort Maginnis. And damn if he doesn't know where the blame lies, and it's not, by God, on Tam. At his spurt of anger, the pickup wobbles dangerously, and it takes all Hube's attention to keep from sliding into the ditch.

In Fort Maginnis the city crews have sanded the streets, and Hube can let his anger simmer closer to the surface, but he's concentrating on keeping a lid on it as he parks in the lot back of the high school and walks around to the big double doors on Juneaux Street and opens them on mostly silent corridors and removes his hat.

About four o'clock, Mrs. Eckles had written in her note, *after classes are dismissed for the day.* Hube hears the sound of his own bootheels on the composite floor and the faint hiss of warm air through the ceiling vents. He feels conspicuous in his sheepskin coat and Levi's and boots and knows he's sure the hell out of his element here.

Mrs. Eckles's room is on the second floor, so Hube climbs the stairs as far as the landing, with its big window, where he pauses to gaze at the distant blue outline of the Snowy Mountains and steel himself with thoughts of the Sun Creek country. Nothing to be done, though, but cowboy up and face the situation, so he climbs the next flight of stairs and finds the door numbered 212 and knocks.

Mrs. Eckles, Helen—although he's never been brave enough to call her that, even though they've had coffee together a time or two—answers the door.

"Hube," she says.

Hube thinks she looks calm and composed, considering everything. She's in her fifties and a little overweight, with curly reddish hair and brown-rimmed glasses. Over her shoulder Hube sees Tam sitting at a desk with her head down and her eyes fixed on her clenched fists. His Tam.

"Come in, Hube. Please have a seat."

Mrs. Eckles indicates one of the front-row student desks, next to Tam, and Hube sits, feeling awkward with his Stetson in his hands. Mrs. Eckles pulls up her own chair to form a small triangle of father, daughter, and English teacher. Hube doesn't dare look at Tam, so he looks first at the gold wedding ring on his finger but gets no answer and then looks at the electric clock on the wall above the teacher's desk as its second hand makes its inexorable slow sweep. It hasn't quite reached the top of the hour when Mrs. Eckles speaks.

"Tam tells me she hasn't seen a doctor, but she thinks she's due in early May."

Hube gives the barest of nods. It's all he can bring himself to do. His world has exploded out of shape and gotten colder in the last twenty-four hours. Ever since. His Tam. Told him.

"Mr. Bowen," says Mrs. Eckles, and Hube looks up and sees the red-haired woman as substantial and unmoving as the boulders of the Sun Creek country. "Mr. Bowen, Tam has the Patrick Adams scholarship, and she has too good a mind to waste. And you and I are going to see that she gets to use it."

During the past summer, Tam's life seemed to have swapped ends like an ornery bronc doubling back on his own tracks in spite of his rider's spurs, except that wherever Tam's runaway life swapped ends toward, it wasn't back down its own tracks.

The second week of June of that year: glorious! Sunlight over the Sun Creek country, crystal water spilling under the bridge, and new Hereford calves staring with unblemished white faces as Hube and Tam skirted their pasture on horseback. Tam wasn't riding the linebacked buckskin mare that summer because the buckskin mare had been sold, and Tam came close to tears to see her loaded into the stock rack on a truck belonging to a rancher over in eastern Montana who needed a good gentle chore horse his kids could ride. The rancher had paid Hube good money for the mare after he watched Tam ride her and show how well she handled.

Tam didn't let her tears fall over the buckskin mare. Crying wasn't something ranch kids did. *You can't cry over every little thing.* No, Tam sucked up her tears, but she did write a poem about the mare. Writing poetry was another place she'd found to pour her feelings.

She had a lightning stripe down one foreleg,
her belly was fawn-stippled, her eyes were flecked,
hazel, liquid, and sad in the depths.
She could never stand to be petted.
She was never really my horse,
But I have never had any other.

No, that summer Tam was riding a slab-sided three-year-old bay gelding Hube picked up cheap and thought he could make into a cutting horse. He snubbed Tam and the gelding for several rides, rode beside them several times without the halter and sub rope, and then told Tam she might as well ride on her own now. Told her she'd be all right on the gelding as long as she kept her mind on what she was doing.

So here was Tam, riding the bay gelding across the Sun Creek bridge, listening to the sound of mountain water and the slab-sided gelding's hooves on the bridge planks, and this June turned out to be glorious because, except for the beautiful thoroughbred horse part of it, Tam's fantasy came true and left her breathless.

Allen, riding toward her with sunlight in his hair. Had she conjured him?

He looked sulky, although he showed some interest when he saw Tam. "Where're you headed?" he asked.

"Nowhere in particular," Tam said, trying to keep her voice light. She touched the gelding's mane and reined him in from the interest he was taking in Allen's mare. "Just keeping his saddle blanket wet."

From Allen's blank look, it was clear that *wet saddle blanket* was a concept he'd never had to consider. On the other hand, Tam was a girl his own age. He reined his mare to ride beside her along the verge of the graveled county road.

"Nowhere in particular is where I'm headed too," he said. "Might as well have company on the way."

Tam heard the complaint in his voice, something next to miserable—*Allen, miserable?*—but for Tam the grasses of late June, dappled with white starflowers, the mountain chokecherries bending with clusters of green fruit, the fragrant junipers spreading their needles over the slope above the road, took on their own radiance. Never had the world seemed so present to her, never had the immediate moment seemed to shine and dance around her.

8

The forks and bends of the ridge trail remind Tam how well she once knew her way along it. She couldn't have drawn a map of the trail while sitting in her study in Portland, but now, in the resin-scented air and the unhurried rhythm of hoofbeats, her hands remember which way to rein the mare and where the bend will lead. It's a form of imprinting, Tam supposes, of a once-familiar landscape on her body.

The trail climbs above the Heckman—Warceski—ranch buildings, follows the crest of the ridge past Zenith's place, and continues until it will circle to overlook Bunce Simmons's house and barns and corrals. Long ago Tam rode this trail with Hube on their way to visit Bunce and Suze and later with Allen Heckman, during the summer that only seemed to be golden. Now she rides the Hellbitch with James Warceski following on Buddy, like an awkward parody of young Calvin and Vay.

James breaks a long silence. "Do you think Vay will ever be able to ride that mare?"

Tam glances back at him. James is not a natural born-in-the-saddle rider, no Hube of course, but he sits the gelding with an athlete's ease, although Calvin's stirrups are a bit too short for him. She allows herself to admit he's attractive, although his bare head jars her. A ranchman without a hat? Of course, James with his mysterious computer room is no ranchman, whatever else he is.

She has to answer him. "Vay? It's doubtful. She'll have to get over her fear, and that's a hard thing for anybody to do."

"To get over what you fear," says James, and Tam has the sense that he and she are having two separate, perhaps parallel, conversations that she must not allow to converge.

And yet she hears herself ask the question. "What do you fear, James?"

The trail has widened enough for him to ride up beside her, and she catches his naked gaze on her. What has happened to his containment?

"Bunce talked so much about you," he says. "He was so glad Hube Bowen's daughter was coming back to the Sun Creek country."

They ride perhaps another fifty yards in silence and come to a grassy clearing in the pines where a fortress of sandstone boulders juts through the thin mountain soil to overlook the Sun Creek ravine.

"Let's pause awhile," says James. "I don't do my best talking on horseback."

Talking? Over that first lunch in his kitchen, four days ago— canned tomato soup and BLT sandwiches, heavy on the lettuce and tomato, with whole wheat bread—James had been courteous, holding her chair for her and pouring coffee, but careful, too careful, not to make eye contact. Tam, stiff and uneasy herself. What had they talked about? Tam cannot remember a single word.

The next afternoon she hadn't known what to expect when she hiked around the spring to the old Heckman corral, but there was James, saddling horses. As he was the next day and again today.

Now she and James tie the horses to pine boughs and hike fifty feet down through patches of sun and shade to the outcropping of boulders. The air is balmy, with a promise of July deepening ahead and the hitherto silent James actually planning to speak.

It takes him some time. He sits on the boulder with his elbows on his knees and his shirt stretched taut across his shoulders, looking off through the scattered pines to the grove of aspens that hide the creek. The McIntosh roof—well, Zenith's roof—just shows above the aspens on the other side of the current. Bunce and Suze's place out of sight, a mile farther along. Creek sounds, small sounds from the underbrush, the omnipresent surge of wind in the ridge pines. Her own awareness of James's chiseled face, his muscled body.

Suze's words. *He's a terrible man.*

No. Tam doesn't think James is planning to kill her. She'd hardly be riding with him on a remote mountain trail if she thought so. And whatever Suze thinks, Tam doesn't believe he killed Bunce. What Tam does feel is the tension between her and James, as white with electricity as the moment before lightning strikes.

Get over it, she warns herself. *You're past all that. Whatever is on his mind is not your aging body.*

But whatever James's mind is on, Tam is not so far *past it* that she hasn't begun to recognize her own responses. How long has she done without? Since Warren. Warren, who had been the beginning of the end with Rob. The beginning and, she guesses, the end.

"Oh, hell," says James. "He's a worse pain in the butt than ever with Vay gone. I sometimes think that boy's going to be the death of me."

"Calvin?"

"Yeah. I tell myself he's basically a good kid—"

"He's just being fifteen."

"—and if he isn't, that's my fault. I've had the raising of him since he was five."

So this is going to be about Calvin. Tam breathes a sigh of what—relief, she tells herself—and waits while the wind argues with the pines above and behind them.

"Car wreck. Killed our dad. Killed Calvin's mom. She was younger, a second marriage for him. My mom's still alive. She lives in Pasadena."

So James and Calvin are half-brothers. "You two look so much alike."

He nods. "Everybody says so. I was twenty-seven at the time of the wreck, and Calvin—well, he was a little boy with a big brother, and that was how it was for a while. Until it got to where I had to say no sometimes and *Here's how it's gonna be* and *Because I said so.*"

Another pause. "A couple reasons why I moved out here with him. One, it was getting to where Southern California wasn't where Calvin needed to grow up. Too much—oh, hell. I got out a road atlas and virtually stuck a pin in the map of Montana. There's a country song, can't remember its name—*set me down, somewhere in the middle of Mon-ta-na*—maybe it inspired me. But I—hell, I didn't mean to get started on Calvin."

James studies his own clenched fists while Tam waits. The murmur of pines overhead. The—*burst of semiautomatic firing*—

The silence after the burst of gunfire transports Tam into an insubstantial realm where time doesn't count and *now* is where she is, facedown and struggling for breath through crushed grass and layers of earth, with James's weight on top of her. She can hear the horses higher up the hill, frightened at the gunfire, neighing and jerking at their tied reins.

"Zenith, what in hell are you thinking!" James shouts. "It's me and Tam Bowen up here, for Chrissake!"

A scuffling sound, James shifts himself off her, and Tam raises her face from the grass to see bobble-headed Zenith, his blue jeans wet to the knees from wading the creek, with Spotty crawling out of the current behind him to shake water from his red-spotted fur. Zenith carries his rifle pointed at the ground, looking sheepish.

"Sorry 'bout that, James."

James rounds on him, furious. "Zenith, what are you going to do if you actually shoot somebody one of these days?"

"Oh hell, James, I don't shoot to kill."

Tam stifles the giggle that wants to burst at the contrast between the words, remembered from some morning program on Bunce's and Suze's television she watched as a child—*don't shoot to kill!* or was it *shoot to kill?*—and Zenith's untroubled face in its white puffery of curls as Spotty shakes another shower of creek water over James and Tam and then sits down at Zenith's heels, looking profound.

"Damn it, Zenith! Those rounds of bullets you fire have to fall somewhere! Have you ever thought of that? You could kill somebody who isn't even in sight! And if it's Ed Evenson you're worried about, don't be. He took Vay with him to Los Angeles for a week or two, and Calvin's been moping around the place like a lovesick calf."

"Wondered why I saw her horse up here. No, I'm not worried about Evenson. Worst he does is complain. No, it's those two fellers from the old Simmons place, prowling around here, that I don't like the looks of."

Tam's heart twists. Allen and Rob.

"Doesn't mean you can go around shooting over their heads," James begins. Then he hisses, "Hush!"

He has flattened himself over Tam again as Zenith, looking bewildered, sinks to his knees.

Gurgle of creek current, soft sough of wind through pine needles. Tam feels the grit of dust on her face and the tickle of grass fronds before she hears the voices from the trail above. Spotty, too, has stiffened into alert, his ears at the sharp.

"—you see where he went?"

"No."

"The son of a bitch. Whose horses, do you think?"

"Warceski's probably. The bastard. Hey, bet you can't hit that magpie on the branch over there."

A cracking shot, then silence.

The moment lengthens. Still nothing from above, then the voices fading farther up the trail and indistinct. James eases himself off Tam.

"You all right?"

"Y-yes." Tam sits up. She brushes dirt and broken grass off her shirt and sees a bruise from the chunk of sandstone that had been digging into her arm. Her mind tells her it ought to hurt, but she can't feel it. What she feels is the absence of James's weight and warmth and cold damp patches where Spotty shook his coat, wet from the creek, on her.

"Oh hell, I've hurt you."

"Where's Zenith?"

They both look down the slope at empty grass and shale and the glint of creek current.

"He must have cleared out. Are you ready to ride home?"

"Yes."

Tam feels numb, wonders if she is in shock from the succession of events: Zenith and his automatic rifle fire, James pinning her to earth, the frightened horses and the voices from the trail that were Allen's and Rob's. She's so shaken that she isn't sure she remembers how to mount a horse, but her hands untie the Hellbitch's reins from their branch, loop them over the mare's neck, find the stirrup, and prompt her to swing astride. James spurs Buddy to ride beside her in silence. Apparently, her conversation with James is over, but she's too drained to care.

The roof of James's house comes in sight as the trail descends and the timber thins. Tam is just aware she's in the saddle, she's riding the Hellbitch, and she ought to keep her mind on the Hellbitch, but the Hellbitch isn't behaving like the Hellbitch. No, the Hellbitch is easing along as though, with a horse's uncanny empathy for human distress and strange attachment to the human who has dominated her, the Hellbitch is being careful of Tam. When Tam glances at James, she sees that he has ridden up beside her and he, too, is being careful of Tam.

At the corral gate, the Hellbitch stops of her own accord, and Tam starts to dismount and finds James at her side, steadying her.

"Have to unsaddle her," she manages.

"I'll unsaddle her," says James, "and then I'm going to take you home."

He's walking her to his pickup, opening the door of the cab, and helping her step up to the high step to the seat. He cracks a window, hands her a bottle of water, and closes the pickup door on her.

Left alone, Tam fumbles the cap off the bottle and sips water that is warm and stale but unexpectedly life restoring. She drinks half the water, screws back the cap, and leans back in the warm leather seat, feeling more herself but drowsy now. And damn, damn. Allen and Rob. The sounds of their voices.

"I'm going to be stuck out here all summer," complained Allen. "The old man's having a meltdown over my wreck. It was an accident, I tried to tell him, but he's cutting up like I did it on purpose!"

"Wreck?" said Tam, alarmed, her dancing moment in stasis. "*Car* wreck?"

"Okay, maybe I took that corner a little too fast on gravel, but how was I to know—it was just bad luck, and it wasn't like the old man didn't have insurance on it. So just to be an asshole, he won't replace it, plus he's keeping me out here on the ranch all summer where I can't see Shannon or play ball or—"

Tam hardly heard the list of Allen's grievances because her moment lit on just two of his words and shimmered. *All summer.* She would have him *all summer.*

Summer, however, has a way of coming to an end.

"I don't want to hear about it! It's nothing to do with me! You're a big girl, and you knew what you were doing, Tam Bowen! Boy-girl! The only reason I fucked you was because you were all that was available! It's not my fault you got yourself knocked up!"

Tam opens her eyes when James's truck stops in front of her cabin. She realizes she must have slept for a few minutes, lulled like a child by the truck's motion, as James comes around to open the passenger side door for her. When he reaches to lift her down, she's too limp to resist.

"Can you walk?"

"I think so."

But she stumbles, and James catches her arm. "Careful—have you got your key?"

She nods and pulls out the key on a chain she's been wearing around her neck. Waits in late sunlight and the odor of roasting grass heads while James unlocks the door and opens it. And there is her big room, although she sees it as though for the first time, log walls and tongue-and-groove ceiling, river rock fireplace and her unpacked crates of books, because James is holding her, which he seems to realize because he guides her to a futon and sits her down.

"When did you eat last?"

Tam shakes her head—she can't remember. James studies her for a minute, then disappears into the kitchen, where she hears him rummaging. She feels the absence of his arm around her, the lost warmth of his body against hers, even as she hears a clink of plate and bowl, a hum of microwave. Shakes her head again, trying to clear it—is she disoriented, is she in some kind of fugue where she's never been before?

Well, yes, she has. Twice before. When she was seventeen and Allen cursed her. When she was thirty-two and Rob cursed her. Now—a punishment? For being alive?

James returns from the kitchen with a tray. Sits beside her on the futon. "Am I going to have to spoon this into you?"

"N-no."

She takes the bowl, manages the spoon. It's chicken noodle soup from a can, but it's hot and it tastes good. She feels almost herself now that she understands her shock at their voices, understands how the past is linked with the present, and she finishes the soup and looks up to find James's worried eyes on her. One unrehearsed action after another: she reaches to brush back the lock of hair that has fallen over his forehead—what has become of the soup bowl—just as he folds her in his arms and she buries her face in his neck, drinking in the faint sweat odor of his skin as he nuzzles her face, finding her mouth, and she is hungry for him, eager to open for his tongue that traces her lips, asking for her, and no room for thought here, just the perfection of holding and being held until James pulls back.

"No."

She stares at him. He's holding her almost at arm's length now, his eyes searching her face and his mouth slack and vulnerable.

"Not now," he whispers. "Not when you're like this. I was afraid you were going into shock. What happened to you back there? You're not afraid of Zenith, are you?"

"N-no." What to tell James, when she's only known him for a few weeks, when they've never really talked, when she's been lusting after him like a dirty old woman? Even now she's seeing the clean lines of his face, the cluster of dark hair at the open neck of his shirt, remembering the weight of him on her body. Damn it, wanting him to pull her back in his arms again.

"Not Zenith. Just—they took me by surprise, was all."

"Who? Heckman and his son? You know them?"

"I used to. And I wouldn't have come back to Sun Creek if I'd known they'd be here. Maybe Bunce told them I was coming."

James studies her, nods. "That's right, they used to live on my ranch, they told me. They made some noise about it, wanting it back. But Bunce never mentioned them, and as far as I know, they just showed up this winter, staying in town and driving around the back roads. Then Bunce was killed, and Zenith thinks they sweet-talked Suze into letting them move in. Damn it, Zenith's going to get himself in a world of hurt if he doesn't stop his snooping."

He paces from one uncurtained window to another, where the afternoon is softening into twilight, and seems to be counting the tips of the ridge pines. "Wish the hell you'd get some blinds for these windows," he mutters and turns to face her. "I don't like leaving you alone up here, not when you're so unsteady. Maybe I should take you back home with me, and you can sleep in Calvin's room, and he can bunk with me."

"No. I'm all right." Tam rises from the futon, takes two or three steps to show him her balance. "And what just happened—won't happen again," she adds and is startled to see him wince as though she had slapped him.

9

Calvin crouches in the shrubbery outside Vay's window. He's had a long hike in the dark, around the spring and past Mrs. Bowen's cabin, down her track to the bridge, and then along the county road until he could slip under the EVENSON sign that hung from its chains overhead and creaked faintly in the currents of night air. Calvin's breathing is rapid. He hadn't wanted to take the chance of waking James by saddling Buddy and leading him, clip-clop, out of the stable. And then, of course, there would have been the ride home, past the house and waking James for sure.

He had been so sure, somehow, that his handful of rattling gravel on her window would bring Vay from her bed to slide over the windowsill in her bare feet and the limp cotton tee she slept in. With the thought of that tee and his own hands exploring the girl-flesh below it, the forbidden warmth of the folds so different from his own troubling, swelling parts, Calvin feels the stir against his zipper, the insistence on space inside the tight denim of his jeans, and he reaches down to ease himself even as the sounds of the night disturb him. Rustle of leaves in the cottonwoods overhead, the cry of some animal from farther up Sun Creek. *We see him! We've got him!*

Here in the shadows of the familiar, Calvin gradually realizes that something profound has changed about the Evenson house, the barns, the fenced paddocks, and the sheds. Too quiet, too still. Too acquiescent to the sounds from the unspeaking wind, the inarticulate hoots and barks from the hills. Because no shadows fall from vehicles that ought to be parked in the driveway, in the road. Even the little caretaker's house behind the main cabin is locked and still. And Vay has not answered their private signal.

73

In her window hangs a pale square of paper. Something is written on the paper, but he can't read it in the dark, and the paper is taped to the inside of the window, facing out. Break into the house somehow—break the window—Calvin feels his fist fold around a good-sized rock in the flower border. But no, trouble, and not just from James and the law that might get involved. Calvin knows all about that kind of trouble. It's the night cries, the warnings he hears from the dark, that pry his fingers from the rock.

"What has Murray County come to?" Tam screams at an astonished Libarriby Sibidibel.

"Tam!" Larry, whose mouth fell open when she burst into his office, now rises from behind his desk and starts to take her by her arms but thinks better of it. "Can you calm down enough to tell me what's happened?"

"I'm supposed to calm down? When I can't ride horseback through the Sun Creek country without being shot at? Or nearly being caught in the middle of a shoot-out? Has everyone gone crazy?"

Larry starts to interrupt, but the very sight of him further enrages Tam. Larry, with his freckles and his paunch, in his sharply pressed khaki uniform shirt and pants, his perfectly knotted tie and polished badge, even his orderly desk and sunny office. What can Larry know about anything, when his wife probably does the starching and pressing for him and Nona the receptionist dusts his office and straightens his papers?

"When I rode all over that country as a girl and never *dreamed*—" Her white-knuckled drive down to Fort Maginnis to corner the sheriff in his office had done nothing to soothe her, only pitched her anger higher, but she's running out of words. "Never dreamed of being shot at! And Bunce, Bunce of all people, dead!"

"Sit down, will you? Just sit down? Have you had coffee this morning? No, I didn't think so."

Larry sidles past her, closes the door behind himself, and returns in a moment with two full mugs. He's looking wary, probably thinking *hysterical female*. Tam supposes she's walked right into that convenient niche, just the way she walked into *dirty old woman* last night. She sits in one of the leather armchairs that faces Larry's desk and accepts the mug of coffee he hands her.

"Now can you tell me what happened?"

Tam takes a deep breath. After James left her cabin last night, she topped off his chicken noodle soup with a couple stiff jolts of bourbon and fell into an exhausted sleep, only to wake in darkness at three in the morning with anger fueled from the dregs of leftover emotions. Anger that had flamed hotter until dawn, when she dressed and jumped in her car for the drive to Fort Maginnis. Now she sees concern written large on Larry's face, and she lets her breath out slowly and begins.

The afternoon horseback rides along the ridge trail with James Warceski that had become a pleasant routine, interrupted by the burst of automatic gunfire over their heads and followed by the appearance of Zenith. The voices of Allen and Rob as they searched through the timber for Zenith.

"Allen *Heckman*? He's living up there now? On Bunce's place?" Larry shakes his head. "I never thought he'd come back to the mountains."

Of course. Allen had been a couple of years ahead of Larry and Tam in high school, but Larry would have known him, would have known that the Heckmans and the Bowens were neighbors, would have heard all the rumors. He's looking at Tam now with—what? Sympathy? He's a decent man who once was a nice kid who put up with being called Libarriby Sibidibel by one and all. Still. He'll see Tam through the lens of her past.

Suze: *Tammy Lou was a pretty little thing, but she was just like her mother. No good. She had to leave town.*

Now he scrubs at his face with the back of his hand. "What I can do," he says. "I can drive up to Sun Creek this afternoon and talk to Heckman and talk to Zenith and see if I can figure out what the hell is going on, short of a young war breaking out up there. Maybe talk to Warceski, see what his take is. And then I'll see if I can get any sense out of Suze, though I doubt it."

"Thanks, Larry. Hey, I'm sorry I yelled at you."

"Hell, Tam, I can't say that I blame you." He walks with her as far as his office door, puts a hand on her shoulder. "Maybe you should think about getting a room in town for a while?"

"I'm damned if I'm going to be driven out of my own home."

"Figured you'd say that." He shakes his head again. "The old folks gave you one hell of a hard row to hoe, Tam. One of these days, you want to tell me why you came back?"

The hard blue sky of late morning arches over the rocks and ridge pines when Tam pulls up at her cabin and gets out of her car with her arms full of groceries. At least she can have a decent meal, even if she can't decide what else she should do. Lets herself in the front door and looks at the room where she and James—*stop.* She's embarrassed herself and embarrassed James, but what's done is done. Maybe she'll unpack her books today. Use their crates for bookshelves. Actually move into the cabin instead of camping in it.

Instead, she carries her groceries to the kitchen, stows them, and pours herself a shot of bourbon. Tells herself just one. Returns to sit on a futon and stare out the window at unchanging grass and road tracks and underbrush. Notes a pair of finches winging above a stunted lilac bush. If she hung a bird feeder in the window, she could watch finches for entertainment. Allows herself to think about her promise. Her promise to Vay. To ride her horse. Which means hiking around the spring this afternoon and up the slope to the Heckman corral to grain and groom and saddle the Hellbitch.

What is the worth of that promise, when she's close to certain that Vay never can ride the Hellbitch?

Come off it, Tam. You've never believed Vay could get back on that horse. Not from the first day. You rode the ridge trail on the

Hellbitch that first day because James said he'd ride with you. Now you're trying to weasel out of your promise because you can't decide which would be worse, saddling the Hellbitch and seeing James come out to ride with you or saddling her and not seeing James come out to ride with you.

Tam sighs. Yawns. Between the bourbon and her short and troubled night, she's feeling drowsy. Her unmade bed waits for her. There's no hurry. To ride or not to ride. No hurry at all to decide.

She wakens to hear someone pounding on her door. Good God, she must have slept—what—a couple of hours, judging by the slant of sunlight through the window. And now what? She tosses back the blanket she'd pulled over her and sits, groggy, on the side of her bed.

Pound! Pound! Pound!

"All right!" she shouts. Runs a cupful of water from the bathroom sink, throws it into her face. Wipes her eyes, runs her fingers through her hair, and walks more or less steadily from the bedroom to the front door. Opens it and finds herself staring at Calvin Warceski.

"Will you let me come in, Tam?"

Tam takes a step back and manages a nod as she tucks in her shirt and hopes it's buttoned straight, hopes she doesn't look as though she's been sleeping, hopes her breath doesn't stink of bourbon. Then she takes a closer look at Calvin, at his tangled hair and flushed face. Surely not a bruise forming on his cheek—

"Are you all right, Calvin?"

"No, damn it!" he shouts. "Do I look like I'm all right?"

The boy is trembling with rage, on the verge of tears, and what can Tam do but get a grip and try to soothe him? "Come in. Sit down. I'll get you something to drink." She thinks of her bourbon, which Calvin probably would love, and it probably wouldn't be the first time he's tasted hard liquor, but she shakes her head. "Water is all I can offer you. And then you can tell me what's going on."

Calvin stumbles after her and sinks into one of the futons. He's just the age, she thinks, either to do automatically what an adult tells him to do or to throw a tantrum and do the opposite. She fetches him a glass of water from the kitchen, remembering her tantrum this morning with Libarriby Sibidibel. How surprised Larry would be to see Tam now, playing calm reason to Calvin's outrage.

Calvin looks at the glass she hands him as though he's never seen such a thing, takes a tentative sip and then a longer swallow, while Tam sits opposite him and waits until he sets the glass on the floor and wipes his mouth with the back of his hand.

"Well?"

He glares at her. "I fucking hate being a kid! Nobody listens to me. Nobody cares what I think—" There's more, he's spewing anger, while Tam tries to look as though she's listening to his words and not just hearing the noise he's making.

"—didn't have a single goddamn person in this whole sucking state except Vay, and her old man's got her locked up in Los Angeles probably, because her phone just goes to voice, and now she's never gonna get to keep her horse, the old bastard's going to sell it—I can't even *talk* to her, and fucking James thinks he *owns* me!"

"You and James had a fight?"

Nodding, Calvin raises a tear-streaked face. A snail track of snot bubbles down his upper lip. A purplish blotch definitely is swelling on his cheekbone, and Tam feels a stab of anger that itself rouses a memory she long has tried and failed to suppress. Warren Wetzel collaring the fifteen-year-old Rob, slamming him down on a sofa: *Goddamnit, keep a civil tone when you talk to your mother!* Rob, scrambling out of Warren's grip: *Don't try to tell me what to do, you son of a bitch!*

What had triggered that fight? Building to the blow to the boy's cheek? It takes Tam a moment to wonder if she's thinking of Rob's fight with Warren or Calvin's fight with James.

"He's been in a real foul mood lately. He came home yesterday, and he was in a goddamn sulk. Worse even than he's been over shit I've done, and I've done some, believe me. But I didn't *do* anything yesterday except try to talk to him about horsebreaking, you teaching me how, and that's when he started yelling how I didn't know a goddamn thing and I could shut up about it and keep out of his way."

Tam can find no words.

"I kept out of his way, all right. I ran off into the timber until it got dark and kinda chilly, and I—well. I took a walk. Kind of a long one. Then I snuck back and slept in the horse barn with Buddy. Which is where James found me this morning, when he came to feed the horses. That's when—I was tired of being yelled at, okay? I grabbed the pitchfork and—"

"Oh God, Calvin, no!"

"I didn't stab him with it, though he thought I was gonna." Calvin's lip trembles. "And maybe I was. But he hooked my leg out from under me, and he took the pitchfork and cracked me in the face with the handle. Then he left the barn, and I heard him start the pickup and drive off. I don't know where he went."

"Sounds like everybody needs to cool off." Which was what Tam had told herself the day Rob left to live with Allen. "Calvin, have you—I know your folks are dead, but maybe an aunt or uncle—"

"I've got grandparents. I guess. My mom's folks. I don't know where they live. James and they don't get along."

Tam sighs. Thinks of sending Calvin to stay with Zenith for a day or two, but aside from not wanting to drag Zenith into this mess, his mysterious sleuthing likely is dragging him into a mess of his own making.

Or she could drive Calvin into Fort Maginnis, find out from Larry who is in charge of Child Protection Services, and file a complaint, which seems a pretty drastic step.

Like the steps Allen took when he dragged Tam into the custody battle and the no–contact–with–Warren Wetzel order?

Does the fight with the pitchfork in the barn count as child abuse? Or can it be understood as James taking the pitchfork away from Calvin after Calvin threatened him with it?

"Can we ride now?"

Interrupted from her thoughts, Tam stares at him. "What do you mean? You want to hike back over to the corral and saddle the horses—"

"No, no. The horses are here."

"Outside? Now?"

"Yeah. After James left, I saddled them and rode Buddy and led Fancy for you. I just wanted to go riding—that's where it all started."

Tam eyes him. "Did James tell you not to go riding?"

"No. Honest! He didn't, Tam. He yelled how I didn't know anything and I should keep out of his way, but he didn't tell me not to go riding."

She studies him, considering. The defiant set of the boy's jaw, his clenched fists. What was it Zenith had said? *James is a man with a big problem on his hands.* But not a problem she's likely to make bigger by riding with Calvin.

10

The early afternoon is a cloudless blue. Shafts of sunlight pierce the pine boughs and cast uneven bars of shadow and light across the dirt road. Brittle weeds along the ruts and crushed grass where some creature, maybe a deer, had spent the night. A magpie wings down from a pine stub to alight on an aspen bough—Allen's voice: *Think you can hit that magpie?*

Tam drags herself back into the present with a trivial question. There had been no magpies in these mountains when she was a girl, and when had magpies started invading the mountains, looking for someplace better to nest?—while this magpie, dapper in its black and white feathers, cocks its head and studies the riders.

Calvin had been surprised, even agitated, when Tam had reined the Hellbitch down the track toward the county road—"But I saw you and James take the ridge trail!"

Tam hadn't answered. Now she wonders if James had told Calvin about Zenith, his gunfire, and the voices of the searchers. Guesses not. Gives herself over to the clip-clop rhythm of the Hellbitch's hooves, which raise puffs of dust from the dry ruts. Dry, too dry, for early July. June is supposed to be Montana's rainy month, and when had they seen a drop? Tam doesn't want to think what a spark from gunfire might set off.

"Last time I rode up here," says Calvin, as they approach the Sun Creek bridge, "it was with Vay. The day she got the Hellbitch."

Tam remembers, as though from another time, the boy and girl racing on gravel and shrieking with laughter like they hadn't a care in the world. "When does Vay get back?"

"Sometime this week, she was supposed to be. But like I said, her phone's turned off, so I haven't talked to her."

Clatter of shod hooves on bridge planks, again the hooves of Buddy and the Hellbitch, this time ridden by Calvin and Tam. Sunshot current. A crow scolding from deep in the timber. Rising dust from recent traffic on the county road the only trace of a human presence. Tam wonders about Libarriby Sibidibel, whether he's paid any visits this afternoon. Wonders where James has gone. Warns herself not to think about James.

"So why'd you want to ride this direction?"

Tam considers. Shrugs. "People in the other direction I don't want to meet."

Concentration, almost comical, on Calvin's face as he tries to work out which people. "Not Zenith," he mutters. "James says Zenith likes you. But who else—" Then it dawns on him. "Has to be those two dudes at Simmons's."

He waits for Tam to choose their direction and follows when she reins the Hellbitch north on the county road. "I've been watching those guys at Simmons's," he calls from behind her back and kicks Buddy to catch up.

Tam lets his remark go. "Where's the Evenson turnoff?" she asks.

Calvin's lip thrusts out at her deflection. "Just up here a ways. To the left. They've got a big-ass sign."

Sure enough, an arched log atop two poles frames a wide graveled road leading west. EVENSON, burned into the sign that swings from the arched log on chains and says wealth is spoken here.

A well-maintained gravel drive leads past a massive log barn and corrals on the right and an equally massive log house on the left, comes to an iron gate, and continues beyond the gate and out of sight into the timber. Wide, empty verandas, curtained windows. All still and all silent when Buddy's and the Hellbitch's hooves come to a halt on the gravel. Of course, Ed Evenson and his daughter have been away for a week in—where—Los Angeles, Tam remembers.

"Quite a spread."

Calvin gazes from barn to house and back again, uneasy. "Why'd you want to ride here, Tam?"

"Curious, I guess." But she thinks she understands Calvin's uneasiness. Something about the stillness makes her feel as though she's trespassing. Which, of course, she is. "Does Mr. Evenson have a caretaker?"

"Guy named Broome and his wife. They live in the little house back there—but their car isn't here."

Tam now notices the oddity. Not a vehicle in sight. She supposes Evenson would have driven his automobile to catch his flight to Los Angeles, but what ranch, even a hobby ranch like this one, doesn't have a farm truck or two parked around the barn, not to speak of the ubiquitous collection of four-wheelers? Locked in a garage, perhaps, during the family's absence?

Calvin has dismounted. He hands Buddy's reins to Tam. "Back in a minute," he mutters and vaults the gate into the fenced yard. Circles the extended log porch and disappears around the back of the house.

Buddy shakes his head at a fly, making his bridle chains rattle, and the Hellbitch adds a sharp switch of her tail. *Why are we stopping here?*—as clearly as though the horses have spoken. It occurs to Tam that the Hellbitch is showing no signs of recognizing her own barn. Maybe she hadn't stayed in it long enough to think she belonged there, to associate it with feed and water. If given her head, she'd likely return to the old Heckman barn.

Oh well, if we've got to stop here in the sun, as clear as if Buddy has spoken. He stretches his neck to lay his head on the Hellbitch's rump, and she answers his affection with another sweep of her tail. Tam lets her mind wander back to affectionate horses she's known. Remembers a team of sorrel workhorses Hube used to have, a mare and a gelding. Hoping to raise a colt from the mare,

Hube had haltered her and led her to a neighbor's stallion. The gelding, left alone in the corral, had trotted up and down the fence rails all afternoon, neighing frantically for his partner. Strange how Tam can remember the neighing gelding but not whether the mare ever had a colt.

The sun burns hot on her bare arms. She wonders what is keeping Calvin. She wouldn't have thought it would take him more than a few minutes to shelter behind a shrub for privacy, unzip, piss, shake it off, and zip again. Wait—was that the sound of shattering glass?

But now both horses turn to prick their ears and stare as a car turns from the county road to the gravel drive to approach the house. A newish red Chevrolet sedan with Murray County license plates. As Tam watches, the sedan stops under the big-ass EVENSON sign, and a woman in tan slacks and a matching jacket gets out and opens her trunk. Takes out a sign on a stake and a hammer. Hammers the stake with the sign into the sod, facing the county road, *bang*, with an accompanying echo from the ridge.

When she goes to return her hammer to the trunk of her car, she notices Tam and the horses, shades her eyes briefly with her hand, and trudges up the driveway toward them.

"I'm sorry I've been delayed," she says, "but when I drove out here a few days ago to put up my sign, a bear ran across the road in front of me, and I was afraid to get out of my car."

Tam has gone somewhere else for a moment, so struck by the other woman's sighting of a bear crossing the county road and remembering Bunce's letters about wildlife moving back into the Sun Creek country—*crowded out of the high mountains, looking for someplace better, just the way folks are doing*—and also the magpie, she has to pull herself back into the present to realize the woman is addressing her as though she, Tam, is somehow in charge.

She looks more closely at the woman and sees a long anxious face framed by rigidly coifed hair. Gold button earrings and a gold chain. Too dressed-up for the mountains.

"I'm Tam Bowen," she says. "A neighbor. I don't believe the Evensons are at home."

"Well, no, of course they're not. They're—" the woman interrupts herself. Fumbles in her jacket for a small pasteboard card, which she hands up to Tam. "They're already in Los Angeles. I'm Marie Jones. A realtor with Janeaux and Jones. I'm sorry, I thought you might be the caretaker."

"Ed Evenson is selling the place?"

Marie Jones nods, flicks a glance over Tam and the horses. "If you happen to know anyone who'd be interested—but you say you're a neighbor? Do you often see bears in these woods?"

Tam shakes her head. "I grew up here, and there never were bears."

"Wait! You're Tam Bowen? The *author*? I read that she—I mean you—grew up near Fort Maginnis! I've read all your books! Oh, how I wish I'd brought one for an autograph! Could you—"

The Hellbitch shies violently, making Tam growl and pull her up sharply because Calvin has burst around the side of the house, waving a torn sheet of paper. He stops at the sight of Marie Jones.

"Vay's gone," he says in a small voice.

"I know," Tam says, just as Marie Jones says, "Is this your son?"

"Calvin," says Tam, without elaborating, and makes some vague promise about autographing books before jerking her head at Calvin. "We'll go on with our ride now and let you get about your work."

"How do you do, ma'am," says Calvin, surprising Tam with his manners. He touches the brim of his hat as he takes Buddy's reins from her and swings into the saddle. Marie Jones is chattering—"loved your novel, what was its title, about the billionaire and the foster child—" But Tam gives her a half-wave and nudges the Hellbitch after Calvin and Buddy.

Tam's head reels. Calvin's manners. The bear that ran across the county road. The Evenson place for sale. Is the Hellbitch part of the sale? Is Tam an unwitting horse rustler?

"Tam. Look. It was taped inside her bedroom window."

Calvin holds up his sheet of paper for her to see. In large black capital letters: HELP.

Tam and Calvin have ridden toward home, across the county road to follow the cluster of underbrush along Sun Creek as far as the bridge, when the black Chevy Tahoe shoots around the bend with dust rising behind it. Brakes to a stop with a spatter of gravel, nose to nose with the two horses. Tam hears Calvin's angry shout—"What the hell? Crazy drivers!"—as he crams his precious sheet of paper under his shirt, but Tam has caught her breath because an old man in black is getting out of the driver's side of the Tahoe and another, younger, man out of the passenger side. In the elongated moment, just as Marie Jones passes in her red sedan on her way back to Fort Maginnis and stares, goggle-eyed, at the scene at the side of the road, Tam sees the two men are dressed identically—black jeans, black shirts, black billed caps. What on earth are they playing at? *Allen? Rob?*

Tam returns to herself. Yes, she's recognized them. Allen, only two years older than Tam but crookbacked and lurch gaited and wild-eyed, his hair white and stringing to his shoulders. Rob with his crop of blond hair and an unfamiliar shadow of stubble. She supposes they have recognized her, probably have spied on her. But whatever Allen's and Rob's game, they pose no real danger in spite of their silly black costumes. She and Calvin can spur around them, cross the bridge, and disappear into the timber before they can turn their Tahoe around to give chase or even—melodramatic thought—pull rifles out of the Tahoe and open fire.

Sunlight and creek current play the mischief in her, and Tam allows the Hellbitch, all long legs and seventeen hands of her, to take a couple nervous sidesteps toward Allen—Allen, gnarled as an old diamond willow root with eyes that glare at her from under the brim of his cap; Allen, who retreats from the Hellbitch to shelter behind the open car door of the Tahoe. Tam smiles grimly to herself, remembering her teen fantasy of riding up to Allen on a fine black thoroughbred. Allen always was afraid of horses.

"Dad," warns Rob.

Allen straightens his shoulders as best he can, but he has to tip his head back to lock eyes with Tam astride the Hellbitch. He jerks his chin toward Calvin. "This must be your replacement son. You got a father for him this time?"

"This is Calvin," says Tam, as she had said to Marie Jones, and is amused to see Calvin lift his chin and touch the brim of his hat.

"How do you do, sir," he says, and Allen's jaw drops.

—*burst of automatic gunfire*—

The Hellbitch shies violently, trying to get the bit in her teeth, crow hopping in her terror to rid herself of Tam's control and flee, flee, flee, and Tam has her hands full as she controls the mare and brings her to a shuddering halt at the opposite side of the road, with Calvin and Buddy pounding behind her. In her peripheral vision she sees Allen and Rob leaping back into their Tahoe and spinning briefly in reverse, before gunning past Tam and Calvin and around the bend.

As their dust settles on the empty road, Tam looks at Calvin, and he looks at her.

"Zenith," says Calvin.

With his name Zenith crashes out of the underbrush on the other side of the creek, carrying his AK-47 and smiling benignly across the current at Calvin and Tam. Twigs have stuck themselves into his dandelion crown of hair. Behind him Spotty peers out of the weeds and wags his pleasure at seeing Tam and Calvin.

"All good here?" asks Zenith.

As she rides over the crest of the hill by the lone pine, Tam looks across her meadow, recognizes the dark-blue pickup truck parked by her cabin, a hundred yards away, and reins back the Hellbitch without thinking. Calvin rides up beside her and stops, eyes on the alert. Zenith, riding double behind Calvin with one arm around

Calvin's waist and the other holding his AK-47 over his shoulder, points with his chin. Spotty sits down in the track beside Buddy and pricks up his ears.

"James," Zenith says, and Tam nods. She can see James sitting on her front steps in the shade. Probably when he returned from wherever he went in his rage, he noticed both horses were gone and rightly suspected that Calvin was with Tam. Now he's waiting to have it out with both of them.

Calvin, gone pale under his deep tan, looks from James to Tam, and Tam shrugs and nudges the Hellbitch and rides toward her cabin. James will say or do what James will say or do. All she knows for sure is that she won't make a fool of herself over him again.

James rises from the porch steps as they ride toward him. His face is expressionless, but Tam thinks she sees his contained anger in the muscles of his neck and shoulders. Another thing she won't do is worry about hurting him.

"Hoo-woo!" shouts Zenith. "Just the man I was hoping to see!"

He slides off Buddy and stumps toward James with his rifle over his shoulder and Spotty at his heels. James glances at Zenith and the dog, looks from Calvin to Tam. What next? Another fight between the brothers? In front of Zenith? And has Tam found herself in the middle of it?

Well. Her home. Her prerogative. At the hitching rack—a fir pole set across two posts by Hube many years ago—Tam dismounts from the Hellbitch and ties her reins to the pole.

"It was them fellers!" huffs Zenith. "I caught 'em trying to run over Calvin and Tam in their truck. Had to fire a round over their heads to chase them off. I keep telling you, James—"

James's eyes find Tam's over Zenith's head, asks a silent question.

Tam shrugs. "They confronted us. It was stupid. They were dressed up in black, looking like grown men playing ninjas."

She pauses, smiling to herself when she thinks of Allen's fear of the Hellbitch. Yesterday she had retreated into a kind of fugue state at the sound of their voices. Today, even with the glimpse she got of Rob's face wrung with, what—anger, distress, fear even— she feels pretty damned good. She thinks if the Hellbitch really is for sale, she might have to buy her from Ed Evenson. She'll have a corral and shed built on the meadow—and stops herself. What is she thinking? She has a plan, after all, so what is all this about the Hellbitch and corral and shed? Is she going from feeling pretty damned good to feeling elation? Too much elation? She looks from James's face to Zenith's and sees they are watching her in silent concern.

"Come inside, Tam," says James. "I'll make coffee."

Her first reaction is to bristle—*being invited into her own house?*—but no. She won't worry; she'll let Zenith and James worry. Calvin, she notices, has untied the Hellbitch and melted away with both horses. A worry there. But for now she lets Zenith put his arm around her and pat her shoulder as he leads her up her front steps.

11

Late-afternoon sunlight slants across Tam's front room, gilds the wood floor and walls, seeks the dark recesses of the river rock fireplace, and warms Tam on the futon she shares with Zenith. The rush to her blood she had felt earlier—must have been adrenaline—has faded. James has set a tray with mugs of freshly brewed coffee on a crate of books, and now he sits opposite her and Zenith with his elbows on his knees and his chin on his folded hands. He's studying Tam, and she can sense but not guess at the thoughts turning through his mind.

What she might have told him and Zenith but did not. The abridged version of her story. Her young self and the young Allen Heckman. The birth of Rob. Rob's rebellion, his hatred of Warren Wetzel, his running off to live with his father. How much that abridgment would have left out.

"Tam." Zenith's voice retains no trace of his good ol' country boy persona, and his face is grim. "My question is, why do those two fellows have it in for you? James, now, I get that, because they've got that crackpot idea he ought to give them their ranch back, but you?"

Tam shakes her head. Allen had said, years ago, that he wanted her to leave him alone. Get out of his life. Which she has done, for over thirty years. Yes, Rob has written that he wanted her dead, which she isn't, obviously, although she certainly has pondered just where her responsibilities to him lie, if not with the secret stash of pills she brought with her from Portland.

James interrupts her pursuit of a philosophical conundrum as he looks up and speaks for the first time. "I had the impression, back when they thought they could argue me into signing the old Heckman ranch back to them, that they weren't exactly flush with cash in spite of their show of fancy suvs and their guns. Maybe because of their show."

Zenith nods. "I've tried to get Suze to tell me what their arrangement is with her—did they buy the place, and are they making payments? Or are they paying her rent? When I've pressed her, she goes into her senile old lady shell."

James turns to Tam. "You own this property free and clear, don't you?"

Tam looks across at him, meets his level eyes, and tries to focus on his question. "Yes. I inherited it from Hube. It never was worth much, and I don't suppose it is now."

"If they had any sense," Zenith grumbles, "they'd be trying to sweet-talk you, not scare you."

Zenith and James stray into a conversation about the Evenson place, what its price tag likely is now that it's for sale.

"Likely the other side of five million—"

"Of course, it's got better buildings but nowhere near the view that Tam's got—what folks will pay for a view—"

"And what somebody might pay to subdivide it—"

Tam half-listens and watches James as he gathers up the coffee mugs and tray. He and Zenith don't know the half of her assets. Maybe Allen does.

"I've got to go out and try to find my brother," James says to Zenith, "but you'll—"

Zenith nods. "I'll stay with her."

"If you don't like who you are," says Zenith, "you can always be somebody else. I turned into somebody else myself."

Tam and Zenith sit side by side on the futon in front of the river rock fireplace. The speckled dog Spotty has graduated from sleeping on Tam's front steps to sleeping on a rug in front of the cold fireplace, where he thrashes at the rug with all four feet as he endures a rabbit-chasing dream. Tam swirls the ice in her glass of top-shelf bourbon. Yes, she and Zenith are drinking from real glasses now, purchased at the new Walmart in Fort Maginnis—when? she's not thinking straight—with ice broken out of trays in the miniscule freezing compartment in Hube's old refrigerator. She squints at Zenith—her vision seems to have blurred—and tries to focus on what he just said.

"What didn't you like about yourself, Zenith?"

"I was dumb. And young, mind you. Not stupid. I've never been stupid. Just dumb."

Tam thinks it over. The difference between stupid and dumb. Raises her glass to her lips and finds it inexplicably empty.

"Here you go," says Zenith and pours more bourbon in her glass and his own.

"Isn't everybody dumb when they're young?"

"Pretty much. But not as dumb as I was."

"I was dumb," says Tam. Hube's last days. Losing track of Mrs. Eckles. How much she hadn't known about time and what it did. Her eyes are filling with tears that should have fallen long ago.

Zenith is still telling his story. "Spent six years in the state pen down in Deer Lodge. You believe that? Me?"

"No."

"Looks like we need more ice. No, don't get up, I'll get it this time."

Spotty wakes briefly and thumps his tail as Zenith heaves himself up from the floor and pads away, while Tam tries to concentrate through her haze of regret.

"What were you in prison for?" she asks when Zenith lumbers back with clinking glasses and pours more bourbon.

"Statutory rape. Can you believe that?"

"No. I can't even believe you just said that."

"But I did." Zenith sighs and tilts his glass to watch the bourbon run back down into the ice. "My name was Mark in those days, so

I changed myself to Zenith. Because who wants to be somebody named Mark? Who wants to be somebody's dumb Mark?"

"You were somebody's dumb Mark?"

"Dumber than hell."

Tam tries to visualize Zenith with his years stripped away. Thinks he might have been quite good-looking once. Imagines him tall and lean, as he still is, and dark haired. The odd black hair still sprouts from his white dandelion crest. *Statutory rape?*

She must have spoken it aloud because Zenith says, "She was beautiful. She was so beautiful. And they took her away from me."

"She was too young?"

And he nods.

A pause. No sounds from the outer world penetrate the thick log walls of the cabin, but Tam knows the ridge pines are thrashing against the wind that threatens to tear them out by their roots. Tam feels her own roots being torn. The superficial books she's written. Rob. *Rob.*

"I borrowed that book of yours from James," says Zenith, "after I heard Bunce talking about it. Don't suppose Bunce ever read it."

"I hope not."

"What got you into writing that junk?"

"Money."

Zenith looks his question, and Tam elaborates. "I graduated from high school and went to college on a scholarship—"

The Adams scholarship and what help Hube and Mrs. Eckles could scrape together, another part of the story she hadn't told Zenith and James earlier. "After college I had to earn a living somehow. I'd taken a couple of creative writing classes in college, learned a lot about good fiction. But—" She remembers fifteen-year-old Rob's anger: *What the fuck am I supposed to think? My mother wrote this shit-ass book the whole high school is passing around!*

It's what puts food on the table, she screamed back. *It puts clothes on your back.*

And then Allen: *You made your pile writing that trash, Tam! It's dirty money! The least you could do—*

"—I wrote a good novel, but literary fiction is hard to publish, and there's so little money in it. I sort of stumbled over a soft porn romance novel that was a best seller, and it dawned on me that I could write one. So I did, and I wrote an outline for a series, and I got a fifteen K advance. And I thought I was in clover."

"But romance novels? Did you give any thought to detective fiction? Science fiction? Thrillers?"

"I wouldn't have known the first thing about police work or science—"

"And you did know about romance?"

Tam studies the level of bourbon in her glass. Ponders his question. What did she know about romance then, what does she know now? That she doubts the veracity of the happily-ever-after conclusion? Yet still longs for the happily-ever-after conclusion?

"Now what will you do?"

She thinks of the—well, not exactly a journal, a series of musings she's started on her laptop. "I've saved enough that the money isn't crucial now. I took this summer to think it over. At least that's what I told my agent."

"Oh hell," says Zenith from what seems a distance. He reaches for the bottle, ponders something profound, and divides the last of the bourbon between his glass and Tam's. "Although," he adds, "the lovey-dovey stuff isn't junk. Don't let anybody tell you that. It's real."

At the change of his tone, Tam looks up. She's seeing him double, with tears running down both his faces, and she's hearing Rob at fifteen: *Yeah, I read it. Some of it, anyway. I skipped the lovey-dovey stuff—it was enough to make me puke!* She feels tears running down her own face.

"It's real," Zenith says. "I know what's real when I read it. I've been there."

"In love?"

A silence. Vibration of wind against night-dark windows. Zenith puts a hand to his mouth, tries and fails to suppress a belch, and glances at Tam. "I've got a daughter. Saw her once."

Daughter. Once. Tam tries to find a connection between the words. "How old is your daughter?"

"She's thirty-five. She's a singer in a band. One night I saw a poster for the band, the Working Poor, and I found the bar where they were playing, and I sat in the back and listened. She's . . . not as great a singer as her mother was, but she's damned good."

"Did you talk to her?"

"No. Why would she want to talk to me? You got any more bourbon?"

"Under the sink."

She shouldn't, she really shouldn't, and neither should Zenith. But here he comes with more bourbon and ice, and maybe they won't remember what they talked about tonight.

"You think I ought to? Talk to her?"

Tam nods and wishes she hadn't. The river rock fireplace is tipping over, the light spins. Oh hell, oh hell.

Zenith hugs her. "What are you going to do about James?"

Tam wakens to the distant sound of automatic rifle fire and finds herself tucked in her own bed with no memory of how she got there. Her head throbs, and oh, her stomach—she stumbles out of bed and runs for the toilet, where she collapses and heaves a reeking spew of curdled whiskey. Sits for a moment clutching the toilet bowl, flushes, and crawls back to bed.

The next time she wakes, her bedside alarm clock shows 12:20 and her head is killing her, but she manages to walk more or less steadily to the toilet, where she vomits until she dry heaves. Finds her bottle of ibuprofen and swallows three tablets with a little water and hopes she can keep it down.

Had she and Zenith really polished off the better part of two fifths of bourbon? Never again, she promises herself.

She finds her shirt and jeans on the floor and pulls them on. At least Zenith—must have been Zenith—had left her in her underwear. Squints against the full bright daylight pouring through her uncurtained windows, finds cold coffee in the pot James had brewed last night, and zaps a full mug in the microwave. Carries it to sit on a futon with her back to the light and gather what shreds she can of last night's conversation.

Allen and Rob. *What does Tam have that they want? Why do they hate her?*

The Hellbitch! Tam remembers she left the mare tied to the hitching rail all night and most of today in full sun without food or water. She sets down her mug, slopping coffee, and runs to the door.

Silence, except for the eternal roar of the wind through the ridge pines. A distant quarrel among the finches in the aspens. Insects rustling through the ripened grass. But no stamping hooves, no whinny from an anxious mare.

Tam walks down to the hitching rail. Shod hoofprints in the dusty grass around the posts, yes. But no Hellbitch. But also no broken reins tied to the hitching rail. And now Tam sees where hoofprints lead across the grass and down the dirt track toward the spring. Someone has untied the Hellbitch and led her away, someone who is not afraid of her.

Plan or no plan, Tam had picked up a current copy of *Western Horseman* in Fort Maginnis and found herself turning to the classified ads in the back of the magazine. Under Horses for Sale, *Half-Arabian filly*, and a color picture of a beautiful bright bay with the Arab's characteristic arched neck and dish-face. Two years old, halterbroken, and ready to start. A price and an address for a ranch near Livingston, Montana.

She shakes her head. Of course she isn't going to do this.

Instead, she slides her feet back into her sneakers and wanders out of the cabin and down the slope, where the ruins of Hube's horse barn and sheds and corrals have slumped into overgrown grass and thistles as though weary from time itself. Hube's John Deere tractor squats at one end of the collapsed barn, up to its faded fenders in an outgrowth of juniper that seems bent on smothering it. At the other end of the barn, Hube's hay wagon, similarly overgrown. How long since anyone has tried to put up hay on the meadow below the barn? In mountain weather that never allowed for more than one cutting, where no one ever should have tried to ranch—stop it, Tam. Hube always scraped out a living for himself. And for you.

An unexpected thought stirs. Was it this inevitable sinking into disintegration that her mother had fled? The disintegration and the loneliness that Hube's woman, Marjorie, had fled? Tam touches the gold ring on her thumb, the ring that never left Hube's left ring finger, even during his time with Marjorie, even with Mrs. Eckles, until the coroner had slipped it off and handed it to a stricken Tam, who slipped it on her thumb for, well, the time being and left it there.

Well. Tam doesn't have to scrape out a living here. Or go on living here in the shadows of the Snowies, where the peaks of the mountains rise to meet the blue. Where the air smells of pine needles and dust, where the grass crackles at her thighs when she steps deeper toward the ruins. A damned fire hazard is what it is. She visualizes a cigarette butt flung anywhere along the track between here and the Sun Creek bridge, smoldering into flames that leap with whatever wind blows down from the ridge pines, consuming the half-rotted logs of the old barn and sheds along with the undergrowth.

And what could she do but let it happen. Let it consume her heart, *sick with desire*, as some poet or other had written.

Forget Calvin Warceski's face, his eyes filled with his need? Forget the Hellbitch?

12

A good time to catch James is early, Calvin had told Tam. After breakfast he usually sits around for a while, drinking coffee and reading his newspapers. That's when he's likely to pay attention to you. After he goes upstairs to his computer room, he's like he's in his own little world. You bother him then, he'll be on the boil.

Tam tries not to imagine James on the boil. So, early. Maybe six? Six-thirty? When the first light grows in her window, she throws back her sheet and pads into her bathroom, uncovers the creaking toilet, and sits. What a life. Eight hundred–thread–count sheets and a rusting toilet. But the toilet is clean now, even if it doesn't look it.

She washes in water that was hot last night and cool this morn-ing; pulls on yesterday's blue jeans, shirt, and boots; and runs her fingers through her hair. James probably will have coffee. He'll probably share with her. If he's not on the boil already. Or still.

Yesterday had been a total waste. A wasted Tam. She'd lolled around the cabin and the ruins of Hube's barn and corrals through the afternoon and evening, unable to keep any food down but a few dry crackers, worrying about the Hellbitch and promising herself never again to match Zenith shot for shot. Had she told Zenith about the summer that only seemed to be golden? About losing Rob?

What Zenith had told Tam. His daughter. Tam promises herself to think more about the daughter. *And not about romance novels?* asks an invisible demon in her ear. *Why you chose to write romance novels?*

Rather than chance the still-drivable track with her car, Tam cuts through the meadow with dew-dampened grasses brushing at the legs of her blue jeans and pauses for a moment on the rim of rocks overhanging the spring. All fair and clear—another hot day ahead. Is it her imagination, or is the water level of the pool lower than it was a week ago, the flow of the creek not as full? She doesn't want to think about the creek drying up and the pool shrinking, and she picks out a rock ledge to use as a marker for the next time she passes by.

Halfway down the track, a grove of serviceberry brush has set on fruit, and Tam pulls off a cluster of berries, not quite ripe but almost. In another week they will stain her mouth and fingers purple. Their mellow warm scent stirs memories of Suze mixing wild gooseberries into her serviceberry pies to add tang to their blandness. Suze. Whatever dark corners of her mind Suze explores these days. *Tammy Lou was a pretty little girl, but she's like her mother. No good.* Tam guesses Allen and Rob would agree.

Once around the spring, Tam follows the tracks of James's truck up the long slope and across the meadow on his side of Sun Creek. It makes about a half-hour's hike before she sees his house. Beyond the house in full sunlight, the barns and corrals and pasture and, yes, the big black mare grazing beside the brown gelding. Tam breathes relief. Either James or Calvin must have come back for the Hellbitch, unsaddled her, and turned her out with Buddy.

Tam shies away from the thought of Calvin, angry and bruised, and focuses her mind on her errand as she knocks on James's door and listens to the constant roar of wind in the pines as she waits.

Maybe she'd misinterpreted Calvin's idea of *early*, or maybe James isn't even home, but no, his door is opening, and there's James, tousled and barefoot in Levi's and a white singlet, looking barely awake and surprised.

"Sorry!" Tam gasps, barely stopping herself from dropping Calvin into trouble—*he told me to come early!* But James holds the door open for her to walk into Allen Heckman's father's house—what was Allen's father's name? All she remembers is Hube and Bunce calling him Old Man Heckman, who spoiled his son. But no—she warns herself away from the distractions of the past, memories of the old man's scuffed leather-seated chairs, his tooled saddle on a sawhorse that used to collect dust in one corner, and the ancient windup phonograph that sat in another corner. All replaced by James's pair of armchairs and shelves stuffed with books.

James studies her, looking wary. But he offers, "Coffee? I just started some," and Tam nods and follows as, barefoot, he pads back to the kitchen and takes down a clean mug from a shelf. As he pours, Tam finds herself staring at his feet. So pale compared with the deep tan of his face and arms. Straight toes, clipped toenails, defined arches. Young unscarred feet, except for callouses around the heels.

James glances back and catches Tam's eyes on his feet. To hide her reaction, to avoid seeing his reaction, Tam goes to the window and looks out over a lawn that has been mowed but left unwatered and turning brown in the sun. Beyond the lawn, a rail fence and the pasture where the two horses, the Hellbitch and Buddy, graze in the shade of a drifting cloud.

Where is Calvin?

"Is this about Calvin?" says James, and for a moment Tam wonders if she had spoken aloud. No, but James's face has tightened.

"Pretty much my business and his, don't you think? He didn't need to go running to you and get you both into that tangle with the Heckmans."

This isn't the way Tam has rehearsed their conversation. Civil, it was to have been. Nonjudgmental. "It's likely to be Child Protection business," she says, "if it's true you and Calvin fought and you hit him with a pitchfork."

"Is that what he told you?"

"Is that what happened?"

James glares at Tam for a moment, then sets down his coffee mug. "Give me a minute," he says. "Let me at least put some clothes on."

As he disappears up the back stairs, Tam allows herself a breath or two of fragrant fresh coffee. The first few sentences she has planned to say to James. Horses. Calvin. Will James allow Tam to give to Calvin what Hube gave to Tam so long ago?

She becomes aware of faint music on James's disc player, a guitar and a tenor voice—*he rides the wild horses*—when the sounds of James's footsteps coming back down the stairs tells Tam that he's no longer barefoot. Takes a sip of coffee, wills herself to be calm. It's not as though she'd seen him naked, for God's sake. Just his feet. And it's not as though she hasn't faced down an angry man before. No. It's afterward that her reaction will set in.

When he sits across the table from her, she sees he's pulled on a long-sleeved gray cotton shirt and combed his hair. Cowboy boots on his feet. Respectably clad now but grim.

He sips coffee, waiting for Tam to make her move. Waits. Waits some more, while the second hand on the kitchen clock makes its slow sweep.

"Hell!" he bursts. "So, on top of everything else, he went running to you. Cried on your shoulder, did he? Told you what a bastard he's got for a brother? Told you I cracked him alongside his head with a pitchfork? Which I did, by God, and I'm not proud of it, but damned if I haven't had enough of his shit!"

"He needed to talk to somebody. Just as you or I would if we'd lost our only friend."

Tam looks steadily back at him, refusing to flinch from his glare. After a moment he drops his eyes and takes a sip of coffee from a mug that shakes in his hand.

"Who are you talking about? Vay Evenson?"

"Did he tell you her phone goes to voice when he calls? Did he show you the letter she left for him?"

James sets down his mug. Carefully. Tam watches his face struggle from anger to worry to shame.

"So, Evenson's pulling up stakes? He didn't take Vay on some two-week stay-over in Los Angeles?"

"No. We rode as far as their place yesterday and found a realtor staking out a FOR SALE sign by the gate."

James studies the coffee in his mug as though it holds an answer. He's gripping the handle so tightly that Tam fears he'll snap it off. "I don't know what the hell I'm going to do with that boy," he whispers.

"I'm thinking of buying a colt," says Tam, which makes him look up, puzzled.

"A two-year-old, I'm thinking. One with good bloodlines, old enough to start with a saddle and rider. I've found two or three advertisements—" She doesn't have to tell James about yesterday's phone call to the man with the half-Arab filly at the ranch near Livingston. "And I'm thinking of making some visits. But James—"

Now the sticky part.

"I want to use Hube's methods and break this filly to ride—" Oh damn, she hadn't meant to specify the Livingston filly. "Hube used to sit me on a green colt, and he would snub for me with a gentle horse. He and I would ride together, snubbed, until the colt was used to me, and I could ride without being snubbed. That way the colt never learned to buck."

"Snubbed?"

She sees she has to explain. The halter on the green colt, the halter rope looped around the gentle horse's saddle horn. The colt following the tug of the rope, reassured by the presence of the other horse. "What I hope you'll be okay with is my asking Calvin to ride the colt while I snub for him. He's easy and natural with horses, and I think—"

James stares at her in a silence that fills the kitchen until Tam hears a faucet on slow drip at the sink and longs to go and tighten it.

"You want to make a horsebreaker out of Calvin?"

"He'd be helping me." She hears herself rattling. "He'd have something to do for the rest of the summer, get him out of your hair, give him something to think about besides Vay. And I'll need a corral built. Hube's corral fell apart years ago—" Building a new shed, resurrecting the horse barn, mending the pasture fence, all the ideas that had flooded through her the night before.

James still stares. "Will it be safe for him?"

"Well—riding is never wholly safe, but he's strong and agile, and of course he'll wear a helmet." The idea of a helmet gives her pause. Who in the Sun Creek country ever wore a helmet while riding horseback, even spared a thought for a helmet? She can hear Hube explode at the very idea of anything on his head but a felt Stetson. "And he pays attention. He's quick to pick up on instruction—"

"Glad he pays attention to you. What we fought about—" his voice trails off. "Guess it wasn't that much. I just can't depend on him to remember anything."

Tam can't be sure of James's expression—exasperation with Calvin? Exasperation with the dirty old woman who is keeping him from his work upstairs? James, who is too young to play father to a fifteen-year-old.

But he surprises her. "Breaker of horses," he murmurs, and Tam recalls his using the phrase several days ago and wonders at its resonance for him. Her wonder must show in her face because he smiles.

"From *The Iliad*," he says. "*So died Hector, breaker of horses.* Not that I picked it up from Homer. It's the title of a short story by a writer I like."

"So I can take Calvin with me to look at the colt?"

"If you can find him. The last I saw of him was when I sent him after the Hellbitch yesterday. Maybe he'll come home when he gets hungry."

The Hellbitch. What will happen to her? Another unanswered question.

Tam drives southeast on Montana Highway 121 with Calvin in the passenger seat. As fields of wheat begin to give way to meadows and the sharp blue peaks of the Crazy Mountains on the horizon, she feels as though the growing distance from Sun Creek is lifting a weight from her. No need to worry about Allen and Rob, whatever their motives. No need to self-censor her own thoughts. Nothing to occupy her but the empty highway ahead.

Calvin breaks their long silence. "Why are the mountains called the Crazies?"

Tam shrugs. "Lots of stories. Some of them have to do with a crazy woman living alone up there. Sometimes she's an Indian woman; sometimes she's a white woman. Maybe the Indians leave food for her; maybe the mountain men do. Whoever, whatever, she is, she's full of grief, and some have heard her wandering the peaks and howling at night."

Tam's eyes are on the highway that unspools into the distance, but she senses Calvin's concentration. Whatever is on his mind must be unspooling like the highway.

"What's she grieving about?" he asks.

"Oh—the stories vary, but usually she's lost her children. Sometimes they wander off to pick berries and are never seen again; sometimes they're killed by Indians—"

"Is it easy to get lost up there?"

"I've never hiked the Crazies, but I suppose it is. It's not hard to lose your way in the Sun Creek country if you don't know what you're doing."

"Um." Calvin pauses. "I'm just the opposite of her. The crazy woman, I mean. She loses children, and I lose mothers."

Tam glances at him. His face is closed, his smattering of freckles stark against his loss of color. Is he carsick? She sees his tough boy's hands are clenched.

"Do you remember your mother?"

A long pause as Calvin ponders the middle distance. "A little bit," he says finally. "I was five when it happened. The wreck, I mean."

"It had to be hard."

"I guess. I didn't really understand. I don't remember much. It was when we lost Melanie that was hard."

"Melanie?"

"James's wife. She died."

Startled, Tam takes her eyes off the highway and has to swerve and correct her steering. "I'm so sorry," she says, when she can. "I didn't know."

"Nah. Nobody here in Montana knows." He swallows hard. "I never even told Vay."

"Now you've told me."

"Yeah."

When she glances at him, he's looking away, out the window at the jagged blue line of the mountains along the horizon.

"Do we have much farther to go?" he asks after a few minutes.

"No. I think this is our turnoff."

Just outside Livingston, the woman on the phone had told Tam. It'll be a right-hand turn off the highway and then about five miles. You can't miss it.

And yes, here's the turn on gravel that divides hay meadows where scattered bales wait to be stacked and a curve of willows follows a meandering creek. It's good rich bottomland here, far from the thin soil of the Sun Creek country. There will be a bridge, the woman had said, and Tam slows and sees the sparkle of sunlit creek current and a gaggle of ducklings paddling upstream, all very peaceful. And then just half a mile—yes, barns for horses and white-painted fences and a house with a wraparound porch.

Tam parks her car and glances at Calvin, who unbuckles his seatbelt as a man in a Stetson opens a door from one of the barns and approaches their car.

"Mrs. Bowen? Guess you found us all right—" He doffs his Stetson, replaces it. Slightly bowlegged, middle-aged and compact in a gabardine shirt and stockman's pants. "I'm Jay Jennings."

He offers his hand to Tam and then to Calvin, who looks surprised but accepts and shakes.

"I've got the little filly right over here."

Tam and Calvin follow him, while Tam gives herself a sliver of daydream, a ranch of fertile hay meadows and a creek with ducklings and horses in pastures. No harm in imagining a parallel life. Then she's looking over a gate at the half-Arab bay filly that Jennings had advertised in *Western Horseman*, and she catches her breath.

What is it about a horse that shimmers with its vulnerability? Is it a projection of innocence, especially in a young horse who always has been gently treated? No foreknowledge of mortality? Whatever it is, it is heartbreaking. This bay filly with her dish face and liquid eyes, her delicate nostrils that probe the air for traces of scent to tell her—what? That her life is about to change? No way she has of knowing that, and yet she takes a nervous half-sidestep, tossing her beautiful head.

"Lovely," breathes Tam. The filly is a bright bay, black mane and tail, not a white hair on her. Deep chested and long legged, with the characteristic Arab arch of neck. Tam extends a hand, and the filly takes a cautious sniff and flares her nostrils, but she doesn't flinch.

"Halterbroken?"

"Oh, yes," says Jay Jennings, who has been watching Tam and the filly with his thumbs hooked in his belt loops. "And we've been handling her, brushing her, taking care of her hooves. She'll be ready for saddling. Who's going to ride her?"

"What I've got in mind," says Tam, "is my father's old method. I'll put Calvin, here, up on her while I ride his gentle horse and snub for him for several days in the round corral, then out on the meadows for several days—"

"Bowen," interrupts Jay Jennings. He seems to meditate on the name for a moment. "Sure, you're Tam Bowen! You're Hube Bowen's daughter!"

"Did you know him?" says Tam, surprised.

"Don't know if I ever actually met him. But hell, the man was a legend in horseman circles. It's a privilege to send this little girl north with Hube Bowen's daughter and know she's in good hands."

Calvin looks from Jay Jennings to Tam with a face full of questions that he doesn't ask.

"How much do you weigh, Calvin?" Jennings asks him.

Calvin blushes. "Hundred twenty."

"She'll carry you just fine."

Jennings speaks softly to the filly and approaches her with a halter, which she dips her head to accept. "Good girl—good girl—" He snaps the rope to the halter, leads the filly several paces in a widening circle while Tam watches her action.

"Beautiful," she says.

Jennings nods, strokes the filly's neck. "We can go up to the house," he says, "and get the paperwork done. My sister will have coffee ready."

13

In the car again and headed northwest, Tam finds her thoughts turning back to Jay Jennings and his sister. The pleasant gray-haired woman in ranching clothes welcoming Tam and Calvin into a sunny living room and pouring coffee into proper cups with saucers. Calvin had turned his cup suspiciously in his saucer, tasted and winced, and again Tam allowed herself another merest sliver of a daydream, of an alternative life where fences are kept up and horses safely graze and where at the end of a working day is a room like this, with polished floors and comfortable chairs and good coffee.

She had made easy small talk with Jay Jennings's sister, until Jay Jennings himself brought out the bill of sale and certification of the filly's half-papers and a receipt for Tam's check. It wasn't until she and Calvin were on the porch, about to leave, that Jennings said, "See you in a month"—the arrangement being that for an additional fee he would deliver the filly after Tam repaired her outbuildings and corrals—and his sister added, "Take good care of your mother, son."

Neither Tam nor Calvin had corrected her, although they avoided each other's eyes.

Now, as the peaks of the Crazies jut into the sky, Tam thinks yes, if she had given birth to a son when she was thirty-five instead of seventeen, that son would be Calvin's age. As though fate has sent her this boy to—what?—seek forgiveness from? Maybe for a do-over? Allen's jibe: *your substitute son?* She smiles at the ridiculous idea, but she sees Calvin studying the blue peaks of the Crazies as though for revelation, and she takes a chance and says, "Tell me about Melanie?"

Calvin doesn't answer right away, his face stays turned toward the Crazies, but his fists are knotted. Tam drives for perhaps a mile before she hears a small voice.

"Nobody wants to talk about Melanie. James won't."

"Why is that, Calvin?"

Another mile of highway behind them.

"Mr. Leeds said it was too painful for him."

"Mr. Leeds?"

"The shrink James made me see. I was—not behaving very well."

What Tam had seen on James's face the first night he knocked on her cabin door, his struggle between past and present pain she hadn't wanted to recognize. And now here was Calvin.

"What were you doing?"

"I guess the worst thing I did—" He's lost in memory for a moment. Then he snickers. "I stacked all the homework I hadn't done in James's wastebasket and set fire to it. It made a heckuva blaze, and it caught the curtains in James's study. I guess I must have yelled something, *Holy shit*, because James came running, and he yanked my ass outta there and shut the door on the fire and called the fire station."

Holy shit was putting it mildly. "So the house was on fire—"

"Nah, the firemen saved the house—it was just James's study that was pretty much a loss. He lost his computers and hard drives, pretty much everything he was working on. I thought he was going to beat the shit out of me when he realized what was gone. In some ways I wish he would have."

"How old were you then? Was that when James sent you to Mr. Leeds?"

"Three years ago. I was twelve. I'd already been seeing Leeds for a year or so."

There was acting out and acting out, Tam reflects. At least Rob never set a house on fire. Then she remembers the target practice around Bunce's old place, not to speak of the confrontation with the SUV on the county road, and mentally adds, *yet.*

A weighty silence from Calvin.

"You still haven't told me about Melanie."

"What was *your* mother like?"

Tam glances at the boy. "I don't know—I don't remember her."

"Dead?"

"Maybe by now. But no—she left my dad and me when I was a toddler."

"Do you ever wonder about her?"

"No-o—"

Why not? she wonders. When nobody talked about her mother, only the occasional snide remark from Suze. Why hadn't Tam wondered where she'd gone?

The only living person who might have a clue is Suze.

"Tell me about Melanie," Tam says, to give herself the space.

Calvin sighs. "She was nice. James had lots of girlfriends, but none of them paid any attention to me. But when he started dating Melanie, she'd come over to our place and bake stuff and cook, like that. Sometimes she'd drive me to the arcade and play the game machines with me, like James never had time to do. And she talked to me. And she was pretty. She had hair the same color as yours."

"What happened to her?"

A mile's silence grows to two, three, four miles. Just when Tam thinks their conversation is over, she glances at Calvin and sees a tear run down his cheek.

"She fucking died!" he shouts. "She was going to have a baby, and something went wrong. They couldn't stop the bleeding, and she died, and the baby died!"

From Tam's laptop journal:

As I've been thinking about loss and grief, I've found an essay about discovering the intaglio in stone of a horse on a desert landscape; an intaglio hard to discern but, once located, rising to life and the light. Studying the intaglio, the writer is struck by several insights: first, by the craft that went into its making; second, by its realism, suggesting a portrayal of an individual horse; and third, by its vulnerability, not just to forces of nature but by human vandalism. On this third point I linger. While the intaglio certainly is threatened by human vandalism, of which the writer cites numerous horrific past abuses of the desert landscape, isn't the vulnerability a part of the horse's natural state? Think of the Hellbitch, think of the filly, think even of placid Buddy, of their heartrending unknowingness.

Tam's first task when she and Calvin get back to the Sun Creek country is to revisit the ruins of Hube's horse barn and sheds and collapsed corrals in the meadow below the cabin and assess the needed replacements or repairs. The junk and litter spread across the meadow look worse than they seemed on her first visit. How could she have overlooked the ancient mowing machine, the buck rake, the manure spreader, where Hube last left them? The overgrowth of grass and thistles, she supposes. Clearing the meadow, resurrecting the barn and corrals, will be a bigger job than she can handle, even with Calvin's help, and she feels a pang at the thought of Bunce, just the man who could advise her where to start, and she experiences a flash of imagination, like a strip of movie film without beginning or end, of herself and Bunce and Calvin working side by side, lifting corral rails, setting posts—oh, stop. And stop seeing James's dead wife, Melanie, with the gold-blonde hair, as she has seen her ever since Calvin told of her—no. Do what has to be done, Tam. What she has promised Calvin.

So that afternoon Tam drives down to Fort Maginnis, where she can get cell phone service, find a café with a quiet corner booth, order coffee from a waitress in her teens, scan the service ads in the local paper, and start making calls. A man who advertises he'll haul away junk and agrees, yes, he can sell old farm equipment for what it's worth in iron. A roofer who says he'll take a look at her barn and see what he can do. A man who advertises he installs fencing and agrees, yes, he can bring a tractor with a posthole digger and a load of treated posts and set them for a new corral, and yes, he can put a blade on his tractor and bulldoze the rotten wood into the gulch. Better to burn that wood, he sighs, but not while the mountains are as dry as they are. Maybe after first snowfall.

Tam's turn to sigh. Life unfolding ahead of her, through the summer and into the winter. What has become of her plan?

Her last call is to Libarriby Sibidibel.

"Oh, hell, Tam, where are you? Down at the Home Plate? I'll join you."

Two or three heads turn at the café counter as Larry walks through the plate glass doors.

He gets a greeting or two from customers, slaps shoulders, spots Tam in the back booth, and warms her with his cockeyed smile.

He lays his Stetson on the booth's table, crown down, and Tam feels another warmth, of being with someone who knows to doff his hat indoors, who knows how to treat a good Stetson. A cowboy never takes his hat off? Balderdash. Hube would have choked at the idea of walking into the Home Plate without removing his hat.

"So, how've you been? Tried to call a couple times, but I guess you don't get cell service up there. Barb's still waiting for her dinner date, got her books all lined up for you to sign." To the young waitress, "Coffee for me, Carly."

Tam takes a deep breath. Tells him about the FOR SALE sign in front of Ed Evenson's gate, which she sees is not news to Larry.

She takes another deep breath and describes her confrontation at the Sun Creek bridge with Allen and Rob. Sees Larry's eyes change.

"Fine, thanks, Carly," he says as the girl pours his coffee, then turns back to Tam.

"Told you I was going to talk to folks up there," he says. "I talked to Evenson, not a week ago, and he never said a word to me about selling out. Had to hear it from his realtor. I have coffee with

Marie Jones from time to time, just to keep track. Hell. Ed was a big contributor to me at the last election. But all that seemed to be on his mind was Zenith and his damned gunfire. That and trying to keep track of his daughter. He's got a problem with that kid."

Tam nods. She's been giving a lot of thought to Ed Evenson's problem with Vay.

Larry sips coffee, keeping his eyes on Tam. "I got quite a bit more out of Zenith. There's more to Zenith than meets the eye."

Again Tam nods, thinking of what memories she has managed to recover from her drunken evening with Zenith. His statutory rape conviction.

"He spent a few years in the state pen," Larry goes on. "His family pretty much disowned him, but one of his professors at the state college up north stood by him. She visited him, got him taking extension courses. He ended up with a degree in geology, can you believe?" Larry's eyes go far off. "Shows what a man can do when he tries. Zenith worked as an oil field consultant down in Wyoming for years at the time of their boom and made his way back up to Montana when the price of oil rose and drilling on the Highline fired up again. He retired here after production slowed. He's sitting on a pretty bundle of cash."

Tam shakes her head.

"Hard to believe, right? And he's still a registered sex offender. Which is a lotta nonsense. Consensual, as far as I could make out from the records, but the girl was underage. He's never been in any such trouble since."

Zenith, a registered sex offender. His words: *I've got a daughter. Saw her once.*

"He told me about that Wild West shoot-out you and James Warceski found yourselves in the middle of."

Tam represses a shudder at the memory, not just of the gunfire or the voices of Allen and Rob but of her own reaction, having to be helped home. James—*throwing herself at him.* James with his dead wife—

"So Zenith's been prowling around, keeping an eye on you, watching out for you, like. Which is how he happened to turn up when the Heckmans tried to cut you off at the Sun Creek bridge. Helluva situation. I figured I'd better drive out to the old Simmons place and introduce myself."

Larry shakes his head. "Hard to know what to make of them. I remember Allen from high school, a little bit, but he's—" He pauses. "Okay, start over. They acted like they'd pulled something off and gotten away with it. Grinning at each other, *telling me, Oh hell, we were just being friendly, Tam trying to make more of it than it was, just like she always did—*"

Larry tries his coffee, makes a face. "Damned stuff has gone cold. No, I don't know what they're up to. I went to see Suze when I got back to town, but talking to her is like—well."

"Zenith thinks Allen and Rob are stockpiling supplies. He thinks they might be whatever those people call themselves, survivalists."

"He told me that too. Look, Tam—I don't know what to tell you. You could press charges, but for what? Reckless driving? I can't arrest them just because I don't like the way they grin at me. But one thing Heckman said that got me to wondering. Just as I was getting ready to leave, he said, *Tell Tam she's gonna pay me for ruining my life!*"

The money theme again.

"Tam? You ready to tell me why the hell you came back here?"

From Tam's laptop journal:

I catch myself thinking a great deal about men's genitalia. The whole outside-the-body thing. Their packages. The cock-and-balls, the bits and pieces, the dangly bits, the junk. I ask myself if I'm suffering from what Freud called penis envy, but I don't think so—it's more a marveling at their difference from my own soft inward folds. What it must be like for men to go around with it all hanging between their legs. Do you remember the girl who was learning to be ambidextrous?

It was this difference between men's and women's genitalia she drew on when writing the soft porn romance novels that supported her and her baby boy and eventually would embarrass that boy so badly.

That girl's story turned out pretty well, after all. Didn't it? After the boy ran off to his father, she spent years paying child support to the father. She learned to be frugal. And after the boy turned eighteen, she began to save her money and invest it, and now she never has to write another romance novel if she doesn't want to, which she doesn't. Although she's been tapping away at this—journal? Memoir? Will anything become of it? Probably not.

But no, her story has not turned out so well. Romance novels are not the issue here. What is at issue is the lost son, who now lives within a rural mile from her. And another young man, also living within a mile from her, who is the age of that son and is the husband of a dead wife, a man over whom she's made a fool of herself.

For Vay's sake, Tam had resolved to ride the Hellbitch as much as she could during the few days before Ed Evenson was supposed to bring the girl home from his Los Angeles visit, although she had little confidence in Vay's ever overcoming her fear of the mare. Now it's clear that Ed Evenson's so-called Los Angeles visit is, in fact, permanent, and it's unclear what will become of the Hellbitch, Tam falls into a kind of running-in-place routine. During the mornings, while her hired helpers carry out the tasks she's paid them for, hauling off junk and setting corral posts and rebuilding the barn, she works with Calvin on the pasture fence. In the cool of the evening she and Calvin ride together on Buddy and the Hellbitch.

Calvin, strong and tough for a fifteen-year-old, quickly learns how to use wire stretchers, while Tam hammers in the staples that fix the barbed wire to fence posts. Three good tight strands and a rebuilt gate. Tam teaches Calvin how to open a wire gate—stick the bottom end of the gatepost through the bottom wire loop and hug the top end of the gatepost to your shoulder until you can loop the top wire over it—and she has to laugh at Calvin's dismay at the rash of tiny red blisters across his shoulder, like slivers, which break out from his gate opening.

Tam knows Calvin is brooding over Vay's letter—she hears the rustle of paper under his shirt when he pats his heart—and she has hoped he'll talk to her about Vay. But no. He takes Tam's teasing about his blisters in good part, though. Grins, ducks his head, almost like the old Calvin. When he has stretched the last length of wire and Tam has hammered her last staple, he looks back over their completed pasture fence with such obvious pride that Tam hides her urge to laugh. Pride in a job well done—a good lesson for any boy or girl.

The lessons Hube taught her. Lessons she had failed to teach Rob.

By late July, and time to start watching the road for Jay Jennings's truck and trailer with the bay filly, the barn is rebuilt with a metal roof. Tam sets Calvin to shoveling muck and years of built-up manure from the corral. He screws up his face and breathes through his mouth while he shovels, and Tam has another grin to hide as she cleans the little spring with its pipe that fills the horses' water trough.

But her mind wanders around the spring and up the slope to the house where James secrets himself with his computers. What does James think about Calvin's work? The fence building, the manure shoveling? Calvin never mentions his brother, and Tam never asks. But what the hell. Calvin's keeping out of trouble, and he displays no new bruises.

Now that the pasture is fenced, Tam has Calvin lead the Hellbitch home from James Warceski's pasture and turn her out to graze below Tam's barn. She does not point out to Calvin that James has no reason to provide pasture for the Hellbitch and that it's way past time to move her. But Calvin's gelding, Buddy, trots up and down his own pasture for hours on end, whinnying his desolation at being separated from his friend.

"Might as well bring him up here too," Tam tells Calvin. "Let him hang out with his true love. There's plenty of grass."

This evening, with shovels and cleaning tools put away, Tam gets ready to ride in the long July twilight. When she goes out with her bucket of oats, the Hellbitch raises her head from grazing, recognizes Tam, and slowly approaches her outstretched hand. Her good points shine, all seventeen hands of her—her beautifully drawn head and expressive eyes, her long straight legs and powerful quarters. She'll make a fine horse, all right, for whomever can ride her. But what kind of fool must Ed Evenson have been to set an inexperienced teenager on her?

Tam offers the mare a handful of oats and snaps the lead rope to her halter as Buddy crowds up and sticks his head into the oats bucket. He follows Tam and the Hellbitch, trying for another mouthful of oats, and whinnies over the pasture gate as Tam leads the mare into the corral. Sorry, Buddy. You're just going to have to be lovelorn this afternoon. Calvin's not going riding this afternoon. James has driven him to Fort Maginnis for early football drills and tryouts.

Tam lets the Hellbitch finish her oats and is brushing her when she sees James walking down toward the corral. And yes, there's the blue pickup parked by her cabin. James is wearing boots and blue jeans and a gray cotton shirt. Bareheaded. He's not planning on riding, is he? When the summer has worn on and he hasn't spoken to her for weeks? Hasn't so much as shown his face since their tense conversation in his kitchen? Does he think she can't ride the Hellbitch safely by herself? Tam straightens the Hellbitch's saddle blanket, flings the saddle over her withers, and tells herself she isn't waiting to see what James is going to do.

What he does is bridle, brush, and saddle Buddy, never glancing in Tam's direction.

No, Tam isn't waiting for James. She's opened the corral gate and gathered her reins to swing into the saddle when she glances at James, twenty feet away, just as he bunches his own reins and meets her eyes.

Count of perhaps three, while James seems to Tam to be asking her a silent question. Although a passing whisper of air ruffles his hair—*why doesn't he wear a hat, doesn't he know he's supposed to wear a hat? Even Calvin wears a hat*—his face never changes; he withholds his thoughts behind the straight lines of his mouth and brows.

The moment passes. James swings astride Buddy, leans out of his saddle to close the corral gate behind Tam and the Hellbitch, and reins Buddy to follow up the narrow track to the ridge trail.

14

During her week or two of afternoon rides with Calvin, Tam has avoided the county road as well as the ridge trail. Instead, she has rediscovered a maze of faint cattle trails, now used mainly by deer, through the underbrush and pines on both sides of the ridge trail, overgrown since her long-ago days of riding the little buckskin mare through pines and young aspen groves springing from the parent roots. Now she has to flatten herself in the saddle and shield her face with an arm as she ducks the trailing branches. The Hellbitch, being so tall, is not the brush horse the buckskin mare was, but at least she doesn't have the thoroughbred's instinctive urge to rear and try to see over the obstacles of pine needles and dead windfall, and she's learning to duck her head and plunge.

Following these long lost ways of deer and cattle, where that fifteen-year-old girl once rode a buckskin mare, is not a quiet passage. The slap of branches, the crackle of fallen twigs under horses' hooves, the occasional grunts and gurgles of horses' bellies. But without human sounds—whistling, singing, conversation between riders—only a mountain horseman or horsewoman would know someone is passing, much less know *who* is passing, through the timber above the old Simmons place, now the hangout of Allen and Rob Heckman.

Which is how Tam has come to know the comings and goings of the father and son. How they usually emerge from the Simmons house in the early afternoon, piss in the weeds behind the house, and fire off a few rounds at their targets. They favor handguns, she notices, maybe .38 calibers.

Eventually, Allen and Rob will holster their guns and climb into the black Tahoe, where Tam has noted the rifle rack with the twin rifles in the rear window. Tam has shadowed them with Calvin as they follow their graveled road west until they reach the county road, where they turn and travel as far as the Sun Creek bridge, which they cross to the dirt road that leads to the Bowen cabin. But they drive no farther. Instead, they U-turn to face the creek and park in the same shelter of underbrush where Tam had parked the day she saw Vay and Calvin racing their horses on the gravel. There they wait. And wait. Perhaps an hour.

Occasional opening and closing of Tahoe doors, occasional bursts of laughter from their hideout. Checking after they leave, Tam has found their rubbish, mostly beer cans but a few hand-rolled cigarette butts and, sometimes, empty fast-food wrappers. On the first day she and Calvin followed them, Tam had turned in her saddle and caught Calvin's eye and saw that he understood as well as she did how Allen and Rob—*Rob*—had waited to ambush them the day they rode as far as the Evenson place.

Now—again today—Allen and Rob are lying in wait, hoping for another chance at Tam. From her vantage point on the hillside, Tam watches as Rob powers down his window and leans on his elbow to catch a cooling drift of air. She notes that he's grown into a muscular young man, taller than his father, with none of Allen's tendency to a hollow chest. Does he look like Hube? Maybe if she saw him on horseback—but has Rob ever ridden a horse? Even once or twice back then on their rare visits to Montana? Another alternative life spins itself, not of peaceful pastures and grazing horses but of herself giving up the Adams scholarship and staying home with Hube to give birth to Rob in the shame that lingered in the backcountry through the 1980s—would that have been a better choice for Rob? Would he have learned from Hube what Tam had learned?

Tam glances back at James, who has ridden beside the Hell-bitch's flank—Buddy fighting the bit to get closer to the mare—

and she sees that James, like Calvin, understands the ambush, and she also sees he's taken a nasty slash of some thorned branch across his face, leaving a red line of embedded black beads of dried blood.

"Does it hurt?" she whispers.

James touches the scar, examines his fingers for bloodstains, and shakes his head. "It's a long way from my heart."

First words he's spoken to her in days.

By the time daylight has faded into evening, the Hellbitch drips sweat and doesn't spare the energy to shy at the sounds of the woodland, the hooting of an early owl or the branches snapped by some passing creature of the evening. Sweat trickles down Tam's own back and shoulders from her own tension and the remaining heat of the day. When she and James rein the horses toward the Bowen cabin, her mouth feels parched, and she itches under her arms and down her ribs. The promise of water and a cool shower has never seemed so sweet.

At her rebuilt corral, Tam unsaddles the Hellbitch and grains and grooms her, while James takes care of Buddy. She has turned the Hellbitch into her pasture and started to walk up to the cabin when James says, "Tam?"

Tam pauses, turns and looks back. Sees, in the pasture, the flailing hooves of Buddy as he takes a good roll in the grass and between her and the horses, silhouetted against a pale sky, James carrying a saddle in one hand and a bridle in the other and looking like a cowboy without a hat.

"Tam," he says again. "I'd rather be friends than—whatever we are now."

She hesitates for a moment. It's too dark to read his face, but she thinks of the hurt she had seen and wonders when she ever has been able to read his face. And what profit in sorting through the silences of the past days, his unresolved anger at Calvin, at Tam—no, let it go.

"Sure," she says. "Friends."

He walks the few yards to her and slings the saddle over the corral rail. Hangs the bridle from the saddle horn. No rain for days and none expected, no danger for unsheltered leather. Tam thinks he's about to say more, but no. He reaches out and just touches her hair. Turns, opens the gate for her, and closes it behind them. Above them, in the last light, a few black shapes swoop and dive. Bats, dislodged from the ruin of the barn and on the hunt for sustenance.

From Tam's laptop journal:

So. Tam Bowen. What she sees when she looks in the mirror. She's an old woman of fifty. Will she look back from, say, seventy years and wonder at how young fifty was?

Will she defy the old conundrum and the curse of her son for another twenty years?

Zenith's question for her: What are you going to do about James?

Libarriby's question: What are you going to do with the rest of your life, Tam?

"Nothing new about Bunce?" she had asked Larry over their coffee at the Home Plate.

"Nada." He gave her a sharp glance. "You hadn't seen him since—when, Hube's funeral? Still, seems like his death has left quite a hole in your life, Tam."

Tam looked around the diner, where she half-remembered spinning on a stool while Hube drank coffee and caught up on the crops and weather from whichever old farmer had dropped in to shoot the breeze that afternoon. Same counters, same shelves with stacks of glasses arranged in pyramids. Heavy white china cups and saucers. Every table with its red-checked oilcloth, weighted down by chrome napkin dispensers, ketchup and mustard, salt and pepper shakers—wait a minute. *Oilcloth? Still?* When had Tam last seen oilcloth? Had she regressed through the thin gauze curtain beloved by fantasy writers to a time when Murray County largely was populated by *us*?

Bunce. Who went back farther with Hube than Tam herself. Bunce, who remembered the old days. Bunce, who was *us*.

Larry, who went back as far as high school with her.

"High school," Larry said, as though he heard her thought. "The damnedest time of our lives. When we think that's how things are and always will be. There's the star quarterback over here, there's the homecoming queen over there, and here's me."

Tam thought about that. "What were you, Larry?"

He shrugged, embarrassed. "Everybody's buddy, I guess. Skinnier in those days."

"Play football?"

"Tight end. Boring. I'd maybe get my hand on the ball five times in a game. Basketball was better. At least I could jump."

Yes, here was Larry, the long-armed skinny kid who could jump like a kangaroo rat and get his hands around a spinning football while the cars parked on the low bluff above the bleachers honked their horns and flashed their headlights. Tam didn't suppose Larry was doing much jumping nowadays, and maybe he caught the expression on her face because he grinned and patted his paunch.

"Those were the days, and I sure the hell wouldn't do them over again."

"What?" Tam said, thinking to tease him, "all those honking horns?"

"Well—that part wasn't too bad." He grinned again and hastily put his hand over his coffee cup to keep the waitress from topping it off. "Much more of that and I won't sleep tonight. But oh hell, Tam."

Another quick glance at her, a bit of a flush. "Had a hell of a crush on you at one time, Tam."

Her mouth must have dropped open because his cockeyed grin widened. "Thing was—even then. You were—hell, what's the word I want. *Competent.* Walked on your own two feet just like you do now, took care of yourself—and you were killer smart. I remember one time in social studies class, you tackled old Mr. McGee, remember him? My mom had gone to school to him, too, and she always called him Fibber for some reason. Old Fibber McGee. He was ranting about the Supreme Court one day, some decision about a school in Arkansas, and you leaned back in your seat and gave him that look of yours and said, *There's where you're wrong, Mr. McGee,* and told him why. And he started to gobble and stutter, and we guys all thought he wasn't going to be able to go on with class."

Larry laughed out loud. "Never have forgotten that. Hell, you were really sumpin', Tam. And you're still—" he hesitated. "Just as good-looking, maybe better-looking, than you were back then."

As Tam raised her hands in protest, he hastened on. "No, no— don't get me wrong. I'm not coming on to you, even if I used to want to. Barb and me've got a good thing going. And she still wants you to come to dinner and sign her books."

Relieved, Tam cast about for another topic. "Have you and Barb got kids?"

Larry's eyes lit up. "Yeah. Would you believe four? Got two boys at the state college up north. And the oldest girl got married last summer, and guess what Barb's hoping for. Youngest girl, Myah, is still in high school."

So normal. So sane. Tam was asking herself if she envied Larry and Barb's life, when Larry cleared his throat.

"Only stupid thing I ever knew you to do. What in hell did you ever see in Allen Heckman?"

Tam turned over Larry's words, taking them literally. Allen's beautiful face. His silken hair. The way he walked, the slant of his shoulders, his direct gaze. She was seeing a red convertible roar past the bus stop in front of the high school, Allen's hair blowing in the wind, the girl in the front seat beside him and the two girls in the back seat with their hair blowing free. Their screams of laughter lost behind them. And in loving Allen, Tam was not the boy-girl.

Larry's eyes were on her. "You ever wonder why he hung around with the girls? Why none of us guys liked him?"

She forced a laugh. "Because all the girls liked him?"

"Because he was a wuss."

The high school word.

"Yeah. There we were, thinking we knew it all and always would. And now here we are. Here *you* are, and you're somebody. And you've got another good twenty, thirty years ahead, maybe more. What are you going to do with them, Tam?"

Hears herself answer him. "I'm going to try to write something worth reading."

And maybe, maybe, do some healing. Get over herself.

15

So. The next twenty, thirty years that may lie ahead for Tam if she ignores the old conundrum. She brews early-morning coffee and looks around the cabin for anything that needs tending to, anything to put off what she's about to do, which is to charge her laptop and open it. Sipping the first cup of coffee, she circles the laptop as though it's a dangerous animal that somehow has made its way into the great room. Its trap closed, it lies in wait.

Then the phone on her new landline rings. It's Jay Jennings, calling to tell Tam to expect him and her new filly the next day. That's good. Tam and Calvin have everything ready—the corral, the pasture and barn, the hay manger, and even the clean pipe into the bubbling little ground spring that keeps the horses' water trough full. The only question is the Hellbitch. Should Tam cut back, perhaps, on her afternoon rides on the Hellbitch to perhaps an hour instead of three hours? Spend the next two hours on Calvin and the new filly? As much as she hates to admit it, she's not up to more than one three-hour ride a day, not in the heat of July.

Well, she'll give the Hellbitch another long ride this evening and mull the question over. Decide tomorrow when Jay arrives with the filly.

Eventually, however, there's no putting off the laptop and its surly demands for her to return to the journal that has become something other than a journal. Thermos of coffee in her hand and the laptop with its thumb drive under her arm, Tam makes her way along the track through brittle meadow grass to the sandstone outcropping overlooking the Sun Creek spring, chooses a boulder where she can lean back against the trunk of an aspen, in the aspen's rustling shade, and open the laptop to a new file.

The blank screen flashes its cursor at her.

James in the twilight, carrying his saddle on his shoulder.

Formulas for explicit-sex romance novels are what have carried Tam through nearly twenty publications. One of her more successful formulas focuses on a young and idealistic virginal girl who falls in love with an older, more experienced, and disillusioned man. The girl's lot is to endure the man's suspicion and scorn for her purity, often beyond what she can bear. Sometimes she flees him; sometimes she falls deathly ill; sometimes she is abducted so he must rescue her and, through her steadfastness, come to cherish her. The plot is interspersed with increasingly graphic scenes of sexual foreplay until the novel's conclusion, where several detailed pages describe the full-blown climax(es) the reader has been promised from the novel's beginning.

When Tam remembers herself at seventeen, in that drab Missoula apartment with infant Rob in her arms, switching hands to scribble on her notepad when she switched Rob from one breast to the other to nurse, she wonders, as she has wondered ever since Zenith asked *Why romance novels?* if that younger self believed at all in the formula's promise of love and fulfillment after the pages of tribulation. Did a shadow of that younger self believe that Allen still would come to love her? Let herself be carried along by hope?

Was she writing alternate-life-for-Tam novels?

She bends to the laptop, confronts the cursor. Types, *What is it about burros?*

On her way home from Fort Maginnis, after her coffee with Larry, Tam had glanced across the road to a neighboring pasture where two small brown creatures nuzzled each other in a fence corner. Remembering a letter from Bunce—*New folks bought a place by the road, plan on leading burros to carry their packs when they go camping*—on impulse she pulled over and rolled down her window to watch them. Small and shaggy coated even in the heat of July. Their absurd ears, their little brush tails, like a parody of horses—or are horses the parodies of some older form?

As she studied the burros, Tam noted their growing curiosity about her. First one burro, then the other, pricking its long ears toward her, its eyes widening, then taking the first hesitant steps toward her. Tam reached a hand toward them from her car window as the burros leaned their heads over their fence, clearly asking for an ear scratch, and what could she do but get out of her car and slowly walk up to the little creatures?

Now, playing with her cursor on the screen of her laptop, Tam catches her mind wandering in strange ways. Why the linebacked buckskin mare, so many years ago, whinnied and trotted up to the fence when she saw Tam. Because she saw Tam as the bringer of oats, Tam tells herself. And yet. And yet. Was the buckskin mare returning Tam's affection? Or was Tam glossing the mare with her own feelings?

How did it all begin, horses and humans? Tam thinks of those first Aztec warriors, seeing horseback-riding Spaniard adventurers for the first time and thinking they had encountered strange two-headed beasts with four legs and two arms, until they happened to witness the Spaniards dismounting and couldn't believe the evidence of their own eyes: a beast that could separate itself into two creatures.

Types: *Could the Greek legend of centaurs have stemmed from such a sighting? Some ancient inhabitant of the Hellenic peninsula, happening for the first time to sight a rider on a horse and, like the Aztecs, thinking he was seeing one creature? I recall a print of a painting I once saw in an art history book.* The Centauress. *The horse-man, the horse-woman.*

Calvin is spending another day in Fort Maginnis—more football tryouts—so as Tam brushes and saddles the Hellbitch, she's not exactly watching for James to join her, thinks maybe better if he doesn't. Maybe that would mean he's finally decided she's safe with the Hellbitch on her own. Which she is. Tam and the Hellbitch have taken each other's measure. A part of Tam wishes she had made a cash offer for the Hellbitch before the Evensons disappeared. But no, she'd have complicated an already volatile situation. She has her own theory about the Evensons' volatile situation, which only Ed Evenson and Vay can answer.

She finishes saddling the Hellbitch and is leading her to the gate when the blue pickup appears over the edge of the meadow and stops by the corral. It's James, in boots and Levi's and no hat. As always, a fleeting expression that suggests a question he's not ready to ask, but he says nothing, doesn't even make eye contact as he bridles and saddles Buddy, mounts and rides to join her at the gate. And well, yes, she's waited for him.

Tam leads their way to the ridge trail, wide enough at the beginning for Buddy and the Hellbitch to walk side by side in the shade of the pines, while Tam's mind wanders back to the attachments between horses—how is it that following the same trail or grazing in the same pasture creates a bond? A kind of love. The way Buddy, separated from the Hellbitch, had trotted up and down his fence and neighed for her. Leave it to humans to complicate horses' feelings and their own.

The air is still and warm. Insects buzz in the undergrowth, light on the horses' flanks and shoulders and are angrily swished away. Upper pine boughs stir in what currents move aloft. Scent of warm pitch, scent of horses. James and Tam, side by side and silent.

The trail narrows as it climbs the side of the ridge, and James nudges Buddy with his bootheels to take the lead. Tam watches Buddy's hindquarters beginning to lather with the sweat of effort as the grade steepens, watches his tail lash away a fly. Anything to distract her from the back of James's head and shoulders, the damp patch of moisture growing along his spine, the shape of his legs in the saddle.

They've reached the high point of the trail above Zenith's buildings, where sandstone boulders have rolled down the slope and lodged themselves among the pines and where Zenith not so long ago fired shots over James's and Tam's heads. Now James reins in Buddy and dismounts, still with his back to Tam, although he waits until, drawn by the tension between them, Tam dismounts and, leading the Hellbitch, follows James and Buddy down to the boulder where they once had sat.

Silence. Tam thinks even the birds are sheltering in the deepest shade. The boulder is warm under her blue jeans. Bright glints of sunlight between the intermittent flicker of pine needles across her arms and shoulders.

James's thigh perhaps eight inches from hers, the stretch of warm denim where a narrow patch of frayed white threads mark the wear of whatever he carries in his front pocket. She raises her eyes and meets his grave gaze.

What she knows will never happen—happens. His shoulder touching hers as he leans toward her—her eyes closing of their own accord—

He draws back—"Damn."

She opens her eyes. "What?"

"I wasn't looking for this."

"No. I don't suppose so."

His hands are clenched between his knees. "What I did need to tell you—just—well, Calvin. You've done a hell of a lot for him."

Tam hesitates.

"What?" demands James.

"Have you heard anything from Ed Evenson?"

"Ed Evenson? Why the hell would I—"

Tam watches him add uncomfortable thoughts to a total. "God, Tam, he's fifteen," he says finally.

"Yes. And she's, what, seventeen?"

"You think—" A long hesitation. "You think I should try to talk to him?"

"Maybe just give him the opportunity?"

"Hell. I hardly see the little shit. Okay, last couple days I've driven him to town for his tryouts, but otherwise, he runs up to your place, comes home late and worn-out from work—which is good, I don't mean that, but—"

It's the longest conversation Tam ever has had with James, and she doesn't want to ruin it. "He's fifteen," she begins, "and you're what, thirty? Pretty young to have to be a father to a teenager. Have you—"

He glares at her. "I'm not that goddamn young! I'm thirty-seven! Next thing I know, I'll be forty! And what do I have to show for it but that spoiled little jerk whose grandparents don't even want to see him! They say he reminds them of his mother! How can they *not* want to see him, can you tell me that?"

"No," Tam says slowly. "I can't understand that. All I know is that Calvin is a good kid, and he doesn't know it yet, but he's damned lucky to have you."

A silence. Tam is stifling the thought that had burst, unasked for—*at least he's not younger than my son*—when James reaches for her hand and touches it.

"Thanks," he whispers. "Do you think we ought to ride home and see what he's up to?"

In spite of his many distractions—anticipating high school in Fort Maginnis in the fall, fearing the consequences of the letter left to him by Vay, and needing to seem aloof—Calvin's eyes are glued to the road for Jay Jennings's truck and trailer. Tam, hurrying through her morning housework, has to smile to herself at the saunter Calvin affects, his self-conscious stroll past the barn and corral to see farther down the road.

And here is James, parking his pickup by the cabin fence— maybe he as well as Calvin could learn something from the handling of the new filly, he'd suggested to Tam yesterday afternoon, and now she nearly laughs aloud to see that his attention, too, is on the road.

Then—midafternoon—here is the big red Ford truck with the Park County license plates, easing its matching red trailer around the bend by the big pine tree. From her doorway Tam sees Calvin running beside the truck, also Buddy and the Hellbitch crowding their pasture fence, ears pricked and nostrils flared at the scent of a strange horse.

"You think they're hoping for a new friend?" asks James, who has joined Tam on her front steps.

She nods. "Nervous, probably—wondering if it's a friend or foe—" But her mind has skipped to Jay Jennings's point of view, the novelist's habit of getting outside her own head and into someone else's. As Jay sets his brakes and lowers the trailer gate, he sees Tam and James watching from the front steps, Calvin shaking in anticipation. A curious little lopsided family. At the beginning of the summer, she had eaten breakfast at James's table and cast him as the too-young father of Calvin and Vay and herself as the soon-to-depart outsider. What is Tam to James and Calvin now?

Admit it, Tam. You care about those boys.

James glances at her, gives her a tentative smile as they walk together to the trailer, where Jay Jennings leads the filly into sunlight.

Jay Jennings smiles at their admiration, shakes hands with James, who introduces himself. "James Warceski, Calvin's brother. Beautiful horse."

"That she is," agrees Jennings, and Tam pulls herself together and does the country thing of offering coffee and delivering the certified check. It's clear that Jennings puzzles over the relationship between Tam and the young men, when he and his sister had assumed Calvin was Tam's son, but he doesn't ask.

Thirty minutes later, coffee duly poured and enjoyed, Jennings excuses himself. "Gotta long drive home tonight, pulling that trailer." And he's wise enough not to remind Tam to be careful introducing the bay filly to the other horses.

Buddy and the Hellbitch still observe the filly from across their fence, while the filly tramps in place where she is tied to the hitching rail, eager to make their acquaintance. Just as Tam and the Warceski brothers see Jennings off, the filly raises her muzzle and sends a ringing neigh to the other horses, who flinch, back away from their fence, and then, drawn by their curiosity, return to draw their nostrils full of her.

"Kind of like a new kid in school," says Calvin.

"That'll be you soon," James tells him.

"Bleah."

James shrugs. He unties the filly and leads her a few paces. Strokes the arch of her neck as she nuzzles his shirt. "Aw, sweetheart—" He glances over his shoulder at Tam and smiles with his guard down. Pure pleasure on his face.

"Let's introduce her to her new friends," Tam says, to cover the moment.

Spend all the time with her that you can, she had told Calvin. Pet her, talk to her, get her used to your hands and your voice and scent. See if she likes apple slices. Now, as the sun sets behind the lone pine, James and Tam sit on her front steps and watch Calvin and the filly play in the last rays. Buddy and the Hellbitch had crowded up for their share of treats but gradually lost interest and went back to grazing, while the filly arches her neck and butts Calvin for more ear scratching.

"What happens next?" says James. Earlier he had put a six-pack of Henry's in Tam's refrigerator, and now he takes a slow sip from a can.

"Once she trusts him, I'll get Calvin to show her the saddle and saddle blanket. Rub her all over with the blanket, ease it on her back, lead her around the pasture. Make sure she doesn't startle. Same way with the saddle and bridle. Once she's used to that, I'll ride Buddy and lead her around the corral. We won't hurry her, but in a week Calvin probably can ride her while I snub."

"Um—"

"What?"

"Am I gonna have to buy myself a saddle to ride with you now?"

Tam turns to look at him and sees his tentative smile. Smiles back. "I think Hube's saddle still hangs upstairs. Which horse are you going to ride? The Hellbitch? Because I'll need to ride Buddy to snub for Calvin."

"You'd let me use Hube's saddle?"

"Why not?"

"Just—he's a legend."

Tam shrugs. "You'd do better to worry about riding the Hellbitch." She glances at James. "You're not afraid of her, are you?"

He grins. "Maybe I'll ride her around the corral a time or two first. Think I'll do all right after that. Make a change, riding a horse tall enough that my feet don't drag."

He takes another sip of beer, looks down at Tam, catches her eyes. "My dad was twenty-five years older than Calvin's mother," he says.

Calvin approaches them, leading the filly, who nuzzles his shoulder.

"Have you thought of a name for her?" Tam asks him.

"Melanie," Calvin says, and Tam feels James flinch beside her.

16

Tam's fine words to Libarriby Sibidibel, *I'll write something worthwhile*—her first tentative attempts at a journal—have been crowded out by thoughts of horses. Legend or not, someone has to have ridden a horse for the first time. Perhaps a horse like Tam's linebacked buckskin, whose dark line along her spine was supposed to indicate ancient lineage? Or perhaps a proto-horse that looked like the little burro?

How would that first horseback ride have come about?

Dogs, well—easy to imagine an early species of wolf, drawn to the side of the campfire by the warmth of flames and the scent of meat dripping on a spit. Gradually a partnership, a kind of symbiosis, developing. *If you'll feed me, I'll hunt for you. I'll fight beside you. I'll curl up close to you in the cold.*

But a horse wouldn't have been drawn to the warmth of a campfire, even by curiosity. Tam has searched the internet for information about early domestication and learned only that horses probably were used first as beasts of burden, capable of carrying heavier loads than dogs, in what is now the Middle East. She dimly remembers a novel she must have read as a child, of a young girl rescuing a colt from a bog and earning its gratitude—bleah, as Calvin would say. She has no desire to write a cave-girl novel.

Hube's saddle hangs from a hook in the ceiling of the big bedroom upstairs that had been his. Tam loosens the saddle from its rope, shaking her head at the stiffened leather.

"Needs lots of work with saddle soap," she says, and James nods he'll get to it. He gives her a look that backs her off when she starts to lift the saddle and hoists it to his own shoulder to carry downstairs.

Tam has decided—well, after some discussion with James—that his riding the Hellbitch is best begun while she rides Buddy without trying to snub for Calvin at the same time. So they leave Calvin playing with the filly—*Melanie*, Tam remembers—while they bring Buddy and the Hellbitch from their pasture to the corral. Buddy is used to Tam's saddling him, but the Hellbitch rolls her eyes at James.

"Take it easy," he growls at her and rubs her neck until she settles down. Tam nods to herself, James will be all right. Still she watches as he rides the Hellbitch around the corral, then kicks her up to a trot. Hube's stirrups are long enough for James, and he looks more comfortable astride the big Hellbitch than he ever did on Buddy.

"May as well do it," she says, and leans down from Buddy to open the corral gate.

They ride side by side along the ridge trail in the fragrant morning until they reach their place among the fallen boulders. Wait a minute, Tam says to herself. When did it become *our place?*

They tie Buddy and the Hellbitch in the timber, out of sight from the trail, just in case, and hike down far enough to hear the creek current over the soft sough of the pines. Sit together, not touching, on the sun-warmed sandstone.

She senses James needs encouragement. "So?" she says, making it a question.

Creek current, sigh of pines. "Melanie," James says. "Yeah. I married her. A year or two after I started raising Calvin. I'd known her in college, and"—the forced steadying of his voice—"Calvin adored her. We—had—" His flat words laid out one by one in thin pine-scented air. "—three good years. We—she—was pregnant. Calvin was excited."

Tam, having an awful idea now of what she's going to hear, on impulse lays her hand on James's clenched fists and feels solid oak that opens to grip her fingers in return.

"We lost the baby. We lost her. She knew she was dying. Hardest thing I ever did. I told her our baby was all right."

His grip on Tam's fingers now is tight enough to hurt, but she doesn't try to pull away, and she wonders who had been there to offer him comfort—his mother?—and remembers Hube and Mrs. Eckles standing by her.

"Calvin loved her too."

James nods. "Don't know if I can live with that name for his filly. Guess I'll have to. Oh hell, Tam."

Their eyes meet again. His eyes shine with tears. He leans toward her, finds her mouth. A brief kiss, like a pledge.

Tam and Calvin are working the filly, Melanie, saddling and unsaddling her in the corral, when the black Tahoe appears at the crest of the hill by the giant pine, and Tam freezes. Now what the hell? She's aware of the filly's pricked ears and stiffened neck, she senses Calvin's tension behind her, but when she looks for the boy, she finds that he has melted away—*where*—slipping through the corral poles and running for the cabin.

The Tahoe pulls past the barn, parks by the corral. A single figure gets out of the driver's side and walks around the Tahoe to look over the top pole of the corral.

Rob. With the sunlight caught in his hair.

He's not wearing black ninja clothes but ordinary blue jeans and a faded cotton tee with lace-up runners. His face is strained. With anger?

"Beautiful horse," he says in a voice she never would have recognized. It's been eighteen years, after all, since she's heard him speak and then with a boy's words hurled to hurt. She scans this man's face, this man who is her son, searching for any resemblance of Hube there, or of Allen Heckman, for that matter. Finds none. He's a stranger.

"What do you want, Rob?" she says, when she can be sure her voice will remain level.

"I want to talk—to you."

Does he want to ask her why she's not dead yet? Tam doesn't get an answer because a dark-blue pickup roars down the track from the Sun Creek spring and stops with a squeal of tires, nose to nose with the Tahoe, and James leaps out, stiff legged, to confront Rob. The filly jerks back in alarm at human vibrations she does not understand, and Tam automatically reaches to calm her.

Calvin must have run to the cabin to call his brother on her new landline, Tam thinks, and yes, there's Calvin, slinking down the front steps of the cabin to observe the action he's sparked, and oh God what now.

James and Rob glowering at each other from ten feet apart. James perhaps the taller by an inch or two of the two men and wider shouldered. The air bristling between them. The corral fence between them and Tam and the filly. The filly, vulnerable in her young beauty, nudging Tam's shoulder with her nose and snorting. *Do something*, she's asking. *Make this stop.*

"Rob Heckman," says James.

"James what's-your-name."

"My name is James Warceski."

Do something. Tam strokes the filly to calm her, leads her up to the corral fence. "You said you came to talk," she says to Rob. "So talk."

"Here?"

"Why not?"

He hesitates, glances at James, and shrugs. "I might have said—some things that were out of line."

What an understatement, Tam might have said and doesn't. She waits.

"I'm worried about my dad."

When she doesn't answer, he goes on. "Look, I've got better . . . things to do than . . . hang around these hills . . . shooting holes in trees. Can't we settle . . . this?"

"Settle what?"

He glances from Tam to James again. "Dad wants . . . his home ranch back. If he can't have . . . his home ranch, he says he'll take . . . the Bowen place. He says you owe him," stumbling over her name, "you owe him . . . Tam Bowen."

"Are you out of your goddamn mind?" says James in a voice that sounds remarkably reasonable, as though he really wants to know the answer.

No, Rob's not out of his mind, but Tam's beginning to think Allen must be out of his goddamn mind.

Rob takes a deep breath, makes a placating gesture with his hands. "Look . . . from his point of view. My . . . *she* . . . tricked him into getting . . . her pregnant. Tried to . . . ruin his life for him. There've been . . . times, oh hell, the . . . child support the state . . . forced her to send him was—all the income we had . . ."

Rob is saying more, but his voice is drowned out by Hube's furious bellow in the back of Tam's head—*the goddamn lying little sonofabitch*—and Tam isn't sure whether Hube means Allen or Rob. From the corner of her eye, she sees Calvin has stolen back down to the corral to listen.

James interrupts Rob—"Maybe your dad thinks Tam tried to trick him, but it didn't work, did it? He didn't marry her, did he?"

"No, but . . ."

"And maybe he really thinks I owe him his ranch back, but I don't believe *you* think that. I think you know that what's-his-name I bought the place from, Dallas Claiborne, bought it from your grandfather, all legal with the deed drawn up and the check cashed, which I can show you. And I don't know what happened to the cash your grandfather got from the place, but Claiborne used what I paid him to buy a share in a golf course. Maybe you and your dad should ask Claiborne to give you his golf course."

A silence. Magpies scolding over something in the timber, maybe a dead squirrel.

"He's my *dad*," says Rob in a different voice, a long-ago voice that Tam does recognize, and she surprises herself with the wave of sympathy she feels, the need to comfort the hurting child. Before she can find words, James is speaking.

"I've got beer in Tam's refrigerator. Come on up to the cabin with me, where we can sit down and talk. That all right with you, Tam?"

And Tam nods and watches the two young men turn from the corral and walk together toward her cabin. Arms' lengths apart. Not friendly, not quite hostile.

Calvin sidles through the corral poles and joins Tam. "What do we do now?"

"We saddle Buddy, and we ride him and Melanie."

Time enough after their ride to call Libarriby Sibidibel.

Tam and Calvin ride side by side along the track toward the county road. Drifts of afternoon clouds above them, a bird in flight vanishing into deep timber. That bird's-eye view might see that Tam leads Calvin and the filly on a tight snub. Melanie had flinched and sidestepped when she felt Calvin's weight on her back, but she was reassured by Buddy's familiar scent, and she stepped out beside him for a dozen rounds of the corral and then several circles of her familiar pasture. Now she paces alongside him on the dirt road, not at all like a green filly but like the well-mannered horse she will be. Tam smiles to herself. Calvin had been more apprehensive than the filly at this first saddling, although he tried hard not to show it. Clamped lips, white knuckles on the saddle horn as he stepped into the stirrup and swung astride her.

But Tam's thoughts are elsewhere, even as Hube growls at her from the depths of shade—*Keep your mind on what you're doing, you got a green horse and a green kid on your hands*—and she feels the magnet tug of her cabin even as she and Calvin ride farther from it. What's happening there—what's happening—at a flutter in the underbrush, some small critter, the filly shies against Buddy, jolting hard against Tam's leg, and Calvin utters a small sound even as Tam reins in Buddy and waits for the filly to calm herself. *Damn it, Tam, keep your mind on what you're doing!*

"You're fine," she reassures Calvin, and he manages a smile.

At the bridge over Sun Creek, Tam hesitates. Should they cross the bridge and chance a ride along the county road, where traffic might spook the filly? Or should they turn back toward her cabin and interrupt whatever James and Rob—she can't imagine, doesn't want to imagine, a scene between James and Rob. Hube is in her head, he wants to horsewhip somebody, and she's arguing with him, his words and hers blurred by the chuckle of creek current, when the rattle of an approaching vehicle turns her eyes downstream toward a rising cloud of dust that follows a truck with a dome light over its cab.

The driver has seen her and Calvin because the truck slows and pulls off on the verge. Murray County Sheriff's Department emblem on the door that Libarriby Sibidibel opens and gets out. Walks slowly across the bridge toward Tam and Calvin.

"Nice horses," he remarks as he touches his hat to Tam like the courteous man he is. Full navy uniform, boots and badge. And the sheriff's department truck. He's on official business, then.

"On my way to the Simmons place," he says. "Got a call—" He interrupts himself, lets his eyes drift over a peaceful scene. A sunny afternoon, the two riders on calm horses, even the filly showing no more than a prick of her ears with curiosity about the stranger. "Don't suppose you've heard anything, Tam?"

Heard anything. Without intention Tam's eyes slide to meet Calvin's, just as his eyes meet hers.

Larry hasn't missed their shared glance. "What?"

What, indeed.

"Just strange is all. Rob Heckman. He showed up at my cabin just as Calvin and I were saddling for our ride. He must still be there, or he'd have passed us on the track. He's driving the Tahoe—"

Larry's eyes move from Tam to Calvin. "And you are—"

Ever well mannered, Calvin touches the brim of his hat. "Calvin Warceski, sir. I'm James's brother." Unnecessarily, he adds, "Tam and I are breaking this filly to ride."

"Real nice filly." Larry looks her over, turns back to Tam. "What did Rob Heckman want?"

Tam hesitates. Hears the unhurried creek current, the never-ending distant roar from the ridge pines, the blessed sameness of the Sun Creek country cast into relief by the strange behavior of its occupants. The behavior of her son. A man she doesn't know, a man who once was her baby.

"I don't really know, Larry," she admits. "At first I thought he'd come to spin that story of his and his father's, that they're entitled to the ownership of the old Heckman place again. But he seemed—"

"Angry?"

"Maybe. Uneasy. Said he was worried. He's in my cabin now, talking to Calvin's brother."

Larry seems unhurried as he considers what Tam has said. But Tam feels tension from—what? That Larry isn't moving from his tracks, although he has left the county truck's engine running, that he hasn't told her anything about the call he got—whatever is happening at the old Simmons place.

"I think if I were you, Tam," Larry says, "I'd take the kid and ride back the way you came, maybe take a side trail if you hear that Tahoe headed toward you. Wouldn't want it to spook that nice little mare. I'll give you a call later on, probably tell you all's good, nothing to worry about. Take care, now. Good to meet you, Calvin."

17

Tam and Calvin meet no Tahoe as they ride back toward the bridge. All quiet except for the clip-clop of unshod hooves in road dust and the squeak of leather, the rumblings of horses. Tam keeps an eye on Calvin and the filly, but the filly seems almost as relaxed as Buddy, and Calvin is focused on the tips of the little bay's ears, as he should be. What is he thinking about? Is he remembering his drill? What to do if the filly unexpectedly panics and shies into Buddy, fighting the lead rope, trying to flee whatever absurd rustling of underbrush or flight of bird alerts her horse brain to unspeakable danger? Or is Calvin turning his thoughts, as Tam herself has been trying not to, toward the two young men who are—doing what? Sitting in her cabin? Talking about what?

"Why is he so mad at you?" Calvin asks suddenly.

Tam glances at him, but he's still looking straight ahead. The filly has flicked back an ear at the sound of his voice but keeps her steady pace beside Buddy.

How to answer. "It's complicated," she begins. "I was seventeen—" She hesitates. Her suspicions about seventeen-year-old Vay and Ed Evenson's sudden decamping with her for Los Angeles. Decides to change course. "His mother was too young to be a mom," she finishes. "She probably wasn't a very good one."

"You?"

But now Calvin has turned toward her, his face written with a naked anguish so like the anguish on James's face when he told of losing his wife and child. The filly, responding to the boy's flood of emotion, lays back her ears and crowds against Buddy, crushing Tam's leg against Calvin's.

"Watch your horse!" Tam warns.

Calvin croons to the filly—"Melanie, Melanie"—and soothes her with the pressure of reins and bit. On a steady pace again, he mutters, "Don't see how you'd ever be a bad mom."

It's Tam's turn now to float out of mind, unseeing of Buddy's steady ears or the patterns of sun and pine needle shadows across the dirt track ahead. Her kitchen table in the miserable two-room apartment in Missoula, spread with typed pages, pens and paper clips, textbooks with dog-eared pages, her water glass, and Rob's sippy cup. All the girl wants to think about is the sentence she's been trying and failing to frame on the essay for her advanced composition class. What she doesn't want to think about is the whining two-year-old at her knee, his soggy diaper, his plea—

Want up! Want up!

When she offers him his sippy cup, his face knots and reddens.

No! He flings the sippy cup, which bounces on his mother's stack of typed pages and loses its cap—somehow left unfastened by the girl with her mind elsewhere—and slops milk across the pages, the textbooks, the pens and paper clips—

No! screams the girl. She's out of her chair, she's shoving the toddler away from her, shoving so hard that he backpedals and falls hard on his bottom, his face showing his bewilderment—

No. Keep your head in the present. Tam slips back into the daylight world around her, the smell of horse sweat, the leather saddle under her, and the working muscles that have carried her around the lone pine on the knoll, the track ahead to where James's truck still sits nose to nose with the black Tahoe and where the two young men wait on the cabin steps, looking as unaware of each other as two strangers sitting on a park bench and waiting for a bus.

"We'll unsaddle," Tam tells Calvin. The filly hasn't had much of a first ride, just the few miles to the bridge and back, but what else to do? Rein up the ridge trail, pretend she and Calvin haven't seen James and Rob, and hope they don't meet Allen, looking for his son?

So the familiar. Unsaddling Buddy and the filly, brushing them, measuring out their oats, turning them into their pasture.

Beginning the long walk to the cabin.

The toddler's face. Rob watching her approach, his face troubled.

Ten feet from the cabin steps, Tam stops. Looks from Rob to James. Wind soughing in the ridge pines, horses whickering in the pasture as Buddy and the filly get reacquainted with the Hellbitch. Calvin, hovering and anxious.

James lifts an eyebrow at Tam, as neutral as though he hadn't kissed her yesterday. "You want to talk here or inside?"

"Here's good."

"You can sit where I've been sitting, then. Have your talk." James stands, leans against the railing with his arms folded.

Rob looks alarmed. "What am I supposed . . . to tell her?"

"Tell her what you told me."

"Maybe," says Tam, "the first thing you ought to tell me is why the sheriff is on his way to the Simmons place, which you've been renting. Why he got a call reporting a disturbance there."

"*What?*" Rob's face loses color. "Where . . . the sheriff . . . how did you . . ."

"We met him on our ride. He warned us to stay clear."

Rob is on his feet now, seeming undecided if he is talking to Tam or to James. "Look, I gotta . . . I can't stay. I gotta get back up there . . . maybe you'll talk to me after . . . after . . ."

He gives it up, stares at Tam and swallows, then heads for the Tahoe, running. Tears its door open even as he's digging keys out of his shirt pocket, leaps in and pulls the big SUV in a tight two-point turn back on the track. Roars away.

Silence, more or less. The diminishing growl of the departing Tahoe. The dust cloud settling back down on the track.

"Jeez," says Calvin.

"Yeah."

Tam turns to James. "What did he tell you?"

James seems to consider. Looks from Tam to his brother. "The guy's got a helluva mess on his hands. I'm beginning to feel like I've got one too. Come inside where we can get out of the heat and this damned dust."

The great room is blessedly cool and quiet. Sunlight falling through the windows in patches, the pine odor from the fresh boughs Tam has arranged in the river rock fireplace. She collapses into a futon and holds her head in her hands.

"It's Rob's story to tell," says James.

"No." She breathes out. "Tell me."

James hesitates. "Does Calvin know any of this? Do you want me to run him outta here?"

"No." Tam eyes Calvin, who shifts nervously. "Come sit with me?" she asks him, and he does.

James is pacing back and forth. Goes to a window, looks out at the yard and empty track, returns and sits opposite Tam and his brother. "Like I said, a helluva mess up there. Sheriff didn't tell you more?"

"No. But he was worried about something."

"So." James turns from the window and unloads on Tam. "All this—what—*history* you've never told us. Who else knows?"

"Hardly anybody. Bunce and Suze Simmons would have known. Libarriby—I mean Larry—the sheriff, knows, but that's because he and I were in high school together. When it happened."

"Hell." James stands with his feet apart, his arms crossed. Glares at Tam. "Seems you had a boyfriend. Fellow by the name of Warren Wetzel. He and your *son*—Rob—had a big blowup, ended with Wetzel beating the crap out of him. Rob being about fifteen at the time. He left you and went to live with his father from then on."

Tam nods.

"This Wetzel guy still in the picture?"

"God no."

"Heckman had moved around a lot, but he was living in Billings when Rob moved in with him. A helluva life for a boy when his father couldn't keep a job, couldn't keep his nose clean. Why the hell did you let him go?"

Tam finds her own fists clenched. None of James's business, about the attorney, eighteen years ago, who had advised her that a judge would take a teenager's request for a change of custody parent into account, the same attorney who had pointed out the damage she would do to her boyfriend, that aspiring young assistant professor, Warren Wetzel, by bringing a battery charge against him. No. Water under the bridge. Over and done with.

"Heckman's father kept him and Rob afloat for a while, that and the child support checks you sent him. Rob graduated high school, did a year or two at the college in Billings, ran out of money and had to drop out. He's pretty bitter about that."

Of course he would be bitter.

"Found a decent job, though. Worked several years for the postal service. Then his grandfather died, and he and his dad were in clover for a while. The money from the ranch sale, I suppose, and whatever else the old man had accumulated. You didn't know any of this?"

"No. I never heard from them after I stopped sending support checks. They moved around quite a lot, and I wouldn't have had an address. Well—except—"

No. She stops herself. She will not tell James about Rob's letter to her this spring. Or what it had done to her. She will not. She's feeling a kind of detachment, almost an out-of-body sensation, that what is happening to her cannot be happening. Like Calvin's putting his arm around her shoulders now, drawing her close—the boy's had a growth spurt this summer, he's taller than Tam now—and she wants to laugh through her tears. Calvin, comforting her. Calvin, the same age Rob had been when he turned on her in fury.

James sounds calmer now. "The hell of it is, I ended up feeling kind of sorry for the bastard. There he was, with nobody in the world except you—I suppose Hube was gone by then? And a dad who was a jerk on his best day and a brainless jerk at that. Then you bring home this *Warren Wetzel* guy, and he and the kid tangle, and the kid runs off to make his point but also to find comfort somewhere—kinda like another kid I know—"

"God," Tam breathes, and feels Calvin's arm tighten around her.

"So they go from living on child support and handouts to inheriting the old man's pile. *Quit your stinking job*, Rob says his dad told him, *we got more important things to do*. And it made"—James shakes his head—"made sense to him for a while. Get back the old man's ranch, hole up and stock up and prepare for what, the end of days, I guess. They planned to practice holding off the invaders. Only problem they had, I got in their way, and then you got in their way. And I guess they thought you'd scare easier than I would."

Shakes his head again. "Must have forgotten what they knew about you."

Calvin speaks for the first time. "So, are they crazy or what? You shoulda seen them on the county road, James, dressed up in black and acting like they were gonna run the horses over."

"I think Rob thinks his dad is crazy. Cracked. Whatever. But Rob? More brainwashed than crazy, I think. But Tam—he talked about Bunce."

"Bunce?" Tam realizes she is shaking and that James suddenly is crouching beside her.

"Get her some water, Calvin."

And she catches a glimpse of Calvin's scared face as he jumps to obey.

"Tam. No. He didn't say his dad shot Bunce. Didn't see it happen. But he's afraid he did."

"*Why?*"

"He said when they first came back to Murray County, his dad tried to—how did Rob put it? Said his dad told him he'd known Bunce Simmons when he was a kid—"

"Which he did, of course," Tam whispers. Calvin is pushing a glass of water into her hand, making her hold it. "But—well, Bunce and Hube thought Allen was a lazy spoiled brat—and Bunce wouldn't have thought he'd improved."

"Apparently not. So—what's his name, Allen, tried his charm on Suze, and that worked out better for him. Next thing, Bunce ends up dead and Allen and Rob are moving onto the Simmons place. Here, sip your water."

Tam sips. Straightens her back. She is *not* going into—where—into a fugue again. She is not giving crazy Allen that kind of power over her. Nor Rob! What was James's word for him? *Brainwashed.* Convinced by his crazy father that invaders are coming—the federal government? Socialists? Out-of-staters? The zombie apocalypse? No matter. Maybe at first the fifteen-year-old boy thought it was exciting. A real-life video game played with his father, who was so much more fun than his strict, rule-making mother.

His hateful letter. *I wish you were dead!* And she—admit it, Tam!—had been on the verge of accepting her role in their real-life video game by coming back to Montana with her secret stash of pills and giving herself the gift of a last summer in the mountains.

Bunce. Had his death shocked Rob out of the video game and back into reality?

Tam realizes that James is talking to her. "You're all right? Better now?"

"Yes. Better."

Calvin, looking anxiously over James's shoulder—"I don't think she's had anything to eat today."

"Hell. And neither have you." James brushes Tam's cheek with his fingertips, meets her eyes for a moment, and stands. "Keep talking to her, Calvin. I'll see what she's got for supper."

"I'm all *right*," Tam snaps, and Calvin blinks but sits down beside her on the futon.

"Yeah you are," he agrees, "but we didn't get much of a ride today."

"We'll do better tomorrow."

Tam hears James opening cabinet doors behind her, opening the refrigerator and closing it. Wonders what he'll find that's fit to cook. When has she last shopped?

"I think James wants to ride with us," says Calvin. "You think he'll be okay riding the Hellbitch?"

"Better than Vay, at least," Tam says and is relieved when Calvin chuckles. Resilient, that's Calvin.

Rob. He's thirty-three now, he's nearly as old as James, and where is his resilience? This afternoon he had seemed—frayed. Running to the Tahoe, wheeling away on squealing tires and a cloud of dust. Maybe not unraveled but getting there.

James's words. *He's got a helluva mess on his hands.* Tam's thoughts fly back to Libarriby Sibidibel. What is happening at the high end of the ridge trail?

The afternoon has darkened into early evening, and through the uncurtained window, Tam sees a light bobbing down from the ridge trail. Someone with a flashlight? James has seen it, too, because he leaves his search for ingredients to watch.

"Wish to hell you'd hang curtains over those windows," he mutters, "and I wish to hell I hadn't left my rifle in the truck." When the knock comes at the door, he glances at Calvin, and Calvin nods at the unspoken signal.

But bounding through the door that James opens is Zenith's dog, Spotty, wagging and bowing and happy to see friends. Right behind Spotty is Zenith himself, carrying a lantern and a picnic basket and squinting in the lights of the great room.

"Anybody hungry?"

18

"You think I could learn to cook?" says Calvin.

Tam shrugs. "Maybe. But you'd better talk to Zenith or your brother about teaching you. I'll stick to teaching you to ride."

"Have you ever known how to cook?" he persists.

"Well—survival level, I guess."

What had she cooked for Rob? Toast and scrambled eggs. Hamburgers. Macaroni and cheese out of a box. Salad greens out of plastic packages. Picking up a pizza on the way home from work, which didn't count as cooking but happened on nights when she was so tired from telephone soliciting all day and studying for mid-semester exams all night, after finally, finally, getting the boy to go to sleep. What an excuse for a mother Rob had had.

What had Hube cooked for her? Fried meat, mostly venison. Fried potatoes, fried onions. Sometimes green beans from a can. Tam pulls herself away from dreams of Hube's kitchen, fire blazing in the woodstove and Hube with a dish towel tied around his waist, heating grease in a skillet.

Raised you to be a boy, he did!

Libarriby's word for her: *competent.*

She was real good, as Hube said, at sticking on a horse, but she never learned to ride a bicycle, so she couldn't teach Rob how. She never learned to swim, so she had to send Rob down to the YMCA. Now she makes an effort and finds herself back on her futon beside Calvin, being offered a plate of something succulent, chunks of salmon on noodles in a lemony sauce. Calvin already is digging into his own plate of salmon.

"Comes from working around the oil patch all those years," Zenith explains, as though he has been part of the discussion of cookery from the beginning. "Had to learn. That or live on fast food."

The afternoon has darkened into early evening. James turns from the window, where he has been watching the horses. Watching, Tam understands, for any signs of disturbance. Their eyes meet, and he is asking a question of her, but she can't read it.

He turns to Zenith. "So what were you doing? Hanging around the Simmons place, looking for trouble?"

Zenith grins, his white curls bobbing as he straightens from serving food to Tam and Calvin and ladles up a plate for James. "Trouble's always good to find. Been looking for it all my life."

James returns to the room, to the windows that look out over the trail. "What did you find this time?" he asks over his shoulder.

"Suze Simmons's sister, Em. What's her last name, anybody know? She was in that old car of hers, buzzing along in the direction of Suze's old place. I wouldn't have thought she could see well enough to make out the road. Maybe she uses pings and echoes, like a bat."

Tam has a brief flash of Em as a bat, hanging from a rafter, and has to fight down the urge to laugh.

"What did she do? Try to run you down?"

"Nah. I wasn't trying to hide, just standing by the county road with Spotty there. I don't think she saw me when they passed. Probably couldn't see as far as the borrow pit."

James turns, gives Zenith a level look, and waits.

Zenith squirms. "James, you want a chunk of bread to go with your fish and noodles? I baked it this afternoon. I baked a lemon pie too. Brought it here with me. No, no, I was just taking a walk with Spotty, minding my own business, like you know I always do—"

"Sure you do. What happened?"

Zenith lays down the loaf of bread he's been slicing. When he looks up, he has shed the country clown persona. "Went on with my walk, and yes, toward the Simmons place. And maybe I was taking a few more pains not to be noticed, but I was curious as hell why that old lady was on the road. Hell, I didn't think she even drove anymore. I know she and Suze order their groceries in by phone."

A practiced storyteller, he looks around at his audience of three to gauge their reaction. "Once I got within sight of the house, I kept to the timber. Told Spotty to lay down and be quiet. Watched Em park the car by the gate, watched her get out and hobble up to the door. Saw the Tahoe was gone, didn't see who answered the door but thought it must be okay because she went inside. So there I was, with nothing much to do this afternoon but watch the clouds float by. I hung around, told Spotty what a good dog he was, maybe kicked up some pine duff in front of some ants just to make them go around it—thought what I'd do if I were ant sized and all of a sudden a big old high hill turned up in front of me—and then I heard the gunshots from inside the house. A string of them."

He waits, satisfied with the response he's getting from James, Tam, and Calvin.

"What happened?" demands James.

"Oh, I made tracks through the underbrush, found a deer trail and followed it out of sight of the house. Didn't have my gun with me, or I might have been a little braver. But I did have my cell with me"—taps his shirt pocket—"and I called the sheriff."

"You get cell phone service up there?" Tam can't help asking.

"Pretty good, up as high as the Simmons place is. Then I waited around a while, saw the sheriff drive by in his big outfit, then an ambulance, waited some more, but nothing much happened, except the Tahoe showed up and the young man ran inside, and after a while the ambulance left, and then the sheriff left. And then I walked home."

"It's a wonder you didn't walk up to the door and knock, offer them lemon pie," says Tam, and Zenith smiles at her, but the clown is gone.

"Em was still there when you left?"

"Her car was still parked by the gate. I dunno, maybe they were having indoor target practice. Hate to think about Em's aim. Suze, now, might not do too bad. Strange she didn't come along, now that I think about it."

Time was when Suze would have done more than all right, Tam thinks, remembering Suze and her shotgun and the chicken hawk on the wing. Zenith's eyes are on her. Thoughtful. A depth of experience there. When he asks, "What is that young man to you, Tam?" she hears herself answer.

"My son."

"Why didn't you tell me?"

Tam and James have walked as far as the boulders above the spring. The heat of the afternoon lingers in the sandstone, but cooler air rises from the creek current.

"Why?" His fists are clenched, and he's glaring as though in search of something to punch.

Tam shrugs. "I wasn't just keeping it from you and Calvin—"

"*Calvin* knows?"

"I didn't mean to tell him—it just slipped out. Because I never tell anyone. I suppose some people know I've got a son and no husband, but they don't ask."

"Did that Warren guy ask if you had a husband?"

"I—not exactly. I think he put two and two together. Look—I was lonely, and Warren was an asshole, and it ended badly."

"When he beat up Rob?"

Tam wants to nod. Wants to let James think so. But no. She may have withheld plenty from him, but she's not going to lie to him.

"No. We hung on for another couple years. It was—rocky."

Rocky, not a strong enough word. A couple years during which she phoned and phoned Allen, pleading to talk to Rob, hating herself for caring so much. And Warren, simmering with resentment. "Why wasn't she pleading with *him* not to leave her when he left? When he came back? When he left again?"

Left, flinging the words over his shoulder: *You're too damned old for me, Tam!* Tam had been all of thirty-four, although she already felt old, and she believed him. Warren? He was twenty-nine. He went on to find a younger woman, he did. His new woman was nineteen, he told Tam in a triumphant email.

James is looking across the pool to the opposite hillside, where a pair of crows hop from branch to branch, picking out a roost to settle down for the night in a rustle of aspen leaves. Aspen leaves turning brittle before their time in the heat and lack of rainfall. Higher on the ridge, the pines turning rusty. Probably from the pine beetles moving from western Montana to destroy the bark and kill the trees.

"I want to think you trust me," he says with his back turned.

Hube's bellow reverberates through Tam's head: *Don't be spillin' your guts, girl!*

"I do trust you, James. I'm just not—very forthcoming."

"When I read that book you wrote, I thought—thought you had to be—"

Tam forces a smile. "Experienced?"

"Sophisticated maybe. I never would have expected to see you in a corral with a green horse."

"No. What I've got is an imagination and a way with words."

"Hmm."

Another long silence, until he says, "I need to get out there with a chainsaw and take down all I can of those damned rusted-out pines. Chop 'em up for firewood or maybe talk to the guys that use the boards for custom paneling and furniture. I've heard they make a fancy finish."

"Furniture."

They walk back to the cabin in the failing light. James is silent, and Tam's head spins with thoughts that won't coalesce into a narrative. The horses are three silhouettes in a corner of their pasture, heads down, hipshot, and comfortable.

"I need to go home," says James when they reach the steps. "Calvin's probably already there. If he's snooping in my computer room again, I'll wring his goddamn neck."

Tam nods.

James's truck waits in the shadows, but he doesn't move. The moment lengthens.

"Are we still friends?"

"Friends," Tam says, and he bends and kisses her mouth, and then he walks away, into the shadows to his truck.

The twin red dots of James's truck have vanished, but Tam sits alone on the cabin steps. Thinks the best thing for her might be to move back to Portland. Lets herself imagine it. Loading her car with what she can carry, stopping in Fort Maginnis for gas, and driving west, driving away from thoughts that won't coalesce into narrative. Telling no one. Well, perhaps calling Libarriby Sibidibel, once she's safely on the interstate highway, assuring him she hasn't met with foul play for him to have to investigate. *Foul play.* She turns the words over, considering the various meanings she can wring out of them.

A sudden movement in the pasture. The Hellbitch flings up her head from sleep and points her ears at the cabin. Tam feels a power surge, as though some invisible equine radar has passed between her and the mare. Words. *Driving west. Telling no one. Foul play.* Waking the Hellbitch, who sends back her distress by pawing the sod and neighing a long ringing call to arms.

By the time Tam is on her feet, Buddy and the filly also are awake. straining over the pasture fence and stamping. Tam detours to the barn for the feed bucket and carries it down to offer handfuls of oats to each of the horses in turn. She pats their necks, feels their tension easing as they crowd each other for another helping of oats. The Hellbitch, dark and lofty against a dark sky, leans over the fence and nuzzles Tam, then lays her head on Tam's shoulder. Its weight and warmth bear Tam down, root her own feet in sod.

Just as, long ago, the little linebacked buckskin mare laid her head on Tam's shoulder, and Tam had felt the weight and warmth, the good pungent odors of horse sweat and horse droppings, steadying her in place. And then she had watched the pickup truck with the stock rack that was driving the buckskin mare away, she had watched the dust settle on the track behind the pickup truck, and she hadn't cried, because a horse trader's daughter couldn't cry about a horse.

Just as she now understands she isn't going anywhere.

19

The dawn has been greeted by a joyous round of AK-47 fire and a flight of crows as frantic as though they are hearing the blasts for the first time. The horses, on the other hand, lay back their ears and pace uneasily to greet Tam when she comes to fill their water tank and pour their morning oats into their feedboxes. She hears their unspoken sentiments: *We wish he'd quit doing that!*

She is straightening from the feedboxes when the single occupant in the black Tahoe drives past the lone pine on the crest and on down the track to the cabin. She and the horses watch as Rob gets out of the Tahoe, walks up the cabin steps, and knocks on the door.

He waits, then seems to feel the several pairs of eyes on him and turns. Sees Tam, seems to consider, then walks toward her and the horses, with early sunlight falling on his fair hair. A grown man in a dark shirt and Levi's and laced sneakers who would not look out of place walking in downtown Portland. Who would not look like one-of-us when there still were enough those-of-us in the Sun Creek country to observe him.

"Good morning," says Tam, when he stops at the other side of the fence.

Rob nods. His eyes are on the horses, especially the Hellbitch, who looks back at him, ears at the alert but eyes dark and calm.

"She's a big horse," he remarks.

"Seventeen hands," says Tam, and when Rob looks his question, she adds, "Five feet, six inches at the withers."

"Taller than you are."

Tam cannot think of a response to that without sounding inane, so she says nothing. She fondles the Hellbitch's muzzle when the mare dips down her head. Rob seems to have taken an interest in the landscape, from the immediate scene of track and cabin, horse barn and pasture, to the distant pine forests rising to the distant blue of the Snowy Mountains. Nearby rustle of aspen leaves, distant roar of ridge pines. A hawk, dark against blue, sailing ever higher on a thermal current.

"Um . . . James . . . said I should . . . talk to you."

Tam feels a quick kaleidoscoping of thoughts rearranging themselves in patterns she had tried to describe to her laptop last night in the file she thinks of as her non-journal. Libarriby Sibidibel's warning, veiled as suggestion. Zenith. Shots fired inside the Simmons house.

"So talk," she says.

Rob raises his hands in a gesture that might be a plea or might be a protest at having a conversation across a barbed wire fence with the woman who gave birth to him, who seems more interested in her giant horse than she does in him.

"Dad's lost it. And we're broke."

The filly, shaking away a nose fly and snorting. Buddy, wandering off a few paces, nipping grass. The Hellbitch at Tam's shoulder.

"Nobody . . . got hurt yesterday," Rob says. "But that old woman. Dad . . . thought . . . she was threatening him, and I guess she . . . thought he was . . . threatening her. And now there's a line of bullet . . . holes across the back wall and some in the floor." He clears his throat, choking up. "The sheriff was already there when I got home. Somebody must have called him. Dad . . . ." He breaks off, tries again. "The sheriff . . . called for an ambulance. No . . . nobody . . . ."

He meets Tam's eyes for the first time. "Nobody got . . . *hurt*. The ambulance . . . was for Dad. He, well . . . they . . . said they'd bring him down from whatever, do detox on him, I guess. He was . . . screaming for me to save him, and the old woman . . . ."

He shakes his head as though to clear it. "She was screaming about rent money and self-defense, and hell, I . . . met her months ago, can't tell her from her sister. Sheriff arrested her."

Tam shakes her head. Tries to picture the scene. Libarriby disarming Allen, disarming Em—and while the ambulance crew loads Allen and straps him down. Libarriby handcuffs Em, Tam supposes, puts her in the rear seat of his truck, and follows the ambulance back to Fort Maginnis. The novelist in her itches to write the scene. Knows her feelings are, what's the silly contemporary word, *inappropriate*.

"I . . . can't pay for any of this," says Rob. "Ambulance. Whatever they . . . do with him. He's my *dad*." Chokes again, turns his back to Tam for a moment, recovers. "I know James . . . owns the ranch, I know it's not the Heckman ranch now. But it's my dad! He's been my playmate! He's always . . . been on my side! And I can't . . . do a goddamn thing for him!"

Tam sighs. Gives the Hellbitch a pat. "Come up to the cabin with me," she says. "I'll make coffee."

Calvin lurks in the aspen grove above the spring. He'd been on his way to help Tam with the horses that morning when he'd seen the black Tahoe pull up to the cabin and the asshole Rob Heckman get out and walk, probably up to the door, which Calvin couldn't see from his position in the aspens. Soon Heckman returned and looked around and must have spotted Tam in the pasture with the horses because now he walks down toward her.

Calvin fumes. He can see that the asshole and Tam are talking, but with too much open ground between him and them, he has no way of sneaking close enough to overhear what they are saying. Unless they're both so absorbed in what they're talking about that they don't notice him—but no, better not risk it. And better not risk running home to alert James, which would take him fifteen minutes or so. Anything could blow up in fifteen minutes, and damn it, he doesn't need James to fight his battles for him. Although—Calvin has to admit it—the conversation between Tam and the asshole doesn't look particularly dramatic or threatening, not a situation Calvin needs to rescue Tam from, just a man and a woman talking. And all three horses look peaceful, which they wouldn't if quarreling were heated or gestures abrupt and angry.

But fuck! She is *his* Tam, not the asshole's Tam. The asshole who ran off and didn't speak to her for years and then wrote her a letter that broke her heart. Oh, yes, Calvin, born sleuth and secret rifler through other people's boxes and drawers, knows all about that letter.

Shit! They're walking back to the cabin together.

But even as he swells with rage at their apparent intimacy, Calvin sees his way to close in on them. The cabin has windows, after all. Uncurtained windows. And patches of juniper and hawthorn brush around the cabin to conceal his approach.

He's on his hands and knees part of the way, breathing the scent of seed heads and dust. Then he's squirming on his belly under haws that droop their killer thorns and blackened berries just over his head. Closer, closer to the window, inching over shortgrass and gravel that is loud in his own ears. And now he's reached what somebody long ago must have planted as a lilac hedge, the blossoms long dried to rust in summer heat, the heart-shaped leaves a screen through which he can listen to voices through the open window. The stronger male voice with the curious stutter, the less distinct woman's voice.

"—who owns the Tahoe?"

"Dad. Well, he makes . . . the payments on it. Or he's . . . supposed to. I don't think he's . . . opened a checking account here in town."

"—repossession?"

"Ask . . . him about that, he'll . . . laugh and tell you they . . . have to find him first."

"—you don't have money of your own?"

"I'd . . . saved some while I . . . was working. It's . . . long gone now."

It's dawning on Calvin that he's gone to enormous trouble to eavesdrop on a discussion of personal finance, when the talk takes a more interesting turn.

"—the guns—"

"Yeah, they're . . . worth something, but go . . . near his guns and he . . . really will go apeshit."

Guns. Apeshit. Calvin inches closer to the window, raises his chin from the detritus of decayed lilac leaves. Now he can see the back of Tam's head, her familiar fall of tawny hair, and over her shoulder the asshole's face. And Calvin sees, in the split second, in the shape of the asshole's eyes and the lines of his mouth and nose and the color of his hair, the indisputable recognition that this man is his mother's son.

A split second that brings the asshole to his feet with a roar. "Who's out there?"

Calvin scrabbles backward in a rattle of branches and leaves that sounds enormous in his own ears. Enormous also is the sound of a window sash being thrown up and the sound of a large somebody landing on the very sod where Calvin has been crouched and listening. The sound of somebody's running strides behind him.

Frantic, Calvin finds his footing, immediately trips over a low-hanging branch, and, oblivious of the wicked thorns, dives for sanctuary into the nearest clump of hawthorn brush. Hugs his knees and shivers, counts his wounds and prays his pursuer won't think he's worth the damage the thorns can inflict.

"I know you're in there, you little shit."

Calvin doesn't dare to breathe. Through the hawthorn leaves, he glimpses the lower part of a blue-jeaned leg ending in laced sneakers. The leg isn't moving, well yes, it takes a sideways step or two, followed by a rustling in the weeds.

Then—*yeow!* The sharp end of a pole, driven through the hawthorns, attacks Calvin in his ribs. Calvin rolls over, squirms deeper into the hawthorns on his stomach, but not before the pole jabs him in the butt and draws another involuntary yelp.

"You coming out, shithead?"

Maybe he should give up, crawl out—Tam probably won't let the asshole kill him, but—but hell, Calvin is where he is because he wanted to *save* Tam, to rescue her from her asshole son, not be rescued *by* Tam! Hell, oh hell! Using his forearms to protect his eyes, oozing blood from numerous stabs and slashes, Calvin emerges into bright sunlight on the other side of the hawthorns, bounds to his feet, and runs.

The thud of running feet behind him only spurs him to run faster. At the edge of the sandstone boulders above the pool, he steals precious seconds to kick off his cowboy boots, feels fingers grasping for his shirt and belt, tears himself free, and leaps and dives.

Not the smartest stunt he ever pulled. The pool is shallower than it has been in previous summers, and Calvin himself taller than in previous summers. His dive grazes the crown of his head against the boulders below the water, *Oh God, this is it*, but his natural buoyancy carries him upward to the sunlit surface.

Someone is screaming.

"Kid? You okay?"

But Calvin is blinded by dazzle and floating in a cold cradle of water, in a strange peace. Sounds of bubbling springwater below him, sounds of current around him, sounds of strokes nearing him. Then an arm around his shoulders in what he vaguely recognizes as a lifeguard's hold. He's being towed against the current that spills into Sun Creek. Hears voices—the asshole's voice—

"Can you lift him out?"

"Yes," he hears Tam say.

Her hands raising him from the water. Sandstone beneath him now, sun warmed and solid. He wants to lie down, but he's being beaten on his back and shoulders, he's spewing water, he feels as limp as a bundle of rags. Now Tam leans above him, her hair falling about her face, brushing his face.

"—concussion?"

"We'll need to get him checked out," he hears her say. "If you'll wait with him, I'll call his brother."

Tam's face disappears. Calvin aches with the loss. Squints against the dazzle of sun through aspen leaves. All the colors of the sun. He tries to count—red, green, gold—but he's being interrupted.

"What the hell were you doing, kid?"

"Purple," he answers.

"I never meant to hurt you. Oh, hell."

"Gold."

"Mild concussion," says the doctor. "We've sedated him, and we'll want to keep him overnight for observation. He's got welts on his face and arms like he's been in a fight with a wildcat, so we've got antibiotics in the drip to ward off infection. But we also found strange wounds—as though he'd been speared—and we've given him a tetanus shot."

Tam, seated by the IV pole at Calvin's bedside, views the scene in the hospital room with strange detachment—herself and James on either side of Calvin's bed, the IV pole with its drip and tubing attached to the needle in the boy's hand, like a lopsided family confronting an outsider who cringes by the window.

James, on his feet—"You fucking bastard."

Rob, who has propped himself on the windowsill, says nothing but makes a hopeless gesture with his hands. He had taken off his shirt and socks and wrung them out before pulling them on again and following Tam and James to the emergency room in Fort Maginnis, but his shirt and Levi's are still wet and plastered to him, and his hair hangs in forlorn damp strands.

"I'll go," he says, as James glares at him. "I'll leave you to it." But he doesn't move.

"We've filed a police report," says the doctor, as though in reassurance. He nods to Tam, James, and Rob in turn and leaves the room, shutting the door behind him.

A silence.

"I don't—" begins Rob and breaks off in the face of James's fury.

"You what? Didn't mean to chase him down and beat him up and then try to drown him?"

"Stop," says Tam. "Just stop," and she rises to her feet as James turns his fury on her, but there is no time for anything else to happen because just then comes a quick tap on the door, which opens on Libarriby Sibidibel in full uniform.

20

In the cool of the evening, Libarriby has helped Tam brush and grain the horses and pump their trough full of fresh water. They hadn't spoken much on the drive from Fort Maginnis, beyond his "Need a lift home, Tam?" and her nod, because she'd ridden from the cabin with James at the wheel of his truck and Calvin cradled in her arms. Now, with the three horses drinking their fill at the trough and the early flight of bats, black against a darkening sky, the sheriff has accepted Tam's offer of a drink and walks with her to the cabin.

"Helluva week." He sighs and sinks heavily into a futon, beer in hand. "Like a war going on. Old women and kids."

"What happened at the Simmons place? Can you talk about it?"

He shakes his head. "I wouldn't have believed it. All those shots fired and neither of them hurt. Em was too blind, I guess, and Heckman was too wired. I took Em's pistol, damned little Saturday night special, away from her before she knew what was happening, and I rapped Heckman a good one in the throat to slow him down and take his rifle. Wondered afterward why nobody was dead. Including me."

Tam resists the impulse to see comedy in the scene. Nothing funny about it, nothing at all.

"But *why*?"

"Apparently, Heckman missed a rent payment to Suze. Maybe quite a few rent payments. Suze might have been all right with it—I think she's a little sweet on Heckman—but Em got all steamed up. Old guy next door said they'd had a helluva screaming fight, and then Em slammed out of the house and leaped in her car and roared off. He says those two old women are nowhere near as senile as they make out to be or as decrepit either."

"What's going to happen to them?"

"Not much. I called the EMTs to come and get Heckman, for his own good, and I took Em back to town in handcuffs, in hopes of making an impression on her, and I let her go on Suze's recognizance. Hope she and Em don't kill each other. Confiscated all the weaponry I could find and signed it in at the jail."

He takes a deep swig of beer, contemplates the bottle. "Don't expect anything to come of it. They can try charging each other, I suppose, but none of them's got money enough to go far with it. Judge would likely give Em a suspended sentence, maybe lock Heckman up long enough on a firearms charge to sober him up. What happened here this afternoon, that's something else. Main thing is whether everybody's stories match up."

Tam nods.

"Well. Thanks for the beer, Tam. I gotta git, or Barb'll be wondering what happened to me. And you're coming in for dinner one night, we haven't forgot."

From the front steps of the cabin, Tam watches Larry's taillights out of sight. Turns to step inside, pauses.

Silence. Even the roar of the ridge pines seems muted. From the hawthorns above the cabin, a whitetail doe and her twin fawns emerge like shadows of themselves, slipping down to the pool to drink.

Even after the near-comic relief of Libarriby's account of the shoot-out at the Simmons place, Tam still is shaken by her memory of Rob's focused anger as he—no other words for it—*hunted down* Calvin, drove him out of the hawthorns with a sharp stake, chased him to the brink of the boulders over the pool—

Yes, he chased Calvin to the brink, but then he dived in after him. Swam back with him, pounded out the water he had swallowed, breathed mouth-to-mouth until the boy stirred—and Tam had watched, helpless, thankful for Rob's help, thankful that at least she had sent him for swimming lessons because she'd never learned to swim and couldn't teach him herself.

Why all the rage? Rage that had driven Calvin to eavesdrop, the killer rage that had driven Rob after him, James's rage when he saw his brother's wounds.

For comfort Tam wanders down to the pasture, for the placid warmth of big bodies sleeping on their feet, the odor of horse sweat and horse droppings. The Hellbitch rouses as Tam reaches the fence, watches her for a moment, seems to perceive no harm, nuzzles Buddy, and closes her eyes again.

"Don't let anyone else be killed," Tam finds herself whispering to the goddess of horses but is answered by Hube: *What are you going to do to stop the rage, girl?*

What can I do?

What you've always been good at. Stickin' like a burr to whatever horse you have to ride.

Tam wonders what he means. Remembers her last glimpse of Rob's face at the hospital as she was leaving Calvin's room.

"I'll help you if I can," she had said, and Rob held her eyes for just a moment before he closed the door behind him.

Bunce. Rob thinks his father shot him.

No answers, not from the drowsing horses and not from a doe and her fawns, slipping back to their bedding ground in the last of the light.

Tam opens her eyes on the familiar tongue-and-groove ceiling of her bedroom, closes her eyes again. Had been one of those nights when she slept in snatches, knowing she'd slept only because she remembered dreaming, fractured dreaming that seemed to pick up where it had been broken by her waking. Now, in morning light, she tries and fails to connect the strands. Mending something, surely she had been mending something with glue that never seemed to hold.

And—yes, what had broken into her dream this time. Knocking at her front door.

Real knocking, not dream knocking. Tam rolls out of bed, discovers she had slept in her T-shirt, pulls on her blue jeans, and steps into her sneakers. Hurries barefoot to the door and opens it to find James, his face tight and his eyes bloodshot from lack of sleep.

"Calvin?" she exclaims.

"He'll be all right." His voice rasps, used up. "They're going to discharge him this morning. I've been home to fetch him some fresh clothes, thought you might ride back to town with me to pick him up."

"I've got the horses to take care of—"

"I'll give you a hand, won't take long."

"Coffee?"

"I'll drive by Steffi's window for coffee when we get to town."

He sounds too tired to answer her, let alone to brush and grain and water horses, but he walks a strike ahead of Tam down to the pasture, gets a brush and curry comb out of the tack box, and starts on Buddy, while Tam pours grain and pumps fresh water into the trough. He's moved on to the filly by the time Tam begins to brush the Hellbitch.

She turns the unanswerables over in her mind. Here she is with three horses, with only one—Buddy—that can be considered reliable. The Hellbitch and the filly needing regular long rides to keep them from sliding into bad habits, the filly still too green to ride without someone snubbing. When will Calvin be ready to ride again, will Calvin ever want to ride again—

"Stick like a burr," she tells the Hellbitch, and James glances at her.

They finish with the horses in silence, put combs and brushes away, wash up at the horse trough, hike back to James's truck.

He drives with his gaze fixed on the track. Tam combs back her hair by running her fingers through it, wishes she'd had a moment in the cabin to groom herself as well as the horses had been groomed. Oh well.

Familiar stands of pine and underbrush roll past the windows, the sky to the west hardens to blue. And now James is turning on the county road, driving past the burros' pasture toward Fort Maginnis. When she steals a glance at his profile, she thinks he looks—not angry, not preoccupied—just empty. Lines from a song she has sometimes heard on her car radio. *Hang on to the hope—at the end of the rope—will be a little more rope.*

As he had promised, James turns into the alley behind US Bank and drives up to Steffi's window, which is little more than a hole in the wall offering hot drinks. He digs into the console of his truck for change to pay for the coffee, hands her cup to Tam.

"Thank you."

He says nothing. Drives on.

The waiting room at the hospital in Fort Maginnis is hushed, the kind of hush that suggests frenetic activity in its unseen depths. James hands a paper sack with fresh clothes for Calvin to the nurse at the desk, who dispatches it upstairs with a candy striper.

"Dr. LeTellier is just checking him one last time," the nurse assures James, who nods and retreats to a far corner of the waiting room. "We'll have him downstairs soon."

Tam sits on a plastic chair, one of a row of plastic chairs. Opposite her is a man buried in the *Fort Maginnis Daily News.* When he lowers his paper, she sees it is Zenith, and she feels a rush of reassurance. When he smiles at her, she gets up and goes to sit beside him, and he lays down his paper and puts an arm around her.

"Just hang in there, Tam. You're doin' fine."

—hang onto the hope—

Zenith wears his sagging blue jeans with suspenders and lace-up boots, but his shirt is clean and pressed, and he has combed his white curls into some semblance of order. "Calvin's gonna be fine.

I went up and talked to him a little bit this morning. His pride's pretty dented is all."

"Why all this anger?" Tam blurts. "I saw it, Zenith. Rob. Enraged. Going after Calvin as though he was about to kill him—"

Zenith nods. "But then he jumped in and pulled him out of the pool."

So Zenith has heard the whole story, either from James or from Calvin himself. "And now James—" She looks across the room, sees him with his head in his hands. "I've never seen him like this."

"He'll be all right." Zenith tightens his grip around her shoulders. "And why all the anger? When you've got three young men here, all in situations running out of their control, all scared and all frustrated? I've seen it happen on the oil rigs—something goes wrong and the roughnecks lose their heads and start swinging. Their age, I'd a done the same. Did, in fact. And then we got a couple-three genuine crazies stirrin' up trouble. That goddamn Em! I'll tell you, Tam, Larry Seidel is one helluva man to wade into her fracas with Allen Heckman and come out of it in one piece."

"Allen," Tam remembers. "Is he still here in the hospital?"

"I believe they've got him strapped down somewhere. Rob told me there's talk of moving him to a detox center. Question is where the money's coming from. Wouldn't surprise me if they turned him out on the street. One more homeless person."

Tam absorbs this possibility. "Rob's still here?"

"Think he's up on the third floor, tryin' to talk sense to his dad."

But a stir at the bank of elevators at the rear of the waiting room distracts both Tam and Zenith. James has gone to meet the middle-aged nurse who pushes the wheelchair carrying Calvin, who, Tam is relieved to note, looks fairly normal in his clean shirt and Levi's and cowboy boots. He's not happy about the wheelchair, however. "I can walk!" she hears him insist.

"Hospital regulations," snaps the nurse. Not hard to guess she's had enough of Calvin.

James nods to Zenith but says, "Are you coming home with us, Tam?"

"Yes, she's coming!" shouts Calvin. "We're riding this afternoon because we missed our ride yesterday, which is bad for the horses! Especially Melanie! Tell him, Tam!"

"*Horseback riding?*" says the nurse, shocked, and Tam feels Zenith's withheld laughter shaking his big body.

"Better go," he tells her. "Don't worry about Rob. I'll talk to him soon's I find him."

"I'm going riding!"

"Like hell you are!"

From her doorway Tam observes the standoff between the two brothers and resists the urge to laugh at the comic resemblance between the older and the younger as they square off in anger. Testosterone at work, she supposes, remembering Zenith's explanation, with Calvin almost as tall as James. She remembers another of Zenith's remarks: *James is a man with too much on his hands.*

But any urge to laugh is stillborn when Calvin turns to her. "Tell him, Tam!"

Now both brothers glare at her, challenging her to choose between them, and Tam looks from one to the other, searching for words. Before she can find them, James speaks.

"His doctor told me! Two weeks of rest! And then *limited* activity! And that's, by God, what's going to happen!"

"*Not!*" shouts Calvin. "Tell him about Hube, Tam!"

"You're not Hube," says Tam. She's found her words now. If James is the too-young father of this lopsided family, she's the too-old mother who still carries the weight of authority. "You're not Hube, and you'll follow doctor's orders. If I have to lock up those horses to keep you off them, I will."

James's gaze has shifted from Tam to Calvin. "So that's that," he says.

Calvin's mouth has fallen open. Tam endures the hurt in his eyes because she has to.

A few seconds pass. With a contorted face Calvin picks up a loose chunk of gravel, and Tam puts a hand to the doorjamb, but he doesn't throw the stone at her. Instead, he turns and hurls it as far as his strength will send it in the opposite direction.

"Right!" he shouts and runs toward the timber, arms pumping and legs churning in his wrath.

A silence, except for the wind quarreling with the ridge pines.

"Um," says James. "What did Hube do?"

"What? Besides raising me?"

Tam pulls her mind back into the present. "Oh, what Calvin said. It was a long time ago. I was about twelve. Hube's horse caught him off his guard and threw him. He came down hard on his head. Told me later it's true what they say about seeing stars. So what does the damned fool do but get back on his feet, shake his head, like to clear it—of course, he hadn't let go of the bridle reins, he'd never do that—climbs back on that ornery horse and yells, *You want to buck, damn you, buck*, and goes to quirting him within an inch of his life. That horse was begging to stop before Hube got done with him."

She pauses. She is seeing Hube's face as though it was yesterday. Contorted with rage. His arm rising and falling with the quirt like an out-of-control automaton. "Only time I ever saw him dumped. It was scary as hell."

"Did he—"

"Have after-affects? Yeah. Not that he complained to me, but he told Bunce the next day he'd had a headache so bad he couldn't sleep, and Bunce said something like *You damned old fool* and drove him to town to ask the doctor for pain pills. And that was the end of it, as far as I ever knew."

"One tough bastard."

"He was that. And I probably shouldn't have told Calvin about that episode. We'd been talking about never giving up—oh, hell. Hube was a lot of things, but he wasn't perfect."

He'd stood by Tam through thick and thin, but no, he wasn't perfect.

"And when Calvin is fit to ride again, he's going to wear a helmet. I never should have let him argue me out of it."

"So now we've got horses to ride. Do I have to wear a helmet?"

21

It's James who rides Buddy and snubs for Tam on the filly. Along the ridge trail. James had glanced at Tam, shrugged, and made the uphill turn. What with Allen in the hospital and Rob watching over him, they won't have to worry about running into trouble.

"Did Calvin come home last night?"

"I think he slept in the hayloft. I saw him slinking around the corner of the barn early this morning. He probably had to take a leak. When he sees I've gone, he'll sneak into the house and raid the kitchen. Damned if I know what to do about him."

Tam shakes her head. The course of the summer seems only to have driven everyone into angry corners. Well, not Libarriby Sibidibel. And not Zenith. She thinks about the exceptions from rage she has just made. The class clown from high school and the would-be mountain man with the AK-47.

"Another thing that happened. I picked up my mail last night on my way home, and there was my letter from Ed Evenson."

Tam steadies herself for a moment on her saddle horn, notes with an abstract part of her attention that the filly is trotting sedately beside Buddy. It'll be time soon enough to free her from the snub.

"Was it what I thought?"

"Yeah."

They ride in a silence broken only by the wind in the pines and the steady clip-clop of horses' hooves in the dust of the ridge trail. When they reach the high point of the trail where the sandstone boulders have rolled down the hillside, James reins Buddy to a halt but makes no move to dismount.

After a few minutes, Tam asks, "What did he say?"

"For me to pay for the—procedure. Damages is what he called it."

A rustling in the underbrush, perhaps a porcupine moving to cooler shade. The filly pricks her ears toward the sound, but she doesn't flinch or spook. Tam strokes her neck. Easy, girl. You're nothing but a baby yourself.

"How old is Vay?"

"I think she's seventeen."

Another silence. James seems to have taken an interest in studying the trail ahead. "Too goddamn dry up here in the timber," he mutters. "And all that beetle kill in the pines. Scares me."

Then he turns in the saddle and looks Tam in the face. "Calvin won't be sixteen for another couple of months."

Tam lets the implications sink in. The age of consensual sex in Montana is sixteen. By law Vay has committed statutory rape upon Calvin.

"Does Evenson know that?"

"I don't think so."

A mountain wren swoops down to a pine bough, eyes the riders and horses for a moment, loses interest, and swoops off again.

"What are you going to do?"

"I don't know."

He adds, "In the middle of last night—I couldn't sleep worth a damn—I got up and got a beer and sat on the back porch for a while. I thought maybe the thing to do would be to send Evenson his check, hope that's an end to it and Calvin doesn't have to know a damn thing."

His eyes are on Tam now, and she realizes she's being asked a question.

"You don't want to press charges."

"Hell, no." He gives a bark of a laugh. "By the time Evenson's attorney and mine went after each other, paying Evenson his so-called damages will be cheap at half the price."

Tam ponders his ugly words. "I think Calvin has to be told."

James scrubs at his eyes with his hand. "You think?"

"He may not be legally old enough for consent, but he needs to know there are consequences to what he does."

She pauses as the filly snorts and dips her head to brush a fly from her nose. One of those consequences—and time rolls backward, she sees herself at seventeen, listening to Hube and Mrs. Eckles arguing in the next room. What would she have done, at seventeen, if she'd thought—*known*—she had a choice?

"Has Vay had"—Tam hesitates, chooses the word deliberately— "had the abortion? Or is it yet to happen?"

James shakes his head. "Sounded like yet to happen. Of course, Evenson's letter took a few days in the mail to get here, so who knows."

Another thought crashes down on Tam. "You didn't leave that letter where Calvin could find it?"

And sees James's stricken eyes.

On their return from their ride, Tam somehow isn't surprised to see the Tahoe parked on the track by her cabin. She glances at James.

"It's you he'll want to talk to. I'll take care of the horses," says James. "I'd just as soon not go near the guy for a while."

So Tam slips out of the saddle and watches James lead the filly behind Buddy to the pasture gate. Then she crosses the track and stops, looks back and sees James has led the horses into the pasture and closed the gate behind them. He glances once in her direction as he heads for the barn to fetch the curry combs and brushes.

Rob sits in the driver's seat, idly polishing the steering wheel with his thumb. He looks up as Tam approaches the open window of the Tahoe, then looks away. His thumb jerks and moves faster on the wheel.

"Is there news?" Tam asks after a moment of feeling the undeflected sun burn down on her shoulders. She supposes she smells of horses, and what she wants more than anything is to escape to the cool of the house and have a long iced drink followed by a shower.

But Rob nods. Slowly. "Yeah. Dad. They're keeping him . . . in the hospital . . . a while longer. I don't know how much . . . longer. They don't tell me much."

"How long has he been using?"

He shrugs. "Ever since I've . . . lived with him. Never as bad . . . as this, though."

Tam can tell that James is keeping an eye on her and Rob as he brushes the horses. A trickle of sweat is crawling down her back. Prickles sting her face and neck. She feels part of an uneasy triangle, James with an eye on her and herself looking at Rob, who looks only at his own thumb polishing at the steering wheel.

"Rob," she says, "I need to get out of this sun. Will you come into the house for a little while, have something to drink?"

He takes a moment to answer. "Yeah," he finally says.

Tam waits for him to climb out of the Tahoe, then leads the way up the steps and into the cabin. She sighs at the relieving cool and heads for the kitchen as Rob looks around the open space of the great room. The cold river rock fireplace, the futons, the bare floor, the new bookshelves.

"The log walls . . . make a big . . . difference," he remarks.

The first words he's spoken that Tam hasn't had to pry out of him. She takes time to rinse out the dishcloth and pass it over her face and neck before she opens the refrigerator and breathes in its escaping air.

"Do you want a beer?"

"Um . . . sure."

She hands him a bottle and sits down on a futon with her own glass of water. Rob stands, looking everywhere but at Tam, finally sits on the other futon.

This man she gave birth to, this man who is a stranger to her. Who speaks one word pausing before it follows another word, forming strange jerky sentences, as though he's out of practice using his voice. Do he and Allen talk? What have they talked about? Or has Allen talked while Rob listened? Remembering the teenaged Allen, she thinks that might have been the case.

She takes a long draft of water and sets down her glass. "Rob. I told you I'd help you if I could. But I won't know how to help you if you won't tell me."

"It's . . . hard."

So. Drag it out of him. "Do you need money?"

A nod, his eyes fixed on his untouched bottle of beer.

"How much?"

"Enough to . . . live on until they . . . release Dad."

"Are you still staying at the Simmons place?"

"No. The sheriff . . . padlocked the house. Padlocked the . . . gates."

"So a room in Fort Maginnis? Close to the hospital?"

A nod.

"All right," Tam says. She stands, collects her glass to carry to the kitchen. "There's just time for me to shower and change these sweaty clothes and drive to town before the bank closes. Do you want to follow me?"

When she turns, she finds Rob staring at her with a face so drawn that her heart turns over. Thinking of nothing, driven by the need to comfort him, she holds out her arms. Finds herself holding a trembling man who grips her as though he will never let go.

Hears the tap on the door, sees over Rob's shoulder the door opening and James looking in. He takes in the scene, withdraws, and closes the door behind him.

The behavior of the Hellbitch the next morning is what Tam notices first. The mare's pricked ears, her tense muscles, her interest in something or someone beyond Tam's vision. Tam scans the pasture fence, pausing on clumps of haws or junipers. The overgrown grass, dried to brown. Notes the need to go around the place with an axe and a scythe to reduce the risk of wildfire to the buildings. The kind of work she would have set Calvin doing.

Sighs. If only.

Wait—had she spotted movement in the barn door? She follows the direction the Hellbitch's ears are pointing.

No. Surely just a shadow.

A shadow of what? *Calvin?*

Tam lets the Hellbitch's halter rope fall and walks as far as the pasture gate, still carrying the curry comb and brush. Studies the half-open barn door and the wedge of sunlight that falls across the barn floor. All seems still, unchanged since she went to fetch the grooming tools and the bucket of oats earlier this morning.

She pushes the door farther open and walks into the familiar warm scent of worn leather and cured hay. Nothing stirs except for a few strands of hay that float down through the trapdoor from the loft, drift briefly in a shaft of sunlight, and settle on the barn floor.

Something in the hayloft?

Tam approaches the ladder to the loft, which still is shadowed from early-morning sun. Peers up into the gloom, puts a boot on the first rung, the second, when she is struck in the face forcefully enough to send her falling backward from the ladder. Stars spin in her vision, merge and separate and merge again in a pattern in red and purple.

"Tam?"

The stars are gone, although the rafters under the loft revolve when she opens her eyes. James's face revolves with the rafters.

"Tam? You okay? What happened?"

She struggles to sit up, leans against James's shoulder. "What happened?" he repeats.

"Something—fell out of the loft."

"There's nothing on the floor that wasn't here yesterday."

"Then I don't know." She shakes her head, then regrets it. Goes back to what she last remembers. The Hellbitch. Ears pricked toward the barn.

"I thought I saw a shadow at the barn door, and I left the horses and walked over to investigate." Doesn't say *Calvin*.

"Did you see anything? Hear anything?"

"I don't think so—James? What's going on?"

"Damned if I know." He stands, leans down to gather her up. Carries her back into brilliant sunlight that makes her close her eyes. When she opens them again, James is setting her in the passenger seat of his truck and snapping the seatbelt around her.

"Where are we going?"

"Emergency room. To get you checked out."

"But I'm—"

"Going to act like Calvin about it? Here, take a look at yourself." He pulls down the passenger-side visor so Tam can see herself in its mirrored backing.

Two blackened eyes and a crust of dried blood around her nose.

"You going to tell me a hay bale rolled itself over and fell out of the loft and knocked you silly? And then it kept rolling down to the pasture so the horses could eat it and not leave a trace?"

"Where is Calvin?"

"He's home. Acting like a shit, but home. And he didn't have anything to do with what happened to you because he was in the house when I left, and he couldn't have beaten me to your place on foot."

"I didn't believe he did. Hurt me, I mean."

James glances at her, keeps driving.

"Mild concussion," says the emergency room doctor on call, who is Dr. LeTellier again. A youngish dark-faced man, straight black hair to his shoulders. Tam vaguely remembers something about his family. First-generation settlers in Murray County, she thinks.

"What the hell are you guys in the Sun Creek country doing to each other up there?"

"Hell if we know," says James. "She'll be all right?"

"With rest. But what it looks like—" Dr. LeTellier pauses, looks straight at James. "With the bruising to her face, bruises on her back and shoulders, it looks to me as though somebody hit her hard enough in the face to knock her down and knock her out. What with this being the second case of concussion you've brought me this week, I have to wonder—"

"No!" cries Tam from her seat on the side of the emergency room gurney.

Both men turn to her, James with tightened lips and rising color, Dr. LeTellier frowning. Tam gropes for the threads and fragments she can draw to the surface. Finds one.

"James didn't hurt me! I'd have seen his truck when I walked up from the horse pasture to check out the barn. And maybe he—maybe somebody—could have sneaked up and hit me on the back of my head, but he couldn't have hit me in the face without my seeing him."

Adds, after a pause, "And we know who hurt Calvin."

Dr. LeTellier shakes his head. "She's good to go. Keep her hydrated, make her rest, but don't let her go to sleep before tonight. And don't bring me another concussion case in the next few days."

Tam walks from the emergency room to the hospital lobby without faltering, although she concentrates on the effort and senses James hovering at her shoulder. Once inside the lobby, she stops short because rising to his feet is Rob, and his shock as he sees her is enough to remind her how battered she looks.

"Holy . . . what the hell happened?"

"Found her in the barn like this," says James shortly. "She was just coming around. Doesn't know what happened."

Rob glares at him. "She looks like somebody beat the hell out of her!"

Tam has had all she can stand of men talking to each other over her head. "I know what happened to me! Something—*somebody*—fell out of the hayloft and hit me in the face!"

James and Rob look at each other, look at Tam. "Somebody?" says James.

"Like you said! Nothing on the floor of the barn that wasn't there yesterday! And that nonsense about a hay bale rolling itself off? So what does that leave?"

"*Who?*"

Tam shrugs. Her head hurts in spite of the hydrocodone tablets she had been given in the emergency room, but she'll be damned if she takes another. "How should I know? Everybody's accounted for. Allen might be angry enough to hurt me, but he's here in the hospital and under guard for his shoot-up with Em, and Rob's been here with him—"

"You're sure about that?"

"Same as with you. I would have seen his Tahoe when I walked up to the barn."

Rob seems to struggle with speech. Gestures toward Tam with both hands. Finally, "I . . . came downstairs because the nurse . . . told me you were here. I wanted to . . . to . . ."

The stammer, if it is a stammer, overcomes him, and Tam takes him by the hand and leads him over to the window, while James glowers at them.

"The nurse . . . told me you . . . were hurt."

Tam manages a smile. "I'll live. How's your father?"

He shakes his head. "They . . . say it takes time. I . . . ." Long hesitation. "Wish I . . . could do something for you."

"Come out to the cabin when you can. You can talk to me."

Rob's face lightens. "Yeah," he says.

22

"If it was a somebody, he'll have left a trace," says James. After parking his pickup on the track, he has led Tam to the cabin steps and brought them each a glass of iced water.

"But who? Can you see Zenith climbing up there and jumping out? While Spotty was doing what? Waiting for him at the foot of the ladder with me?"

James gives a snort that almost could be a laugh. "Not hardly. I don't know—it'd have to be somebody wandering around on foot. Maybe a homeless person looking for a place to crash?"

"This far from town? It's a long walk from anywhere."

"Well—" James sets down his empty glass and stands, scanning the hillside above the track.

"Where are you going?"

"To look for tracks. No, you don't have to—"

"I'm fine!"

Tam follows James to a point halfway between the cabin and the barn, where he stops and studies the drying grass and weeds. Shakes his head. "Too much tramping through here—me on my way to the barn, then out again with you. Let's see what the grass looks like on the other side of the track."

Tam stares with him at the hillside. Brittle grass that barely moves with the light wind, clumps of hawthorns and junipers climbing up toward the pines. And a clear line of broken and flattened grasses to mark where someone in a panic has run for the timber.

Libarriby Sibidibel parks his truck opposite James's pickup on the track. The official force of the light bar across the cab of the Ford 250 and the Murray County Sheriff's Department emblem on its door are like a warning of what is to come.

"Did you call him?" Tam asks James.

"Yeah."

They wait on the cabin steps as Larry shuts the door of the cab and walks across the track toward them.

"Holy hell," says Larry. "Honey, you look like somebody beat the hell out of you."

"Thanks so much."

"We found his tracks," says James, indicating the hillside, and Larry wanders over to take a look for himself.

"What was the point of calling him?" Tam asks. "He's wasting his time driving all the way out here."

"He'll need to file a report."

Larry returns, shaking his head, and accepts Tam's offer of a cold drink. "Helluva thing. You got good locks on your doors, Tam?"

James shows him around, pointing out locks and grumbling about uncurtained windows.

"Good work," Larry allows. "You going to stay with her tonight?"

"Yes."

"No," cries Tam, and both men turn and glare at her in a way that stiffens her spine and her hackles. "We'll talk about that," she warns, and turns to scan the dirt track and the hillside.

"Dry as hell out here," says Larry a few minutes later, as he takes his leave, and Tam remembers her note to herself about scything and raking up the foliage around the buildings, even as James says, "I'm going to round up my brother, and we'll get grass and weeds cleared."

She and James wave Larry off and watch him make an expert three-pivot turn to head back down the track. It's not until the sheriff's dust begins to settle behind him that Tam trusts herself to speak.

"I. Do. Not. Need. You. To. Take. Care. Of. Me."

"Tam—"

She turns on her heel, takes the next step, and feels herself sway. The next moment James has swept her up and is carrying her through the great room and into her own bedroom, where he lays her on her bed. Pulls off one of her boots, then the other.

"What are you—I'm all right!"

"You're not all right. And you're damned well going to stay on your bed until I can find Calvin and come back here, if I have to take your boots with me to keep you off your feet!"

He glares down at her, his anger quivering off him.

"Anything you need before I go?"

"No."

She turns on her side with her head on the pillow and listens to the sounds of his bootheels as he stamps back through the house and slams the door behind him.

The afternoon has lengthened when Tam opens her eyes. Realizes she must have slept in spite of all warnings. The house is silent, feels deserted. For a moment or two, she plays with the notion that she has slipped into a coma from sleeping after a concussion, died, and come back to the familiar world as a ghost. How would she like being a ghost? Would she be invisible, might she move among the living and note their doings? Catch the *somebody* attacking the living Tam?

Stop it, Tam. Anyone would think you're planning to write a supernatural thriller.

She pads in her stocking feet into the great room, looks out the south window. Beyond the barn someone in dark jeans and dark shirt is scything down the overgrown grass and weeds. Calvin? But no. This figure is hatless, with a shock of fair hair. Could it be—

But yes. When she looks out the opposite window, she sees the black Tahoe parked in the track. Rob.

Tam searches out her sneakers—has James really taken her boots?—fills a thermos with water, and walks down the track toward the barn. Rob looks up from his work and waits, leaning on his scythe.

"Hot work?"

"God, yes." He flicks sweat from his brow with his fingertips, takes the sweating thermos and drinks deeply.

"How did you know I needed this work done?"

He takes another deep swig of water. "I saw the undergrowth when I was here the other day. Later, when the sheriff dropped by to try to talk to Dad, he got to talking about fire danger up here. I thought—" He hesitates, looks squarely at her. His eyes, so much like her own that she might be looking into a mirror. "You said you'd help me. And you did. Will you let me help you?"

Tam doesn't trust herself to speak. Nods.

Rob takes up his scythe again, swings it through another patch of overgrown and drying grass, starts to take another swing and stops abruptly, looking past Tam so intently that she, too, turns to look.

"Did you see that?"

No, she hasn't, but she does hear the dull thud of the shed door closing, the sound released and fading into transparent air as though she had imagined it. Followed by a challenging neigh from the Hellbitch, who has galloped up to the pasture fence.

Rob strides up the slope toward the shed, still carrying his scythe, and Tam hurries to catch up. The distant roar of ridge pines, the crunch of her footsteps and Rob's in the overgrown grass, no other sounds. Rob reaches the door of the shed before Tam does and pulls on the latch, but something is blocking it from within.

He glances back at Tam, who shrugs. No reason why the shed door would be locked. The shed itself is ramshackle; she'd considered having it bulldozed for burning with the rest of Hube's falling-down outbuildings, but the roof had been sound enough for him to store God knew what, boxes and kegs and trash bags stuffed and tied shut. Tam had shaken her head over his junk, but she couldn't bring herself to get rid of it without sorting through it and in the end hadn't had the energy to do more than close the door on it.

Rob pauses a moment, sizing up the door. Wood planks held together by slats nailed across them, hung from ancient iron hinges. In one motion—*ninja*, thinks Tam—he raises a foot to the door and delivers a smashing kick that pulls loose its hinges and leaves it sagging open.

Gloom. Shadows of junk. A whimper.

Tam and Rob exchange glances.

"Who's there?" Rob growls. The taut lines of his back and shoulders, his fist clenched on the handle of the scythe, flashes Tam back to the day he chased down Calvin with a pole. No one answers, and Rob motions Tam to the side and jerks the door farther ajar, until sunlight falls through it to illuminate junk and shrouded spiderwebs and a trembling dark-haired girl crouching behind a crate.

Tam gasps. "Vay!"

"You know her?"

"What do you think you're doing back there, Vay? Come out!"

"No! He'll kill me!"

Tam glances back at Rob. He's a fearsome sight, all right, in his black T-shirt and jeans, which must be his leftover ninja clothing, with the scythe in his hands and menace on his face. "Back off," she says. "You're scaring her."

Sobs from Vay as Rob retreats around the corner of the shed.

Tam settles into soothing mode, a tactic she'd once used on Rob himself. "Vay," she croons. "Vay. Nobody's going to hurt you. Are you hungry? Thirsty? We've got a thermos of water, and there's food in the cabin, and you can take a shower—I know you don't like being so filthy—"

And indeed, as Vay takes a tentative hands-and-knees crawl from behind the crate, Tam sees she is caked in grime, face and hands and clothes, her hair in tangled strings. As she staggers to her feet and falls into Tam's arms, it flashes on Tam that the girl is not noticeably pregnant, however far along she is. Or has she had the "procedure"? Shelves the thought, shelves any wonder how Vay has gotten here, let alone why she is here. Patting the girl, coaxing her back from hysteria, is enough for now.

When her sobs subside, Tam leads Vay out of the shed with her arm around her shoulders. Thankfully, Rob stays out of sight, although Tam notes his shadow falling into the heavy grass at the end of the shed.

Then the slow, hesitating walk down to the cabin. Once inside with Vay, Tam wonders if she dares let go of her. But no, Vay feels limp and defeated in Tam's arms; she can be eased down onto a futon with a shawl pulled over her and water brought to her, which she gulps like a little girl.

"Not too fast—how long since you've had anything to drink?"

A dismal shake of her head.

A silhouette outside the window, Rob standing watch.

Once Tam manages to coax Vay into the shower and lay out clean clothes of her own for the girl to change into, she returns to the kitchen to heat soup and hears the front door crack open. Rob's head appears, assessing the situation.

"There's somebody else out here," he says in a low voice.

Tam sets down the unopened can of soup and goes to the window. "Where?"

"Up along the timber line."

Tam studies the hillside, sees nothing but familiar rock outcroppings, clumps of juniper, and gently blowing grass. The pines point skyward, undisturbed.

Rob is shaking his head. "Lock your doors," he says, "And I'll be around a while longer, see how many weeds I can whack down."

Tam hesitates. "Is your father better, that you can leave him?"

He shrugs. "About the same. Out of his head most of the time. The nurses finally told me to leave, that they thought he was agitated by me. Be another week, they said, before we'd get anything rational out of him. So I thought I might as well do something useful."

He grins suddenly. "One thing about mowing down weeds, I can work off the worry, and when I look back, I can see I've accomplished something."

23

Tam has heated the soup and set out bread and butter on the kitchen table when she hears the sound of the shower stop. A few minutes later, Vay sidles out with wet hair and bare feet, looking uncomfortable in Tam's flannel shirt and jeans. Her eyes light on the food.

"Go ahead," says Tam, and Vay doesn't wait for another invitation but drops into a chair at the table and falls on the soup like a starving person. Pauses in spooning soup just long enough to tear off a chunk of bread from the loaf Tam baked yesterday, slather it with butter, and rip into it with her teeth so fiercely that Tam half-expects her to growl over it. Tam shakes her head. Not *like* a starving person. Vay is a starving person.

"How long since you've eaten?"

Vay stares at Tam over the spoonful of soup that is on its way to her mouth. "Dunno," she mutters after she swallows. "Day before yesterday, maybe. Calvin was—" She drops her eyes, clutches the soupspoon in one hand and winds the fingers of her other hand in her wet tangle of hair.

"Slow down, you're going to make yourself sick if you keep eating so fast. Calvin was supposed to do what? Bring you food?"

But Vay clamps her mouth shut, shakes tendrils of hair to shield her face.

"How long have you been out here?"

Silence.

A sudden surmise. "Was it you in my hayloft yesterday?"

Silence.

Tam ponders her options. What she wants to do is call Libar-riby Sibidibel and turn the whole problem over to him to solve. He'll get in touch with Ed Evenson—the realtor, Marie Jones, will have Ed's phone number if no one else does—and probably hold Vay in juvenile custody until her father can come back to Montana and collect her. Tam seems to remember James saying that Vay is not eighteen yet, so her father will have the say over her. But Tam also fears that the instant she goes to the telephone, Vay, now revived by a shower and a little food, will bolt like a wild thing for the timber. Rob, scything grass and underbrush around the barn—she wishes she'd kept him in the cabin as backup.

Movement past the kitchen window catches her eyes. The dark-blue Ford pickup, parking in the track outside the cabin. She watches James get out and walk out of sight, headed for the front door. Then his knock, and Vay's head shoots up.

The door, of course, is locked. If Tam goes through the great room to open it for James, she will have given Vay her chance to run out the back door.

The hell with Vay! Barefoot and malnourished, Vay can't run far. Even if she manages to hide in the timber, she'll soon have a sheriff's search party after her, and, God knows, Calvin. Whatever he's up to.

James has knocked a second time, more insistently, by the time Tam opens the door. He scans her face, searching for what, she wonders.

"Is Calvin here?"

"No, but—"

James interrupts her with a yelp. "What the—" and dashes off the front steps. Tam runs out in time to see the small fleeing figure of Vay, who indeed has escaped out the kitchen door. James runs after her, but Rob, who tossed aside his scythe and has a head start, rapidly catches up with Vay, whose bare feet slow her uphill flight through sharp grass and loose rocks. Arms flailing, she's just short of the timberline when Rob dives and brings her down in a flying tackle.

By the time Tam and James reach them, Vay is fighting Rob's hold on her, kicking and scratching and biting until he gives her a hard wallop on her butt that makes her howl. Still, she struggles, gripped not just by Rob but by terror stark on her young face.

James gasps when he sees her. "Vay!"

"Jam-*eee!*" she cries and, as Rob releases her, flings herself into James's arms. He holds her, automatically stroking her shoulders, while she sobs.

"Who the hell is she?" asks Rob.

Tam wonders where to begin even as she quells the urge to wring the girl's pretty little neck. Vay. Vay and the Hellbitch, neighing from the pasture fence. Vay and Calvin. Vay, who now has plastered herself to James as she sobs.

"Oh, Jamie, Jamie—"

"She's a runaway," Tam says. "James, could you bring her down to the cabin while I call the sheriff?"

A fresh burst of sobs from Vay. "No! No! Don't let them take me, Jamie!"

James, looking stricken, meets Tam's gaze over the top of Vay's head. Tam shakes her head, and James glances down at Vay and scoops her up in his arms. Carries her down the slope toward the cabin with his head bowed over her.

Rob looks his bewilderment at Tam. "She . . . has to be the one in the hayloft. Nobody else it could be."

"Unless it was Calvin. James's kid brother. James can't find him."

"Seems like there's a whole helluva lot going on up here that I don't have a clue about."

"I know the feeling."

A pause as they continue to walk. Then Rob says, "You like him."

"Who, James? No, I—"

"You do. And you . . . don't like her. Or the way she's . . . making over him."

Tam starts to deny the feelings, stops. No. She doesn't like Vay. Never has. What had Zenith said about her? Spoiled rotten? Trouble? Tam had tried to help Vay with the Hellbitch out of—what—pity, she guesses, but not from liking. Now James walks with Vay in his arms while she wraps both hers around his neck. Yes, Tam admits she's irked as hell at the girl. More than irked, downright angry.

"Why did you . . . never write to me?"

Tam stops walking, turns to stare at Rob. "What are you talking about?"

"I used to . . . wait for your letters. Couldn't . . . believe you wouldn't . . . answer mine. But not when . . . when I wrote I'd graduated high school, not when I started college, not when I had to drop out . . ."

"Rob, I didn't get any letters." Well, the *I wish you were dead* letter, but—

Their eyes meet. "You did . . . write?" he asks.

"Every week at first. Then—well, eventually my letters began coming back, marked 'address unknown.'"

But Rob's eye is caught by movement at the bottom of the slope. "What's he doing?"

Tam turns, sees that James, with Vay in his arms, has walked ahead of her and Rob, and now he is opening the door on the passenger side of his pickup. "James," she shouts and runs toward him. "Wait! Where are you taking her?"

James sets Vay on the seat of the pickup, turns and glares at Tam. "I'm taking her home with me! Can't you see she's scared out of her mind? Why did Heckman think he had to throw her down and pound on her?"

"*Don't* take her home with you! Don't be alone with her! Can't you see the position you'd be putting yourself in?"

James's jaw twitches, his eyes blazing. "She's just a kid! Can you feel any compassion at all for her, or are you so involved now with your precious son that you can't see he's a bully and a brute? When you watched what he did to Calvin?"

Tam tries and fails to bite back her anger. "She's a seventeen-year-old runaway! You told me about the letter her father wrote you. Has she had her *procedure* yet? Does Ed Evenson think Calvin got her pregnant? Or does he think *you* did?"

Vay whimpers. "Jam-*ee*—" and he takes her hand and holds it before turning back to Tam. Starts to speak, stops, because Rob is standing at Tam's shoulder, and Tam feels the surge of antagonism like an electric current between the two young men.

"We have to call the sheriff," she says in as calm a voice as she can manage. "A seventeen-year-old is a ward of her father's. He'll—"

"Jam-*ee*! Don't let him take me!"

"We have to call the sheriff," Tam repeats, and a new voice speaks.

"I already have."

Zenith, walking up the track toward them as though on one of his usual strolls. Spotty at his heels, cringing at the conflict he can sense radiating between the humans. Meanwhile, the wind roars its own complaint through the distant ridge pines, cumulus clouds drift in slow motion across the sky, the indifferent sun beats down on the track.

"Let me talk to him, Tam," says Zenith. "He'll take it better from me."

Tam nods. Turns and walks up the steps to the cabin. Opens the door on the relief of cool air. Glances out the window at the track where the two men stand by the open door of James's pickup with their backs to the cabin and their heads together in a conversation that at least looks peaceable.

Oh, James.

Yes, Rob. I do like him. Too bad this happened.

Rob has followed her into the cabin, and now, as though she has spoken aloud, he answers her thought. "Hell of a situation."

She shrugs, she doesn't trust herself to speak.

"*Is* Calvin the father?"

"I think so. Almost certainly."

Out on the track in the blaze of sunlight, Zenith and James continue their conversation. Like watching a silent film, Tam thinks. Zenith unhooks a thumb from his suspenders and gestures toward the ridge trail, James leans into the pickup, says something to Vay, turns back to Zenith.

"How old is Calvin?"

"Fifteen."

Rob winces. "When I was fifteen . . . oh, hell. I was embarrassed, well, mortified when your books . . . got passed around at school. Gave you . . . every kind of grief I could think of. I got in that knock-down-drag-out with Warren whatshisname . . . and then Dad . . . he promised me . . ."

"Yes." She thinks James looks more relaxed, his shoulders less tense as he speaks to Zenith.

". . . a whole lot I still don't understand . . . ." But Rob breaks off because rolling into view of the window is the white Dodge Ram with the Murray County sheriff department insignia on its door and the light bar on its roof. Libarriby Sibidibel.

As Tam and Rob watch, the sheriff gets out of his vehicle and walks around it to face James, who stands with an arm barring the open pickup door, where Val cowers on the seat. A uniformed female deputy jumps down from the high seat in the passenger side of the official Dodge Ram and joins the sheriff, who is talking to James. As always, the thick log walls of the cabin mute their conversation, but Tam catches sight of Zenith watching the action with his elbows comfortably propped on the old hitching rack. Spotty, at his feet, also studies the unfolding scene.

James takes a sudden step toward the sheriff, his anger written across his face, and Tam hears Rob's drawn breath. "Not good," he mutters.

Oh God, Tam prays. Don't hit him, James.

Before her eyes Tam sees Libarriby Sibidibel transformed into the full authority of the county sheriff, straight-backed, with his hands on his hips where a holstered handgun is strapped. She sees James's eyes drop to the handgun, return back to the sheriff's face. Sees him take that step back, although his arm still is braced across the open passenger door, protecting Vay.

More conversation, muted by the cabin's log walls. The female deputy has joined James and the sheriff. She ducks down to see Vay under James's arm, seems to be talking to the girl.

Abruptly, James turns and walks a few feet away from the pickup, his back turned and his body rigid, his fists clenched and his head bowed. Watching from her window, Tam realizes she is holding her breath. Lets it out slowly as the female deputy holds out her arms to Vay, who shrinks away. More words exchanged, then suddenly Larry and his deputy each have Vay by an arm and are half-walking, half-dragging her toward the sheriff's truck. Vay's mouth opens in a silent scream as they push her into the back seat of the Ford and close the door.

James has turned to watch as Larry takes the Ford in a three-point turn in the track and drives away. As dust settles on the track, James sees Tam and Rob watching at the cabin window. Makes an angry gesture with his fist, slams the passenger door of his pickup, which has been hanging open, gets behind the wheel, and roars away in a spatter of flying dust and gravel.

The track, barn and shed, the slope up to the timberline, the pines pointing skyward. The horses drowsing in their pasture. All serene.

A tap on the door, which opens before Tam can reach it. A hat sails past her with momentum that causes it to slide several feet on the hardwood floor before it comes to a stop at Rob's feet. He stares down at it.

Tam shakes her head at his expression. "Come in, Zenith," she calls, and in he walks, carrying a bottle of bourbon, with Spotty at his heels.

"It's an old western custom," Zenith explains to Rob. "Maybe more of a joke. If you're not sure of your welcome, you toss your hat through the door. If it comes sailing back, you'd better leave."

Rob shakes his head.

"Zenith, this is my son, Rob Heckman," says Tam, and Zenith tramps up to Rob with an extended hand.

"We've met," he explains, "but pretty informally."

Rob's face is a study, and Tam has to choke back a laugh. Informally, indeed. Some fragment of her familiar self is reminding her that at least she can laugh after the rapid succession of events within a week, each worse than the last. She turns to the kitchen to fetch three glasses and ice, sees Vay's soup bowl and plate of bread and butter on the table, and chokes back what is more of a sob. Spotty has followed her, his eyes reflecting her distress, and she pats him on the head for the comfort of it before she returns to the great room.

Rob still stands by the window, but Zenith has made himself comfortable on a futon. He arranges ice in the glasses, pours bourbon with a liberal hand, offers a glass to Tam and to Rob, and leans back.

"So," he says. "Here's how it all went down."

24

Tam awakens the next morning blurry from Zenith's bourbon. Pulling on a robe, she stumbles as far as the kitchen and finds coffee waiting on its burner and a note.

Went back to town to check on Dad. If no change, I'll come back and hack more weeds.

She had persuaded Rob not to drive back last night but to sleep on a bed improvised by her and Zenith by pushing the futons together and supplying it with an extra blanket and a pillow from her bed. Zenith had waved to them as he stumped homeward, followed by an annoyed Spotty at being wakened from a comfortable sleep. Tam hadn't heard Rob make coffee or drive away, but she's almost sure she had roused at Zenith's gunfire salute at dawn. Maybe that's what had wakened Rob.

Now she pours herself a cup of the coffee and carries it out to the front steps to observe the morning and the mark of yesterday's traffic across the track. The light movement of air from the pines is cool on her face and bare arms, but it smells of baking grass and timber. Another hot dry day ahead.

Rob. James.

No. Don't think of them. Think of horses. Horses who need to be watered and grained and groomed. Horses that missed their saddle blankets getting wet for two whole days, which won't have done the Hellbitch or the filly any good.

Well. She might as well get started. Finish her coffee and return to the cabin to get dressed in yesterday's clothes, which are the cleanest she has, now that Vay has been driven away wearing her spares. Foresees a trip to the Laundromat in Fort Maginnis.

When she walks down to the pasture a few minutes later, all three horses wait at their fence with their ears pricked, expecting breakfast and attention, and she is struck as always by their beautiful lines and their trust as the Hellbitch nuzzles her shoulders before turning to her oats.

No, too much she can't block out, starting with the blow someone—had to be Vay—struck by jumping from the hayloft and knocking her down. Or James, watching the sheriff's truck out of sight and then spinning clods of dirt and gravel behind his wheels as he roared homeward. She wonders if he's found Calvin yet.

Calvin. As though the thought had conjured him, there he stands.

Except for the horses' interest, she might have thought him an illusion born of the turmoil of the past few days. But no. He walks across the pasture toward Tam, picks up a curry comb, and goes to work untangling Buddy's mane.

"Where have you been?" Tam asks when she has finished brushing the Hellbitch and turned to the filly.

"Around."

"Have you talked to your brother?"

No answer.

Tam shrugs and goes on grooming the filly, who leans into the brush strokes with a contented pleasure that Tam envies. She gives the filly a final pat, picks up the brush and curry comb, and starts walking toward the barn.

The boy's voice behind her. "Are we going to ride?"

She stops and turns. "You want to ride with me?"

Calvin meets her eyes without flinching, although the way he stands, with his booted legs a few feet apart and his arms stiff at his sides, suggests he's braced for whatever Tam may hurl at him. She notes as an aside that he looks as though he's lost weight and that he's been sleeping in his clothes.

"Yes," he says, and his gaze doesn't falter. "I want to ride with you."

Tam reins Buddy up the slope to the ridge trail, now that no threat looms from the Simmons place, what with Allen incapacitated in the Fort Maginnis hospital and Suze and Em under something approaching house arrest. The filly falls into her familiar rhythm beside Buddy, the clip-clop of their hooves a soothing counterpart to the tension between Tam and Calvin. At least the boy seems to keep a part of his mind on Melanie—when a whitetail doe crashes off through the underbrush, he automatically checks his reins to steady the filly—but Tam only can guess what else preoccupies him.

They are riding past the slope where boulders crop out from the underbrush—sun-warmed sandstone boulders that contain memories Tam tries to blot out—before Calvin finally speaks.

"What did they do with Vay?"

Tam remembers Rob's warning: *There's someone else out there.*

"You know the sheriff came for her?"

"Yeah, I was watching. I saw him and the lady make her get into the sheriff's car."

"They will have turned her over to Child Protection Services until her father can come for her. She hasn't committed any crime"—well, except for jumping down from the hayloft and blackening Tam's eyes—"if that's what you're worried about. She hasn't been arrested. But she's being held because she's a minor, and her father is responsible for her."

"He's a bastard. Did she tell you what he did?"

Tam ignores his question. "How did she get back to Montana?"

"Hitchhiked. She was—some guy picked her up—" Calvin interrupts himself. His emotions are being transmitted to the filly, who snorts and sidesteps into Buddy.

"Watch your horse," Tam warns, and Calvin collects himself and reins in the filly.

"Melanie's doing well, isn't she?" he says after a few minutes.

Tam nods. "I think we might try her off the lead rope in the corral after we get back this morning. If she does well, we might take her out of the corral and off the lead rope tomorrow."

Another pause. "Tam? What happened to your face?"

She is considering what to tell him when he asks in a tight voice, "Was it James?"

"God no," Tam says, startled. "Why would you think that?"

"Because—" he hesitates. "I snuck into the house yesterday afternoon. After, you know, the sheriff drove away with Vay. I was looking in the refrigerator when I saw James drive up, and I knew he was all worked up from the way he was driving, tearing up the road and then squealing his brakes, and I didn't have time to do more than hide in the broom closet. Figured he'd beat the hell out of me if he found me."

Tam winces.

"He was slamming around the kitchen, cussing up a blue streak about Rob Heckman, what he'd do if he got his hands on the son of a bitch, what he thought of you—" Calvin blushes. "I think he put his fist through something because I heard it break. Then I heard him go upstairs, and I came out of the closet and ran."

"No," says Tam after a moment of intensity that vibrates between her and Calvin. "It wasn't James. And it wasn't Rob, in case you're wondering. He didn't know who you were. Or why you were lurking, looking through windows. Or why you ran."

"But you know who hurt you. Don't you!"

Tam doesn't answer. Knows her silence is a confirmation. Spurs Buddy to a faster pace, and the filly, surprised, trots a few strides to catch up.

"Ready to try her off the lead rope?"

All had looked serene around the cabin and track when Tam and Calvin returned from their ride with horses sweating and lathered. Tam felt her own skin prickling with heat and runnels of moisture, and from the appearance of Calvin's flushed and dampened face, he, too, felt the effects of their ride. Now, with the sun overhead and beating down on the shadeless corral, she wonders whether the boy is up to a longer workout. How long a rest after a concussion was he supposed to have had?

But Calvin's face lights up. "Sure!"

Tam leans from the saddle, unsnaps the lead from the filly's halter. "Ready?"

He nods, his glow rises not just from sweat but from anticipation. Tam nudges Buddy, who begins a weary plod around the corral, and the filly, used to hours walking beside the gelding, follows without prompting from Calvin.

"We're doing it," whispers Calvin, as though he's fearful the sound of his voice might break the spell, but the filly just flicks a peaceable ear in his direction.

A couple laps around the corral together, then Tam says, "See if you can rein her away from Buddy."

Calvin nods. The filly hesitates, but she's learned the basics of being neck-reined from her days beside Buddy, and she takes a tentative step forward without him. With a length between them, Tam follows on Buddy, smiling to herself at the rigid lines of Calvin's back and shoulders. Guesses he's more nervous about this first solo ride than the filly is.

"Try reining her in a figure eight," she calls when they've completed another lap. And sits back in her saddle, admiring the filly's grace and ease as Calvin reins her around the corral. Notes that she's still awkward in responding to the pressure of the rein on the neck—she'll need hours of work before she's perfect. But—high praise from Hube—she's going to make a saddle horse.

"Let's call it a morning," Tam calls finally, and Calvin dismounts, gives the filly's reins to Tam, and goes without being asked to carry a saddle on either shoulder and fetch curry combs and brushes from the barn.

Scorching sun. A killdeer calling from the lower meadow. Tam wipes her brow and dismounts, leads the two horses through the pasture gate and over to their water trough. Watches as they drink deeply, wishes she had a cold drink. Or maybe dip her own face into the water trough—

The sound of an approaching vehicle. Both horses raise dripping muzzles to point their ears. Dust settles on the track as the vehicle passes the barn and stops. The black Tahoe. Rob.

As Tam watches, Rob gets out of the Tahoe and starts toward the corral almost simultaneously with Calvin's emergence from the barn, also to walk toward the corral. Watches as Rob and Calvin, on their diagonal paths, meet.

A pause as they regard each other from a few feet apart. Rob says something to Calvin, takes a step toward him. Calvin doesn't retreat. Replies to Rob. Tam, too far from them to hear, lays a hand on the Hellbitch, who has trotted up from the far end of the pasture to nuzzle Tam's shoulder. Tam lets out a breath she hadn't realized she was holding.

Rob and Calvin continue their conversation. Rob glances in Tam's direction, turns back to Calvin, asks him something. Calvin nods. Tam hardly believes what she is seeing when the two— young men? boys?—shake hands and walk together down to the pasture fence.

Rob splits off, walking with a direction in mind, but Calvin joins Tam and the horses. Goes to work with a curry comb and starts untangling the filly's forelock. Tam watches for a moment as the filly turns her head toward the boy, arching her fine Arab neck as she leans into him, loving the grooming.

Tam takes the other curry comb and goes to work on Buddy, who placidly accepts the substitute of her for Calvin. Yes, too bad, Buddy, Calvin loves the filly more than he loves you. Tam feels far from placid. With her back to Calvin, bending over Buddy's fetlocks, she says, "What?"

"What?" he echoes.

"You and Rob."

"Oh." A minute passes. Sounds of horses ruminating, sounds of comb and brushes at work. "Nothing much. Told me I surprised him the other day. Well, startled him. Apologized to me."

Silence for some time. Tam combs out Buddy's tail, takes up a brush and finishes his grooming. Then she unclips the lead rope from his halter and watches as he ambles off, picks a spot in the pasture, and drops down to spoil the effect of her work by rolling over.

"Tam?" says Calvin. "You want me to groom the Hellbitch? Or else I'll go back and rake for Rob."

"Go ahead. I'll take care of her."

Back at the cabin, Tam takes a long shower, ridding herself of sweat and grime and at least some of her tension. Calvin and Rob, Rob and Calvin. Out of the shower and towel wrapped, she shakes horsehair and dust out of her shirt and jeans as best she can, dresses, strips her bed, and adds sheets and towels to her accumulated laundry for a trip to Fort Maginnis and the Laundromat.

As she carries out her basket of laundry, she feels the weight of mid-July heat and glances skyward at unbroken blue. No sign of relief from the weather. Shrugs. Nothing to do but carry on.

As she passes the barn, she glances down the slight incline and sees the horses drowsing in the shade of the box elder tree, while the two boys have progressed most of the way around the pasture with their scything and raking without apparent hostility, just guys getting the job done. Wonders what should be done with the piles of dried grass and weeds and junipers, even a lot of the hawthorns. Too dangerous to risk burning. Maybe rake the piles into the ravine on top of the posts and boards that already have been bulldozed down there.

She turns on the county road toward Fort Maginnis and on impulse pulls over at the verge when she reaches the pasture where the burros graze. Gets out of her car and leans on the top rail of the fence to watch them. Shaggy little creatures, comic miniatures of their larger cousins. First one burro and then the other notices her and leave their shade to come for an ear scratching, which Tam obliges.

Sees a man standing at the door of what must be a stable, looking in her direction. When she waves, he waves back and disappears into the stable.

From Tam's laptop journal:

I've been reading a book about horses by a Canadian writer, who seems as curious as I am about the first man who ever thought of riding a horse. The Canadian points out that paleolithic cave art and the ivory and bone horses carved by the men—more likely, in his view, by the women—of prehistory, precede the domestication of horses. Recognizing through their art the grace and loveliness of the horses, the Canadian suggests, those painters and carvers in the dawn of time distinguished between horses as wild prey and horses as spiritual beings.

Laundry. She gives the burros farewell pats and continues to Fort Maginnis.

At the Laundromat she loads washers, wishing she was brazen enough to strip off her grimy shirt and jeans and throw them in. But no, the Laundromat may be empty on this weekday afternoon, but she can't trust that another customer or two won't wander in. She shrugs and inserts quarters, takes out her paperback detective novel and finds her place. A few chapters later the washers have shut down their noisy spin cycle, and she folds a corner of her page—bad habit—and transfers wet sheets and towels, blue jeans and T-shirts and underwear, to their respective driers. Hesitates a moment, pulls her phone from a pocket, and punches numbers.

"Have time for coffee?" she says as Libarriby Sibidibel answers his line.

"Hello to you, too, Tam. Now?"

She glances at the timer on the nearest dryer. "Maybe half an hour."

"Fine. Meet you at the Home Plate."

Like the Laundromat, the Home Plate has few customers. Too late for the noon rush, too early for the five o'clock regulars who choose coffee over a beer at one of the bars. The air smells of grease from the grill and fried potatoes from the deep-fat fryer. Tam sees Larry at his favorite window table, in uniform with his hat properly doffed and hanging from the chair next to him. He lays down the papers he's been scanning when he spots Tam, stands and pulls out a chair for her.

A waitress glides up with the omnipresent coffeepot. "Black for you, Sheriff? And your friend?"

They both nod and wait until she returns to the counter before Larry says, "A little more excitement out your way, Tam."

"Too much excitement."

He smiles. "You wished a handful on me this time, Tam. That Evenson girl is a little hellion. She fought—scratched, bit—took me and Debbie both to wrestle her into the truck. Ended up handcuffing her to keep her there."

"Where is she now?"

"We *wanted* to turn her over to Child Protection Services until her dad can come and get her, but they couldn't handle her. We were lucky the county jail is pretty well empty now, a couple of drunks on the east corridor was all, so we locked her in a holding cell on the north corridor, with either a female deputy or one of those women from CPS keeping her company from outside her cell. One thing, she tore into dinner like a starved wolf, so maybe she'll settle down once we get her fed enough. Ed Evenson said he thought he could get here tomorrow. Don't know how he'll handle her."

Larry shakes his head, and in the lines around his eyes, Tam gets a glimpse of the weary father. And of the experienced father

215

of daughters. "Teenagers. Think the sun rises and sets for them." He sips coffee, sets down his cup and looks across the table at her. "Tam. She had to be getting help from somebody to be living rough as long as she had."

Tam nods. "I think she was hanging around my place for several days. Not that I saw her. Just signs of somebody. Then—" She finds herself reminding Larry about the blow from the hayloft that had knocked her down and, later, the glimpse Rob had had of a fleeing figure. How he'd chased Vay down. Tam adds, "I fed her and gave her clean clothes, but she tried to run again, which is when Zenith called you."

Larry shakes his head again, studies her face. "Wondered how you got those black eyes. Worried one of your new neighbors gave 'em to you."

"No, but—James Warceski got in a big blowup with Calvin over it. Next thing, I've got Calvin skulking around my place."

Tam skirts around the topic of Ed Evenson and his letter to James.

"That who Vay was getting help from? Calvin Warceski?"

"I think so. And I don't know what to do about him. At least today he's been helping Rob cut grass and weeds around the pasture, but I've got to talk sense into him somehow."

"Rob. Rob Heckman. Better for him to cut weeds than sit outside his dad's hospital room. The nurses told him it was pointless, his dad didn't recognize anybody and wouldn't until they got the crap out of his system, and then I talked to him about your tinder problem and told him to go out there with a scythe. He's not a bad guy, Tam, when his dad isn't ranting and raving poison in his ears."

"How is Allen?"

Larry shrugs. "They think he's starting to show signs he's back among us. A few more days will tell more."

She nods.

"Allen Heckman. I'm keeping a rotation of town cops outside his hospital room, twenty-four hours a day. Not so much over that shoot-out with Em, though that's a handy excuse. I just don't want to think about him breaking loose and coming after you. Or after James Warceski. I've heard enough from Heckman's mouth to know his feelings about the both of you."

Tam nods. Finishes her coffee. Reaches across the table and touches Larry's hand. "Thanks," she says.

25

Tam, with her basket of clean and folded laundry in the back seat of her car, makes pit stops for gas and groceries and bourbon and consequently has barely driven beyond the city limits of Fort Maginnis when her cell phone rings, a rare enough occurrence that she pulls over to answer.

"Tam? Larry here. I hope I caught you before you got out of town."

She glances out her car window. "Almost. I just passed the Presbyterian church."

"That's a relief. Tam, is there any way I can get you to come back into town? To the jail?"

A pause. Tam hears women's voices in excited argument with Larry. He apparently turns to placate or remonstrate, she can't tell which, and returns to her.

"The thing is, Tam, Vay Evenson is raising holy hell back in her cell. The girls are afraid she's going to hurt herself. And what she wants—what's she's screaming for—is to talk to you."

Tam takes a breath and lets it out slowly, trying to process what Larry is saying. Asking. "You—want me—" sounding in her own ears as though she's come down with Rob's stammer.

"Sure would appreciate it." His relief apparent in his voice. "If you can't calm her down, I'll have to get a doctor, have him give her a shot of something, which I sure would rather not do."

The only excuse Tam can come up with are the perishables, milk and salad mix, in her car. "Have you got a refrigerator at the jail?"

"What? Oh. Groceries. Yeah, sure, we got a refrigerator. We can make room for whatever you need."

No excuse to give, then. Tam sighs. "Okay." And makes a three-point turn in the middle of the highway and drives back into Fort Maginnis.

At the courthouse Tam lugs two plastic bags from Safeway up the steps to the portico, then down the echoing granite corridor that leads to the annex that houses the county jail. Here she finds Larry leaning over a desk, where a uniformed deputy speaks into a phone. A second deputy sees Tam and leaps to relieve her of her Safeway bags.

"I got 'em, ma'am—it's just a little refrigerator, but we can pull out some of this crap to make room—" He sets out a case of what looks to be cans of soft drinks as he speaks.

Larry is at her side, hugging her shoulders with one arm while he opens a heavy door with his free hand.

"Sure do appreciate it, Tam—" Whatever else he says is cut off as the door opens on a scream that seems not to end.

A woman in jeans and a red polo shirt rises from a chair in the hallway, her hands over her ears. "I don't know how she does it," she shouts to make herself heard to Tam and the sheriff. "She doesn't even seem to stop to take a breath."

Tam resists the impulse to clap her hands over her own ears. Walks, instead, to look through bars of the cell where Vay lies on her back on a cot, screaming her never-ending scream and beating her head against the thin pillow.

"Vay," says Tam. No answer. Of course, Vay can't hear anything through her own screaming.

"Vay!" Tam shouts. No answer, no reaction, no break in the screaming.

How to get her attention. Tam looks at Hube's wedding ring on her left thumb. Uses it to rachet across the cell bars with the sound of a thousand giant fingernails raking glass.

Creecheech! Creecheech! Creecheech! over and over, until the racket not of her own making brings Vay out of her what—trance state? hysterics?—enough to crack open one eye. Sees Tam and breaks mid-scream.

"Mrs. Bowen?"

"You said you wanted to see me."

After all the din, the silence in the cell block is deafening. Vay sits up slowly and swings her legs over the side of the cot, never taking her eyes off Tam.

Tam waits.

"How's Fancy?"

"Fancy—" For a moment Tam is baffled. Then remembers. The name Vay called the Hellbitch. "She's fine. I've been riding her."

"I know. I watched you."

Tam wonders how long Vay had skulked around the cabin, sleeping in the hayloft or nested in the underbrush. Being fed leftovers and scraps stolen by Calvin from his brother's kitchen. Getting dirtier, hungrier. She supposes she should ask the girl. Probably Larry will want to pass the information to Ed Evenson. But the questions Tam wants to ask are about Vay's plans. Vay's future.

"Would I be able to ride her now?"

Tam brings her thoughts back to Vay in the here and now. "Not if you're still afraid of her."

"I only got to ride her once. I never get to do what I want to do!"

"What do you want to do? Other than ride the Hell—Fancy?"

The girl's bottom lip trembles. Tears spill over and run down her cheeks. "I wanted to take her with us. I begged Dad, but he wouldn't even listen, even when I—" She interrupts herself, clamps her mouth closed.

Tam is trying to imagine the Hellbitch in Los Angeles. She supposes it could be done by someone with the money to pay for her board at a stable, for the sake of a girl who can't ride the mare, will never ride the mare—when a thought strikes her.

"You know your father will be here tomorrow to take you home with him. Maybe you can talk to him then—"

"No! No! I won't! I won't! I want to stay here! Jamie will let me live with him if I just—I know Jamie will let me stay! I just have to get back to Jamie! Jamie—"

Tam feels torn between pity and exasperation. "Vay, you're not of age. James is not your legal guardian. Your father—"

"I'm old enough to get married, and my father can't touch me when I'm married to Jamie!" She stares at Tam though the cell bars, smug and defiant. "Because I *won't* go back with my dad—he'll—oh, Mrs. Bowen, I thought you'd help me."

She searches Tam's face for a reaction. When she can't find encouragement, she goes on. Twists her face into a grotesque snarl, pats her stomach. "I won't go back to Los Angeles! How do you think I got this way?"

"Vay, you—"

"Didn't want to hear it, did you. Nobody does. Even Mom! She went off and left me with him, didn't she?"

"Vay," Tam says carefully, "are you telling me your father has been—abusing you?"

"Is that what you call it? *Abusing* me?" Vay hurls the words at Tam. "When he's been *screwing* me? I thought you were different, I thought you'd help me, but you're just like the rest of them."

Tam cannot tell if she's hearing the truth from a trapped and desperate child or a fabrication from that trapped and desperate child. "Vay," she says, "will you tell the sheriff and the social worker what you just told me?"

Sees the wheels of calculation turn in Vay's face. "If I do, will they keep him from taking me home?"

"I don't know. But what do you have to lose by telling them?"

A long silence before Vay nods. "Okay," in a small voice.

Tam waits in the anteroom of the jail, watching the hands of the clock complete their slow turns and listening to the murmur of voices occasionally punctuated by Vay's sharper interjections. At least it sounds like a conversation, not a confrontation. She sighs, letting her tangled thoughts take which direction they might. Can the life she's resumed in the Sun Creek country get any more complex? James. Calvin. Vay. Rob. Allen. Even Zenith. If she had pen and paper, she'd draw a diagram between them, arrows pointing to who is still on good terms with whom. Herself and Zenith, she guesses. Maybe herself and Calvin. Maybe herself and Rob. Vay?

Vay and James. Tam's mind flashes back to a scene in James's kitchen early in the summer, when she sat down for the breakfast he was cooking for her and Vay and Calvin. Calvin and Vay playing their teasing games, Calvin dipping a lock of her hair into the pitcher of maple syrup. And just before that. Vay holding up a CD album with its picture of a grinning cowboy, teasing James about his taste in music. *Ooh! Jamie!*

James's irritation with Vay when she teased him about his CD. Hadn't it struck Tam at the time that his irritation was masking his attraction to his brother's girlfriend? Even when she dismissed the possibility, telling herself it was her own inappropriate feelings drawing her to James?

Vay throwing herself into James's arms, sobbing. *Jam-ee, Jam-ee—*

A plotline unrolls itself, like something she might have dreamed up for a novel. James and Vay. Meeting—where? Behind Calvin's back, of course—but not an obstacle for any competent novelist to find a way around. Calvin easily could be sent—by James, of course—on an errand to a neighbor. To Zenith, say, or even to Tam herself.

Tam's stomach churns. She wishes she'd seen the letter Ed Evenson had written to James, demanding reimbursement for Vay's "procedure." She tries to remember James's exact wording when he told her about it. Had he ever mentioned Calvin's name? Or had Tam jumped to that conclusion?

And now Ed Evenson himself.

With a start Tam realizes that Libarriby Sibidibel is bending over her, trying to ask her something. "Sorry," she manages. Sees lines deepening across Larry's face, sees he looks as exhausted as she feels.

"Just trying to thank you. For coming back here and talking to the girl. Don't know what we'd have done, otherwise."

"So she—"

Larry looks grim. "Spilled her guts, all right. And with Evenson expected tomorrow, it doesn't leave Kim and me a whole lotta time."

"Kim?"

"Kim Katynski. From Child Protection Services." The woman in the red polo shirt.

Tam nods. "So you believe her? Vay, I mean?"

Larry draws a slow breath, lets it out even slower. "Kim and I haven't had time to talk it over. Thing is, Tam, these are serious allegations she's making. It's not a question of believing or not believing. We have to check her story out."

"Did she tell you she's pregnant? Or at least *was* pregnant? Maybe already pregnant when her father took her to Los Angeles?"

Larry's face slackens, his eyes looking inward and his mouth sagging slightly open. "Crap," he whispers. "Oh, crap."

Tam herself feels numb as she waits for Larry to add in his head to a total of three. Which will Vay blame? Who will any one of the three blame in turn? She struggles to her feet as Larry grasps her arm. "You'd better sit back down, Tam."

Larry is grasping her arm. "You'd better sit back down, Tam."

Guides her to a desk chair on rollers, fills a paper cup with water from a cooler and carries it to her. Sits on a corner of the desk. "Gotta sixteen-year-old myself," he mutters.

"Is Vay still talking to—Kim, is it?"

Larry nods. "And Kim's very good."

A silence. Muted voices from the stairs, a deputy and an older man descending into the anteroom of the jail. They nod to Larry and retreat to a desk in the corner. The deputy shuffles through some papers, hands one to the older fellow. Nothing about their interest in the paper seems urgent. Tam feels as though she's watching the two men through a bubble. If she cared enough, she could dream up uneventful small-town lives for them. But she doesn't care.

"Tam? You don't have anything you need to be doing this afternoon, do you? Let's get the hell outta here."

No, Tam guesses she really doesn't. Horses who need riding— but saddling horses and riding would mean reentering the fraught scene of young men and testosterone at her cabin. So she stands, catching herself on the corner of the desk when the chair shows signs of starting to roll under her, and allows Larry to guide her up the stairs and into the clear light of the courthouse foyer.

Larry has his cell to his ear, speaking into it. "—okay, great. See you in ten. Yeah, got Tam Bowen with me—okay, sure."

He closes his phone and drops it into his shirt pocket. "Barb," he says. "We'll go right over. She's been looking forward to meeting you. Says she remembers you from school. We were a couple years ahead of her, you know."

As she half-listens to Larry enthusing about his wife, Tam finds herself guided to the big white Ford with the sheriff's emblem on the door. From the high vantage point of the front seat, she can look down on the roofs of parked cars and the tops of parking meters and watch a pair of pigeons wing down from the eaves of one of the old sandstone stores to light on a sidewalk and saddle ahead of passersby. The peace of pigeons.

Larry turns on Sixth Street and drives into an older neighborhood of generous frame houses set on watered lawns and shaded by cottonwoods and mature oaks that must have been planted years ago. Pulls into the driveway of a white house with bow windows on both sides of the front door. "Hard to believe, we've been living here nearly twenty years now. Our oldest boy was just a toddler, and then Kyle and the girls came along—"

The front door opens on a dark-haired woman wearing blue jeans and a pink T-shirt and a wide smile. "Tam Bowen! On our very own doorstep! Do come in!"

Bubbling, she leads Tam through a small foyer and into a living room, where a bow window looks out over the street. "I'm Barb, of course—I was Barb Monroe, but of course you won't remember me—but I love your books. I've read every one, and I've asked Larry scads of questions about you—please, sit right here on the love seat!"

Tam finds herself seated on rose-patterned chintz, facing a platter of crackers, sliced cheese, and cut-glass pots of dip on a glass-topped coffee table. Shakes her head. Barb must have been a whirlwind of activity during the ten minutes or so of Larry's phone call and his arrival with Tam. Hopes her shirt and blue jeans aren't too dusty for the chintz.

Larry, grinning, seats himself in a rose plush armchair. "That's Barb for you, can't keep her down!"

"I have all your books that I hope you will sign—you don't have to sign them all, even one would be lovely—no, no, not until you've had a chance to relax and share some nibbles with us. Larry and I love our nibbles before dinner. And it's not too early for a glass of wine, now, is it? Larry, I have that new bottle of Chard chilling—"

"You can't beat her, you may as well join her!" Larry patting his paunch, disappears through an archway and returns in a moment with a dark-green labeled bottle and glasses.

Yes, might as well join her. Tam leans back on the love seat and allows Larry to pour her a glass of Chardonnay. Meets Barb's smile as best she can, helps herself to a cracker.

A couple of toasts later—"To old friends!" "To Tam's next book!"—the signing of books, the effects of the very good Chardonnay, and Barb's warmth, and Tam finds herself surprisingly relaxed in this feminine, flowery room where Larry in full uniform and Barb in her blue jeans look, well, oddly clad for their surroundings but thoroughly at home. Tam recalls the pleasant sunlit living room of Jay Jennings and his sister in the midst of their peaceful acres and allows herself another fleeting dream of an alternative life, in which she had stayed in Fort Maginnis and married a man as kind as Larry, who raised Rob as his own— maybe not so much rose chintz in their lives—

But she hadn't, of course. And her fantasy fades as the front door opens behind them and a girl walks through the foyer into the living room. A very young girl. Sixteen? Seventeen? Tawny hair, hazel eyes, a confident athletic walk.

"Our youngest," Larry introduces her. "Her name's Myah."

"Da-ad! Can I have a glass of that?"

"Absolutely not!"

Apparently used to defeat, Myah shrugs and snags a cracker, scoops up a generous load of dip, mumbles something to Tam about being nice to meecha, and takes herself off.

"Kids." Larry shakes his head, his face suddenly sobered as Tam, too, remembers another pretty teenager.

"And not that she's not capable of sneaking down to the kitchen and pouring a glass—" Barb begins, glances at Larry, and breaks off. So Larry carries his work home with him. Barb knows something about the other teenager.

"Another glass of wine, Tam?"

"No—no. I'm driving home. In fact"—she glances at her watch and sees that it is nearly six—"I need to be off. But I surely do thank you for the nibbles and drinks. And you have a beautiful daughter."

"I'll drive you back to your car," says Larry. He and Barb both rise, and after a startled hesitation, Tam returns Barb's embrace. After a summer in the company of men and a boy, she's almost forgotten the ways of friendly women.

"Come again, real soon! We'll have a dinner party!" Barb promises.

Back at Tam's Focus, still parked by the jail, Larry opens the door for her and pauses for a moment, looking down at her.

"At least you look a little more relaxed than when we got here. Hang in there, girl." He smiles and pats her shoulder before turning and walking back to his car. Tam sighs, snaps her seatbelt, starts her ignition, and turns the Focus toward the Sun Creek country.

26

By the time she crosses the Sun Creek bridge and turns on the dirt road toward her cabin to drive through the shafts of sunlight and shadow that fall through the tops of pines, Tam feels her hands back to gripping the wheel after the respite she had felt in Barb and Larry's living room. Tells herself not to idealize the Seidels. And yet. And yet. What she's driving toward.

But when she tops the crest by the lone pine, she sees tranquility and full sunlight. Her cabin as solid as she had left it, the black Tahoe parked undisturbed beside the road. The three horses drowsing in their pasture, in the shade of the old box elder tree, undisturbed by the angry-hornet buzz of a chainsaw as it attacks its way through the underbrush below the barn.

Chainsaw? Rob? Maybe he rented the saw in Fort Maginnis and brought it out here. And if he's working below the barn, he's already cut some serious brush. And yes, there's Calvin, swigging water from a bottle, then giving Tam a wave and straightening to his scythe and going back to work on the overgrown grass.

Tam drives down the slope and parks by the cabin. Feels the absence of James's blue pickup truck like a weight. Lifts the groceries she'd recovered from the refrigerator in the jail out of the car and makes a couple trips back and forth to the cabin to stow the perishables and put away the rest. Another trip for the laundry in its basket, with the package from the liquor store riding along with the folded sheets and towels and clothing. At least these are weights that are real.

The cabin is so quiet that her footsteps echo as she walks back and forth, putting away her clean laundry. Finishing her small tasks, she stands by the rock fireplace, staring at nothing for a minute or two before shaking herself—she could open her laptop and write, couldn't she? Finish the piece about the burros, meditate more deeply about the strange human yearning for beauty that might account for their love of horses.

No. What she needs is hard physical activity. Tam turns her back on the waiting laptop and marches herself out of the cabin into hard bright sunlight. There's another rake in the barn, isn't there?

Tam works a few yards behind Calvin, raking downed branches and scythed grass toward the gulch. Pauses for a moment to wipe perspiration from her face, feels trickles of sweat down her arms and back, breathes in the fragrance of curing grass. Ahead, she sees that Calvin also has paused, waiting for her to catch up to him and almost certainly hoping for news of Vay.

All he says, however, is a withdrawn "Hi," without taking his gaze from the horizon.

Tam waits, finally says, "Hot."

"Yeah."

He stares at the horizon, but the knuckles of his sun-browned hands have gone white from his grip on the handle of the scythe. Just as Tam thinks he won't speak again, he says, "Goddamn hot," and then, after a pause, "What are they going to do with her?"

Tam has wondered how she is going to answer that question. Honestly, she guesses. "I don't know, Calvin. All I know is they'll do what's best for Vay. And Sheriff Seidel is a decent man."

Calvin nods. At first Tam thinks he has shifted his gaze to track a hawk sailing above the bluff beyond the cabin on a thermal current but then sees that he is watching Rob, who hikes up from the bottom of the pasture with his chainsaw.

"Whoa," says Rob as he sets down the saw and strikes sweat from his face. "Where's that water bottle?"

He takes a deep draft from the bottle Calvin hands him, draws a breath, and looks pensive for a moment, then adds, "Hot as hell out here, but I think I've carved a good swath all the way around the pasture and the buildings. What's next? You got another rake, Tam? Maybe rake all this trash into a pile and set backfires around it until the pile's safe to burn?"

Tam considers. "Not much wind today. But maybe several small piles would be safer. We can soak feed sacks in the horse trough to beat out the backfires."

"How about a garden hose? We could hook it up at the tap at the trough and stretch it as far as we can."

Calvin takes a second deep swig of water and starts hiking up to the shed to fetch sacks and hose and another rake, while Rob looks back over the swath of grass and weeds and branches.

"It's good the cabin and the barn have metal roofs, but we can use the hose to wet down the roof of the shed," he says. "As hot as it's been, we'll probably need to hose every day."

Tam nods. August heat, after all. She thinks Rob seems more—what, observant?—and his stammer has become less apparent. Is it the hard work, is it his respite from Allen's diatribes, can it be that Rob has begun to relax in her presence? A tiny bloom of hope grows. Can something good be salvaged from this summer that somehow has tangled itself into a snarl she never could have imagined?

"Rob—" she begins and hesitates, not sure how to continue. "I've been glad of the help. You've done good work here."

He scuffs mown grass with the toe of his sneaker. "I've been happy to do it. Nothing like a good offense with a chainsaw against these bushes—what kind are they, anyway?"

"Mostly hawthorns. And junipers. The ones with berries ripening are chokecherries. And the gray clumps are sagebrush that's crept up here from the prairie."

"—like I was saying, nothing like destroying hawthorns to work my knots out." He lays the chainsaw down on the freshly cut stubble, picks up Tam's rake, and takes a long look across the pasture to the cabin with his Tahoe and Tam's Focus parked beside it, across the gorge of Sun Creek, up the farther timbered slope. Soft summer greens and browns, jagged tips of distant blue ridge pines cutting into the endless sky.

"Beautiful," he says. "I never realized. No wonder you love it here."

Is *love* the word for it? Tam wonders. Supposes it is.

"—I've been thinking. If I could get some kind of job in Fort Maginnis—work for a while, try to save a little—hope I can straighten my dad out some, once they get him detoxed—Calvin was telling me how much work he and you put into the place, how much you had to hire done—could be I could help out here, get to know the place?"

He turns to meet her eyes now, his eyes the color of hers and sunlight in his fair hair, and something stark in his face catches at her.

"Calvin," he says. "He's a damned good kid. You know that, don't you? He's been telling me about you and him. How you're helping him to break his colt, the rides you've been taking—" He breaks off, seeing Calvin hobble down the slope, laden with another rake, a shovel, and a bundle of stiff green garden hose that's trying to escape its coil. "I'd like a chance to know the place," Rob finishes.

And Tam has no words, can only nod and blink back an unexpected film of tears as Calvin staggers up and throws down his load.

"This f—, excuse me, Tam, this *fricking* hose was the biggest goddamn tangle, like somebody wanted to see how big a mess they could make of it—and heavy! I just hope there's enough of it to reach the horse trough so I don't have to try to find some more!"

Tam wakes as early sunlight falls through her window and across her bed. Gropes for her bedside clock—six thirty. Pulls a pillow over her face and dozes, then wakes with a start as her phone rings. Lets it ring. The clock says ten thirty as she untangles herself from her sheet, snatches up her robe, and staggers to the

its and lets flow, feeling the relief of emptying her
en has she ever felt so exhausted, with muscles sore
er knew she had?

es, stands. Wonders how Rob and Calvin are feeling.
The three of them had worked until dark, raking the felled grass
and branches into piles, setting fire to the stubble and letting the
low flames burn downwind until the piles went up like torches.
Dragging the garden hose as far as it would reach to douse every
spark, resorting then to beating out the backfires with wet sacks.
Carrying buckets of water to pour over the burned stacks. Calvin's
and Rob's faces and hands were blackened with soot, and Tam
had known she didn't look any better. But between the three of
them, they had burned a fireguard all the way down from the
track, around the buildings and pasture, and as far as the gulch,
where Sun Creek chortled in the twilight.

"Big risk now is the timberline above the track," Rob had
pointed out as they finally, wearily, put away their buckets and
tools.

"Will you be all right, driving back to town tonight?"

"Yeah—I'm filthy as hell is all. I'll take a shower at the motel
and check on Dad. Probably grab a burger at the drive-in and hit
the sack. See you tomorrow."

"What about you?" Tam asked Calvin as the Tahoe's taillights
disappeared past the lone pine.

He had shrugged. "Walk home, I guess." But he lingered, scuff-
ing at burned-over stubble with the toe of his boot. "Oh, hell, Tam.
I don't know what to say. We've had—I mean, riding with you,
working with the filly—I just hope that's not all over."

"I hope not too. Go and get some rest. Maybe tomorrow will
look better."

He nodded, and Tam watched him trudge away in the dark.

Tam had stuffed her sooty, reeking clothes into a plastic bag and
tied it shut. Then stood under the hot shower a long time, watch-

ing the water at her feet run black down the drain until it cleare. and she felt clean again. She'd pinned back her wet hair, pulled on an oversized tee, poured herself a double bourbon, and fallen into bed.

Now, squinting against the light, she starts coffee and rummages for bread for toast and an orange to peel before she remembers the phone call. Better check. Not many people would be calling her.

The phone on the other end is snatched up in the midst of the first ring. "Tam! Glad to get hold of you! Hell, I hate to ask again, but I've got more trouble here."

"*Larry?*"

His voice crackles with anxiety. "Got a woman here, name of Heather Macclyn, says she's Vay Evenson's mother. She asked to talk to Vay, and Vay started screaming again at the sight of her. I tried, Kim tried—like I say, I hate to ask, Tam, but could you find it in you to come back to town and see if you can calm her down?"

Tam sighs. "I'm beginning to think heaven is not having Vay Evenson anywhere in Montana."

"You won't be any gladder than me to get rid of her."

Tam parks her Focus in the lot next to the courthouse. As she gets out, she sees Larry waiting for her at the top of the steps. He walks down to meet her, shaking his head.

"Getting to be a helluva mess, Tam. I've called the county attorney, and he's meeting me and Mrs. Macclyn in an hour. Big thing now is to get Vay calmed down enough that he can interview her."

"How did Mrs. Macclyn get here so fast? Doesn't she live in California?"

"She said a friend called her. Must have been somebody in Fort Maginnis. Her new husband, turns out he's an attorney, another complication in this damned mess, and he chartered a plane and flew her back here."

Tam and Larry stand for a moment in the heat of direct sunlight reflecting off concrete. The leaves of the cottonwoods around the courthouse shiver, then droop as a soft breath of air wanders through them and dies. Tam longs for the tranquility of horses and the peace and shade of her cabin, even surrounded by the blackened new fireguard. She's wasted too much of her life on paved streets. And now this tangled situation without a solution.

"Guess we oughta walk down to the jail and see if she's still screaming," says Larry. "Beings I got you to come all the way back into town."

A middle-aged couple are seated in the anteroom of the jail, holding hands and looking anxious. They're well-dressed, he in a suit and she in heels and hose. He lets go of his wife's hand and stands as Tam and Larry enter, Tam automatically noting the rhythmic screams coming from the cell wing.

"Adam Macclyn," he introduces himself, "and this is my wife, Heather."

Tam allows Larry to introduce her to the couple, then slips off into the cell wing, where the social worker, Kim, sits outside Vay's cell and knits. Kim has found one way to mute the relentless screams; she's wearing what Tam recognizes as shooter's mitts over her ears. Tam has to smile, even as she rattles on the cell bars with the ring on her thumb.

"Enough of that, Vay!"

Predictably, Vay breaks off mid-scream, and Tam stifles her irritation with this teenager who manipulates the adults around her, including Tam herself, who has driven back into Fort Maginnis like an obedient puppet.

"This is the last time I'm doing this, Vay."

Vay stares at her, bottom lip quivering.

"I mean it. You can scream until you have no throat, for all I care. What will happen then is that you'll be sedated and put into protective custody and kept there until you've shown you can behave yourself. Which does *not* include trespassing on my place or assaulting me or anyone else. Because another time, I certainly will press charges."

"Jamie," Vay whimpers.

Tam winces but steels herself to go on. "*If*, rather than protective custody, you'd choose to go home—either with your father or your mother, depending on how the county attorney decides to proceed—you and your parent can petition a judge to emancipate you."

"What's emancipate?"

"You'd legally be declared an adult. You're seventeen, after all. If you were behaving yourself, a judge likely would be amenable. As an adult, you could make your own decisions. Marry James Warceski if he wants you."

Tam takes a breath at that last suggestion. "You'd also be subject to prosecution, as an adult, if you misbehave—" Was that entirely true, she wonders? All she knows of the law is research she's skimmed for one of her novels. Shrugs. An attorney—whatshisname, Adam Macclyn—could put her straight. Vay can't.

And Vay is listening.

"I could do all that?" she asks in a small voice. "And I could come back and marry Jamie?"

"If he wants you."

"Will you take care of Fancy until I can come back?"

"Yes," says Tam and hopes she doesn't sound the way she feels. "Okay."

"Okay what? Will you talk to your mother? Will you talk to the county attorney like an adult?"

And Vay nods, like the spoiled child she is.

Tam turns to Kim the social worker, taps her on the shoulder until the other woman lays down her knitting and lifts an earmuff. "She says she'll straighten up. I'm leaving."

Kim stares at Vay, gradually processing that her screaming has stopped. "Wow," she says.

"Good luck."

Tam turns to the stairs leading to the jail anteroom. Hears the hollow sound of her own footsteps, the soft murmur of the social worker's voice and Vay's tearful responses. Hell and damn. She emerges into the anteroom to find Larry and the Macclyns, apparently getting used to the sound of silence.

"Holy—" Larry interrupts himself. "What did you do?"

"Told her to behave herself. Told her what will happen if she doesn't."

Heather Macclyn is on her feet, facing Tam. "My fault—my fault—I *told* Ed, I told him, *I don't know how to be a mother!*"

"None of us does," says Tam. She sees another man in a suit, probably the county attorney, who has joined the Macclyns and probably full to the brim with questions for Tam. Tam doesn't care. Doesn't care what the Macclyns do, what the county attorney decides. Because Tam is emancipating herself from the whole miserable, tangled situation. Turns her back on all of it, climbs the stairs out of the jail, and walks out into the relentless sunlight that beats down on the paved parking lot.

27

In the cooling twilight Tam shuts the gate to the horse pasture and walks back to her cabin. An afternoon with the horses, grooming and caressing them in the shade of the old box elder tree, has eased the rage that had driven her flight from Fort Maginnis, gripping the wheel and taking corners too fast on the graveled county road. What she feels now is the dull ache of loss—loss of what—her peace of mind, she tells herself, but it's not that, not exactly.

Whatever. Whatever. Without much interest she rummages for food, then hears a knock on her door and goes to answer.

Zenith, bearing a rich-smelling covered dish and beaming at her. And Spotty, wagging politely.

"Thought you might need some nourishment," Zenith explains. "And hoped you might share some of that top-shelf bourbon of yours."

Tam opens the door wide for him and Spotty, the question at the back of her mind—why would he think she'd feel needy?—firmly stifled. Manages a smile. Food and good company, who could ask for more?

"What have you brought, Zenith? Ah-h. Venison stew."

"Last package in the freezer from the fall hunting," he explains, as Tam lifts down bowls and lays out forks, "and a good loaf of bread."

"Bless you."

Neither speak as they dig into the food. Tam might feel needy, but she's also ravenous. She butters chunks of bread and spoons up mouthful after mouthful of stew in the thankfully cool mountain air of evening flowing through the windows she has thrown open, while Spotty pads between her and Zenith and back again with hopeful eyes. Only when, replete with Zenith's cooking, they have moved down the front steps to the scrap of dry lawn where Tam has placed rocking chairs, with glasses of Tam's bourbon at hand, does Zenith clear his throat.

"Your boys did quite a piece of work on that fireguard. Looks like hell now, all blackened over, but new grass will perk it up if we get fall rains."

Her boys. Rob and Calvin. Tam nods. "I haven't seen them today."

Spotty, who has licked the last mouthful of stew from a bowl, hears something in her voice that brings him to her side to lay his head on her knee. Tam strokes him absently.

"I worry about Calvin," she says.

"Yup."

A rustling of aspen leaves, almost a sound of fall. Maybe rains aren't so far away.

"My girl was his age when we met."

"Fifteen? The girl you loved?"

"Yup. And don't let anybody tell you that feelings aren't real at that age." He rocks back, sips bourbon. "I'm not proud of myself, what I did. Shoulda held back, for her sake, at least. A course, no telling what she might have done if I had. Something worse maybe. She was hellbent on California. And she got there, eventually. On her own. I was in lockup at the time. Got back together with her one last time, after I got out and she came back to Montana. Goddamn disaster."

Tam tries to visualize the young man and the spoiled girl who was not much more than a child. Doesn't have to try very hard.

"Vay is seventeen," she says.

"Heard they were holding her at the jail until her folks could come and pick her up."

"The sheriff was expecting her father to get to Fort Maginnis this evening. But somebody called her mother, and she and Vay's stepfather are already in Fort Maginnis."

Zenith rocks back and forth a time or two in his chair. Swirls his bourbon. "Yup. I'm the one who called Heather. When I heard Ed was coming for the kid."

Tam stares.

"Got to know Heather a little bit, back when she and Ed were breaking up. Don't think she knew a thing about what Ed was doing with Vay, but—"

"How did *you* know?" Tam gasps.

"James told me."

"*James?*"

"Yup. Think he got it out of his brother. Reason they were trying to help her. One of the reasons, anyway."

Tam stares into her glass. Maybe she should get drunk. Maybe that would help. Senses Zenith studying her over the rim of his own glass. "What?" she says.

"Um. Had a pretty good talk with James. It's not Vay he's torn up about. Though he's concerned about her, a course." Shrugs, sips bourbon. "You need to be back on those horses, don't you? Better call him."

"I'd feel like a fool."

"Phooey. Call him."

It must be the bourbon haze. As she meets Zenith's level eyes, she sees the years drop off, an illusion of the aging process reversing itself, until, for a moment, she sees the young man he once was, dark haired and straight limbed, intense and in love.

The moment passes. "Zenith," she says. "Was your girl the only woman you ever cared about?"

A silence that drags on. "Sounds real stupid when you put it like that," he says, finally. "Probly didn't admit it to myself for a lot of years. And not that I never, what they call it now, *hooked up* again, oh, hell no. Oil patch and that. But—" His words trail off.

"Whole hell of a lot I wish I'd done different," he adds after a time. "And a whole lot of shit coming down which I couldn't do anything about, serving my sentence like I was. When I got out—

guess she'd got herself mostly straightened out. Got married to somebody who took good care of her. Still does, I guess. What I don't know—" finishes his bourbon and stands, as Spotty, sensing a departure, lifts his head from his muzzle. "—what I don't know is whether she still sings."

He snaps his fingers for Spotty and walks to the door. "Call James," he says, and disappears into the night.

Another hot August morning, starting early. Tam stumbles out of bed, gropes her way first to the toilet and then to the kitchen, where she zaps a cup of yesterday's cold coffee in the microwave. Sinks upon a stool to wait out the minute or two before the beep. Threads together what she can recall of last night's conversation with Zenith. The main thing that comes back to mind is *Call James*.

Damned if she will.

The hot stale coffee steadies her, and when she sees the black Tahoe pull around the barn and park, she swallows the last dregs, sets the mug in the sink, and runs back to her bedroom to pull on blue jeans and a T-shirt and boots. By the time Rob taps on the cabin door, she's back in the kitchen, starting a fresh pot.

When he joins her in the kitchen, he's wide awake and smiling, and Tam thinks his father must have had a quiet night, although she doesn't ask, just offers him the other stool. In his Levi's and blue chambray shirt with his sleeves rolled to the elbows, a bootheel—*he's wearing boots?*—comfortably hooked in a rung of the stool, and straw cowboy hat doffed and set on the counter behind him, he could almost pass as young ranchman. Tam wonders where he got the clothes, which don't look new, and she must look her question because he grins and says, "I got to talking with your friend the sheriff last night. About a lotta things. Anyway, he asked me what I planned to do while I waited for my dad to detox and face charges. Gave me these clothes. All but the hat, which I bought myself. Or I should say, you bought for me. But they gotta rummage box at the jail, stuff that gets left behind, I guess, and maybe some people donate."

"And then he offered me a job." Rob pauses. "Night janitor at the county jail," and laughs out loud at Tam's expression. "Hell, not like I never had a job before. And it beats sponging on you."

"Rob."

"Nah." He touches her hand as she pours his coffee. "It'll get better."

Tam hesitates, not wanting to hurry what feels like an offer of hope. "Do you ever think about going back to college?"

He nods. "Won't be for a while, though. I can't think that far ahead yet." He sips coffee, hesitant himself. "What would be good, though . . . if you'd teach me how to ride, maybe ride with me a couple hours this morning before I start on that stretch of fire-break above the road?"

Surprised, Tam thinks about it. "Have you ridden much?"

"Never have." Shakes his head. "Never. But I thought—Calvin's not here to ride with you—"

"I haven't seen him this morning—"

"No, because James drove him in to Fort Maginnis early this morning to say goodbye to—whatshername, Vay—before she left with her mother. Also—" eyes fixed on his coffee cup—"they both gave the sheriff DNA samples."

The sunlit kitchen window is not revolving. Tam knows it isn't. She watches it take three or four turns before Rob sets down his coffee mug and catches her shoulders.

"Put your head down!"

"I'm all right," she insists, but he's easing down her head and holding her, and for the moments she allows the room to right itself, his warmth reassures her in a way she never expected to feel from him. Slowly, she rights herself, meets his eyes. A grown man, a stranger. Well, no.

She reaches for her coffee mug, takes several deep and deliberate drafts. Sets the mug down. "I need to go riding. Let the horses clear out my head. Are you riding with me?"

Rob is taller than Calvin, not quite as tall as James. After some thought, Tam decides that Calvin's saddle on gentle Buddy will be the best for Rob's first horseback ride. Calvin's stirrups will be a little short, which will be safer than James's saddle—Hube's saddle, she reminds herself—which would be too long. No point in taking time to unlace stirrups to adjust them, after all, when they will just have to be adjusted back again.

Maybe, she remembers. Her riding days with James and Calvin probably are over.

She shows Rob how to bridle Buddy and throw the blanket and saddle across his withers, then allows him to carry her saddle to the Hellbitch and throw it on her. Good saddling practice for him, she tells herself as she heads for the pasture gate with the Hellbitch at her shoulder and Rob with Buddy following behind.

At the gate Rob catches up and leans into the gatepost to open the gate and drag it aside for Tam and the horses, and she nods to herself. At least someone has shown him how to open a wire gate. Waits for him to close it, shows him how to check Buddy's girth one more time.

"Okay," she says.

"Okay what?"

"Time to mount up."

She swings astride the Hellbitch in the swift movement of her girlhood, turns to watch Rob.

Rob stands with Buddy's reins over his arm, staring up at her. "How?"

Tam bites her lip, breathes in and out. "Put the reins around his neck, the way I've got mine. Keep the reins in your hand as you grab the saddle horn. Put your foot in the stirrup."

Watches Buddy give Rob an appraising look as he follows Tam's instructions with the reins. Grips the saddle horn. Waits.

Wind rustling the aspen leaves, moving into the pines.

"Put your foot in the stirrup," Tam prompts. Is he afraid?

"Which foot?"

Which foot. Rob's words simply will not process themselves for Tam. Which foot. Hube's ghost is howling through the canyons of her mind, whether in hilarity or horror—*his own grandson!*—before Tam can recover herself.

"Left foot."

With some fumbling for the stirrup, he catches it with the tip of his boot and swings up into the saddle. He's reasonably athletic, Tam notes, and doesn't seem afraid of the horse, but he's clearly clueless about the bridle reins, which he's holding in both hands, so when he glances at her, Tam holds up her own reins in her left hand and nods.

"Don't give Buddy so much slack rein. But don' t pull back too hard, or he'll think you're telling him to back up. Yes, that's the idea. Now you can nudge him with your bootheel to get him to move out. Ride him as far as the shed and ride him back. Remember, our Western horses are broken to neck-rein."

She demonstrates by reining the Hellbitch in a circle, then halts her and watches Rob ride up the slope to the shed, noting with one track of her mind that he looks natural enough in the saddle, only a little stiff, while another track of her mind is vibrating at the new landscape it runs on. Riding horseback with this stranger, this adult son returning into her life, no more possible than riding out of her own body. She drags her attention back to the real landscape she's riding through, sees she's automatically turned to ride down the dirt track to the county road. *Woolgathering on horseback*, scolds Hube's ghost. *Dangerous.*

Focus. Dust rising behind the horses' hooves and filtering back down through ripened grasses, chokecherries below the track drooping with bunches of berries turning purple, pines rustling with a breath of wind. Rob, looking grim around his mouth, concentrating on what he's doing, which is balancing in the unfamiliar rhythm of a horse's paces. Not too badly, though.

They've nearly reached the Sun Creek bridge when Tam hears the rumble of an approaching vehicle and reins the Hellbitch to the grass verge on the upper side of the track. Glances back, sees that Rob has done the same. And then looks ahead and sees the dark-blue pickup. James. And Calvin.

Stopping.

Automatic driver's side window lowering silently.

Tam is wondering how best to explain to Calvin why she has loaned Buddy to Rob, when Rob rides up beside her and dismounts.

"Um, she . . . Tam . . . let me borrow your horse so I could ride with her." He rubs his backside. "First time I ever rode a horse. You want him back? I could ride back to the cabin with your brother." Adds, "If you'll let me, James."

James, expressionless, looking straight ahead.

But Calvin has stepped down from the passenger side of the big truck and walks around to join Rob.

"I remember the first time I rode a horse. After we'd moved out here and James got me Buddy. When I got off that first time, I wondered if I'd ever be able to sit down again. And my legs, sheesh."

But before Rob can answer Calvin or hand him Buddy's reins, another vehicle charges across the Sun Creek Bridge and pulls up behind James's pickup truck, honking. And Tam sees, to her dismay, that it is a Murray County Sheriff's truck.

But it's not Larry driving. A younger man, whom she recognizes as the deputy who had cleared out the jail refrigerator for her, hops out and hurries up to Rob.

"Heckman, Sheriff Seidel's been trying to call you! When he couldn't raise anybody out here on the phone, he sent me to fetch you back to town. Your dad—"

Rob whitens. "Oh God, no . . . he's not dead, is he?"

"No, no, but—you need to come with me—" The young deputy glances around at his audience. Calvin's mouth hangs open, as Tam supposes hers does, and even James has turned in the seat of his truck to stare. "I'll explain on the way back to town."

Rob throws Tam one glance she cannot read—is he telling her to stay? Is he asking her to follow?—then climbs after the deputy into the sheriff's truck. Using the grassy slope where Tam once watched Calvin and Vay race each other across the Sun Creek Bridge, the deputy pulls a three-point turn and roars off.

Silence in its wake as dust settles back down. James studies his own hands on the steering wheel, Calvin stands holding Buddy's reins, and the Hellbitch snorts and stamps at a fly. Tam reins her in with automatic hands, as James looks up, still not looking at her, and says, "Calvin, you'd better ride back to the cabin with Tam. I'll meet you there in a bit."

"Okay," agrees Calvin, his voice hardly audible, and Tam looks from him to James and feels the tension between them. Have they been quarreling again? Calvin stands at Buddy's head for perhaps a full minute, then shrugs and mounts the gelding and heels him into a trot down the dirt track. Tam reins the Hellbitch around and follows. At the bend in the track, she glances back over her shoulder and sees the blue pickup still sitting where James had parked it.

Calvin, riding beside her, looks straight ahead and says nothing. Tam feels as though years have passed from the boy who had driven with her to the Arabian horse ranch near Livingston and asked her the story of the Crazy Mountains. What had he said? *I'm the opposite of that crazy woman who lost her children. I lose mothers.* And what he had named his filly. Melanie. And now this further loss.

Heather Macclyn. *I don't know how to be a mother.*

A crack of gunshot. Both horses shy sideways as something crashes through the underbrush and timber on the steep slope above the track, and for a moment Tam has her hands full controlling the Hellbitch and can only hope Calvin is doing as well with Buddy. The next moment a wild-eyed whitetail doe charges across the track in front of them, bolting on three legs into the protection of chokecherries on the lower slope while one foreleg swings limp and helpless.

Tam stares after the doe as thrashing chokecherries track her flight. An out-of-season hunter? In the old days in the Sun Creek country, poaching wasn't uncommon. Tam herself had eaten her share of illegal venison. But in this new Sun Creek country, increasingly populated by well-funded outsiders in search of clean and spacious living, she would not have expected summer deer hunters.

The Hellbitch snorts and shies again, crashing against Calvin and Buddy, and Tam growls at her and reins her back as this time not a wounded doe but a man, and a strange-looking man, leaps out of the underbrush and lands awkwardly in the track.

28

The Hellbitch snorts and shies again, crashing against Calvin and Buddy, and Tam growls at her and reins her back as the apparition with straggling long white hair and ill-fitting clothing leaps out of the underbrush and lands in front of them.

"Where's my deer?" screams the apparition.

In the next elongated seconds, Tam sees he's glitter eyed, and he's brandishing a .22 rifle, not a rifle for deer hunting but capable of real damage, and damned if she's going to let him hurt Calvin or the horses. She claps spurs to the Hellbitch and feels the lunge of the giant mare that closes the gap between her and the apparition, who screams and leaps for the hillside, scrambling back into the hawthorns on hands and knees. Tam can't follow, she's got all she can handle with the Hellbitch bucking under her, fighting the bit and crashing sideways. *Whoa, whoa, damn you, whoa*—is she really getting out the words, is she really sawing on the right rein to force the Hellbitch into a spinning circle, is she really catching glimpses of a white-faced Calvin on Buddy?

"Whoa, whoa, damn you, Hellbitch, whoa—"

Somehow the world rights itself. Pines again point at blue sky, the track settles back in place, the Hellbitch trembles beneath Tam and snorts but no longer in full panic fight-or-flight. And not even a shudder of underbrush to show the flight of the apparition, who had to be, was, *is*, Allen Heckman, but *how*—hospitalized, under police guard—nevertheless, Allen Heckman.

Sound of an engine, rumble of tires on gravel, and James's pickup truck appears around the bend in the track. Catches up to them and brakes to a stop. James steps down, walks around the side of the pickup to look over the scene: Tam on her trembling mare, a frightened Calvin on Buddy.

"Somebody want to tell me what's going on here?"

Calvin looks around at hearing his brother's voice with transparent relief.

"Allen Heckman," Tam explains. The shambling old man who once was a beautiful fair-haired boy she had loved.

James has his phone in his hand. Shakes his head, no signal. "Calvin, ride back to the cabin and call the sheriff on Tam's landline. Might as well keep those boys busy today. I'll keep an eye out for Heckman."

Mutely, Calvin gathers Buddy's reins and throws one look at Tam before he canters off. Asking her what? Telling her he's over his head in troubles? The next minute he's past the bend in the track, and Buddy's hoofbeats fade.

Tam feels a sense of revulsion as sharp as rising nausea. What has caused Allen Heckman to deteriorate to this state? The echoes of Hube and Bunce summing it all up: *Spoiled the boy rotten, Old Man Heckman did.* Tam can almost see their nods of smug agreement.

Bunce.

Allen's strange baggy clothing. She recalls the gray plaid flannel shirt with the sleeves torn out, the ancient denim pants held up by bright-red suspenders. Even stranger than his black ninja wear—*Wait! Was Allen wearing Bunce's clothes?*

A thought with ramifications too frightening to consider.

"Tam?" James breaks through her preoccupation.

"Are you all right? Have you got that damned horse under control? You don't have to stay here. Go home, see to Calvin. The sheriff's boys will take a while to get here."

Calvin. Tam nods.

Once around the bend in the track where James stands, the mountain landscape returns to its ordinary daylight familiarity, which is jarring in itself. The sky as tranquil as though there had been no injured deer and no apparition with a rifle, the pines untroubled by anything but the incessant currents of wind. No making sense of what she has just witnessed. Tam doesn't even try. And then the Hellbitch's ears are pricking up, and Tam hears the hoofbeats of a trotting horse. Calvin on Buddy, returning from making his phone call.

Just as Calvin rides around the outgrowth of hawthorns toward Tam, as though on cue comes for a second time the unmistakable crack of a rifle.

Tam's first reaction is to check for wounds. Both horses flinch but not in pain or panic. Tam hasn't been shot, Calvin hasn't—but Calvin's face has drained of color, and Tam realizes the boy is terrified. Feels her own anger surge. That the Sun Creek country has come to this—frightening children with gunfire. Is James carrying his rifle in its rack in his pickup?—no, no time to think, nothing she can do for James, she has time only to get Calvin out of here.

"This way," Tam snaps, and Calvin seems to wake from wherever fear had taken him and spurs Buddy to follow Tam and the Hellbitch up an old cattle trail that winds up the slope and deeper into timber.

"Tam?" Calvin is trying hard not to let his voice shake. "Where're we going?"

"To get to Zenith."

"Oh."

They crash on, the horses forcing their way through chest-high underbrush and into pine boughs that lash Tam's face. Blood has beaded along a deep scratch on her arm where a pine stub caught her. She doesn't dare to look back to see how Calvin is doing, but she hears from the crash and crackle of branches that he and Buddy follow her. Only another half-mile, and the cattle trail widens into the county road.

Tam hesitates, but the easier ride beckons, and she and Calvin have reached the opposite side of the ridge where the sound of the shot had come from. She reins the Hellbitch out to the road, telling herself she'll head back into the timber at the sound of a vehicle, when Calvin rides up beside her. His face is scratched.

"Almost lost my hat back there in all that brush," he says, trying for casual.

"That wouldn't have been good."

"No."

Tam strains her ears, but all she hears is the clip-clop of horses' hooves and the eternal roar, like distant thunder, of the wind in the ridge pines. And now they've reached the turn-off to Zenith's place, a short slant of graveled road and a new sound, an angry buzz that she recognizes as a weed whipper, and yes, there's Zenith, whacking a firebreak around his house and outbuildings.

He looks up at the sounds of horses' hooves, squinting to see them against the sun, and switches off the weed whipper. Asks, in the sudden silence, "Tam? Calvin? What's going on?"

Of course he couldn't have heard rifle shots above the noise of his weed whipping, either the shot that had wounded the doe or the later shot, which Tam can't bear to wonder about. She swings down from the Hellbitch and turns, giving Zenith his first look at her face.

"Tam! What the hell?"

Tam feels reassured by Zenith's beaming face under its mop of white curls, his bulky presence in old-man's shirt and overalls— *old-man's shirt and overalls like Allen Heckman had been wearing, clothes that were too big for Allen Heckman—Bunce's clothes—*

"Zenith," she says, "something's going on."

Spotty, who has been napping in the shade of the porch, pads up to Tam and licks her hand as Zenith's eyes flick from Tam's face to Calvin's.

"You kids better tie up your horses and come inside where it's cool," Zenith says, and Tam thinks, *Kids?* But she ties the Hellbitch alongside Buddy to the fence in front of Zenith's house and follows him indoors. Calvin has not spoken a word.

"Okay, what?" says Zenith when he's got them settled on his surprisingly comfortable leather couch, with a can of Coke for Calvin a shot of bourbon for Tam, and a worried Spotty curled at Tam's feet. Four solid tongue-and-groove walls around them, bookshelves that overflow with paperbacks, hardcovers, a round oak coffee table and a couple of overstuffed armchairs that match the couch. A window looking out at the road.

"What?" he repeats.

And Tam tells him.

"So you got hold of the sheriff's office?" Zenith asks Calvin when she finishes, and Calvin nods.

"Said they'd send a car—probly take 'em at least thirty minutes, maybe longer—"

They all look at each other. Tam is pretty sure she and Calvin have been riding for at least thirty minutes—anything could be happening by now. Apparently, Zenith is thinking the same thing because he lumbers to his feet and takes up his landline phone. Dials, waits.

The phone crackles an answer. "Gervais here. I need to speak to Sheriff Seidel," Zenith growls. Listens a moment. "Yeah—okay—yeah—yeah, hello, Larry."

A rattle of speech from the other end, something complicated. Zenith listens, his eyes wandering to Tam and back to the phone.

"Yeah," he says finally, "I got Tam and Calvin with me up here. So you'll be out here to my place? Maybe forty minutes? Sure."

Hangs up the phone. Turns to face Tam and Calvin.

Tam tries to read his face. Realizes Zenith has seen a lot in his time. That now he's seeing a profound sadness. "James," she whispers.

"He's alive," says Zenith. Behind Tam, Calvin whimpers, and she reaches back and puts her arm around him. She half-hears Zenith—

"Seidel's on his way out here. Called me from the road. He was relieved as hell I had you two here with me—" He's cradling Tam and Calvin, comforting them with his warmth and bulk. "He'll be able to tell us more."

Tell us more. Tell us more. Tam can't focus on the meaning of the words, only their sounds. Around her are the walls of Zenith's—living room?—lounge, no, *lounge* is an English term, found, in Tam's experience, only in British novels—well, no, *lounge* is a déclassé term, perhaps found in the former colonies. *Sitting room?* Folks in Sun Creek country would have called it their "front room." Nobody left in Sun Creek country to say, *Come on into the front room and make yourself comfortable.* Wonders what Larry's wife, Barb, calls hers. Wonders what language her mind is trying to wrap itself around. How is it that people still can talk to each other?

It's the way things are, snarls Hube.

No, Hube. It's the way things were.

How long she had been keeping her thoughts away from James, how long she'd been standing in Zenith's arms with Calvin huddled beside her, Tam couldn't have said, before Zenith stiffens—yes, at the sound of a vehicle pulling up outside his door—and pulls away from Tam and Calvin. An eye on the AK-47 in its corner, then an eye on the window and a long minute before he relaxes.

"It's Seidel."

29

"What we think happened," says Larry, "is that my boys responded right away to Calvin's call. They didn't hear the second shot, the one that sent you and Calvin scrambling off through the brush and timber to Zenith's place. Too much engine noise and tires on gravel, especially at the speed they were going. When they turned the bend and saw James Warceski's truck, they pulled up behind him and found him in the road. Shot in the throat and bleeding. No sign of Allen Heckman, no sign of a .22 rifle."

"So he's out there somewhere."

Calvin shudders, and Tam hugs him closer. Larry had brought them back to town, and now they sit with him in the waiting area of the emergency room at St. Luke's in Fort Maginnis, drearily familiar by this time to Tam. What about the horses, she'd said to Zenith, and he had waved her off.

"You and the boy go back to town with Seidel," Zenith had ordered. "I'll take care of your horses. You think I never unsaddled a nag?"

"They radioed back to me and requested an ambulance and backup," Larry continues. "I had no idea, of course, what had happened to you, Tam—not until Zenith called and caught me on the road. That was damned good work, by the way, Tam, getting yourself and the boy out of there. I have to admit I was—well. I sure was glad to hear from Zenith."

Everyone looks up as the door to the corridor swings open and the surgeon, still in his green scrubs, with his mask hanging from the strap around his neck, walks across the waiting room toward Calvin. At first no indication of James's condition from the surgeon's expression, then the faintest of smiles.

"Dr. Mohr," he introduces himself. "We've got him stabilized. You're the brother? Would you like to see him for a minute or two?"

Calvin grips Tam's hand. "Can she come with me?"

The surgeon glances from Calvin to Tam. "All right. You'll have to wear masks."

He nods to a nurse, who provides them with masks and leads them through the door and down a corridor to a closed door.

"Just a few minutes," she warns, "and he's still under the anesthetic. Breathing through the respirator. But you'll see he's resting comfortably, and you can come back this evening and he may be able to recognize you."

The sterile room, the hospital bed with a shape under a sheet and a white blanket, a shape whose only movement is the rise and fall of his chest with the even drone of the respirator, Calvin, still gripping Tam's hand, takes a hesitant step toward the bed, takes another step. Tam finds herself counting the rhythm of the respirator. One breath in, one breath out. Another breath in, another breath out. Still counting, she sees Calvin bend over his brother and whisper something.

Then the nurse is at the doorway, motioning to them. Calvin casts one look back at his silent brother as he and Tam leave the room and follow the nurse back down the corridor to the waiting room, where Larry Seidel is just getting up from his chair.

"What did you say to James?" Tam asks.

"Just—sorry for being such a little shit to him." Calvin adds, almost as a question, "I don't think he could hear me."

"Maybe he could." Tam pauses. "Are you going to tell him again when you know he can hear you?"

"Maybe. Yes."

"Are you two ready for home?" asks Larry, and Tam remembers she is without transportation.

"Will you drive us?"

"To my house, yes. No, just listen—it's not safe for either of you on Sun Creek right now. Not until we catch up with Allen Heckman and his whoever-it-was, I was going to say, jail breaker, but I guess it was a hospital breaker. His police guard feels like a fool. Old lady sweet-talked him into helping her get a drink of water at the fountain, got behind him, and conked him one. But he'll recognize her. No, don't say a word about coming home with me. Barb and I've got plenty of room for you, now that we've only got one kid still at home, and she's already made up the beds for you. Besides"—speaking to Calvin now—"you'll want to visit your brother again tonight, right? When he's liable to know you? Hear your voice?"

Calvin has jammed his hands into the pockets of his blue jeans. He exudes his misery as he gives Tam a quick sidelong glance.

"Yes," he mutters, and Tam shrugs. Other words of Larry's are lingering with her. *Hospital breaker.*

"Where is Rob?"

"He's downstairs in the jail. No"—Larry explains at the expression on Tam's face—"we didn't lock him up. I gave him a job, remember? Although I can't pretend we're not keeping an eye on him. Are you prepared to believe that if his dad asked him for help, he wouldn't help him?"

Tam shakes her head mutely. "No," she admits, and she lets Larry take her elbow and guide her and Calvin to the Sheriff's Department truck parked in a blue zone outside the hospital, casting long shadows as the afternoon sun sinks in the west. Where has the day gone? Did Tam really begin today riding horseback with Rob?

Larry pries Calvin's hand loose from Tam's and boosts him, unresisting, into the back seat. Snaps his seatbelt for him. Glances at Tam and shakes his head.

"Kid's like a goddamn zombie," he mutters as Tam climbs into the front passenger seat and snaps her own seatbelt.

The drive to Larry's house seems endless. No one says a word. Finally, the turn on the avenue shaded by mature trees, most of them cottonwoods, a few clumps of birches, even a young oak, then the turn into Larry's driveway, stopping behind a gray Lincoln, which must be Barb's car. Tam opens the door of the truck, slides down from her seat, and sees Larry go to unsnap Calvin and help him down. Is he in shock over the sight of his brother?

Then Barb is opening her front door, calling greetings, all blue jeaned and ruffle shirted. "Tam, so good to see you again—and this must be Calvin—" She seems to take in Calvin's condition at a glance. "Just come with me, honey. I've given you Tony's room. He won't care, he hardly ever comes home now that he's in college—there's a bathroom next door. And Tam, have a seat—" Sweeping Calvin along with her warmth and chatter, she guides him up the stairs and out of sight.

"Damn," says Larry. "You want a drink, Tam?"

"Yes. And I want answers."

Larry walks heavily to a cabinet, lifts down glasses and a bottle of bourbon. "Ice?"

"Please."

He returns, hands her a tinkling glass, and drops into his chair. How weary he looks, Tam thinks. His face drawn and gray. No trace now of the freckle-faced boy, the class clown, and she feels a pang of guilt, which she instantly dismisses. After all, she's not the reason for the new lines in his face. Or is she? Did her return to the Sun Creek country somehow bring down mayhem on all of them? Bunce and Suze, James—*James!*—Allen and Rob Heckman. Calvin. Even Zenith caught in the swirl of violence through no action of his own. Well—unless spying on his neighbors caused it, like the butterfly fluttering its wings on the Horn of Africa—

Larry's voice from the chair next to hers—"Wish I had some for you, Tam. Answers, that is"—while another part of her mind is chasing after an elusive something. Catches it.

"Allen was wearing Bunce's clothes."

Larry has just taken a sip of bourbon, and now his startled eyes meet Tam's over the rim of his glass. "When, Tam? When did you see Allen Heckman wearing Bunce's clothes?"

Tam lets her mind drift back to the frenetic scene on the track. The shot that caused both horses to startle and shy. The whitetail doe, swinging an injured leg, in panicked flight from the timber and down into the underbrush along the creek, followed by the apparition that was Allen in the old man's clothes that dwarfed him, swinging his rifle and babbling something about his deer.

Larry nods. "So he was wearing Bunce's clothes. How did you know?"

"Recognized them. That gray plaid shirt—and the red suspenders, they'd been a Christmas present from Hube. Bunce kept them for good—" She pauses. What had happened had taken less time than the telling of it.

"James caught up with us, sent us back to the cabin—"

And then the second shot.

"Helluva thing," says Larry, and as if on cue, Barb appears at the top of the stairs, leading Calvin, who still looks dazed but who has been washed and neatened, with the broken branches carefully brushed out of his hair.

"Supper will be ready in a flash," says Barb, "and oh, there's Myah!"

Tam sees the tawny-haired girl pause in the door as she takes in the unexpected visitors, recognizes Tam, and stares at Calvin, who wakes from his numb state to stare back. The teens' sudden connection is as clear as though they had spoken the words: *A boy my age! A girl my age!*

Larry interrupts. "Myah, you remember Miss Bowen. And this is Calvin Warceski. His brother's in the hospital, and Calvin's going to be staying with us for a few days. And"—an invisible signal from Barb—"you'd better go and help your mother get supper on the table."

Myah reluctantly heads for the kitchen as Calvin follows her with his eyes.

"Go ahead," Larry tells him. "Ask Myah to give you a Coke from the fridge." He tops off his glass with bourbon and offers the bottle to Tam, who shakes her head. She's going to need to keep her wits about her.

"What a day." Larry swirls his bourbon in the glass, glances at Tam. "I sent a couple of the town cops to Suze's sister's house—Em whatever her last name is, McCracken, I think. They had a hell of a time getting her to open her door for them, they told me, and when she finally did, she acted like she couldn't hear anything they said. They couldn't see any sign of Suze there, and that rust bucket of a car was gone. Damn. Guess I'll have to send the guys back to search the place. And send a couple more out to the old Simmons place. If Suze—"

Larry breaks off. Shakes his head again. "Maybe I've got time for a couple calls before Barb gets supper on the table."

To Tam's disappointment, he palms his phone and steps out the front door, closing it behind him. She can see him plainly, though, as he half-turns, punches in some numbers, and claps the phone to his ear. And she can read the tension growing in his face as he listens—lines drawn hard around his mouth, his eyes fixed on the middle distance. Whoever is talking to him is making Larry a worried man, and Tam longs to know what he is hearing. But Barb has come from the kitchen to look out the window at her husband and shrug and call Tam to dinner.

The walls of the hospital waiting room are a pale dun, with a darker dun molding in the shape of an S curve around the ceiling. Tall narrow windows stretch nearly from the ceiling to the floor, each crowned with S curve molding. Five windows. Tam has counted them several times. They allow a glimpse of sky above the unrevealing gray brick wall of the next hospital building. Tam seems to remember that the hospital's architecture is considered quite contemporary, in contrast to the old Catholic Hospital of the Good Samaritan, which it replaced and which recently, according to Barb, has been purchased from the church and converted into condominiums.

Barb sits in another corner of the long tan waiting room— bench? more of a sofa?—busy with her phone. Larry having disappeared on one of his secret errands, Barb had driven Tam and Calvin to the hospital after dinner. Also Myah, who had decided at the last minute to come along for the ride and now sits with Calvin on the bench across from Tam's and Barb's, showing Calvin something complicated on her own phone. All these things happened—dinner, the drive, the arrival at the hospital, the quest for information, the retreat into the waiting room—but the air of the hospital and the near-silence creates an illusion of time standing still.

But no. Tam realizes a man has cleared his throat to get her attention, a man in green scrubs standing in front of her. The identity badge clipped to his shirt reads RN. From the corner of her eyes, she sees that Calvin's head has whipped around, his whole body on the alert for news.

"Um, ma'am? You're here with James Warceski's brother?"

"Yes, I'm Tam Bowen," she manages. "And I have Calvin Warceski here with me."

Calvin is on his feet, hesitating, taking a step or two toward Tam and the man in scrubs. He glances down at Myah, who smiles at him. Something between them registers with Tam, something as yet unacknowledged.

"He can see his brother now," the nurse is saying, and Tam jerks her attention back to him and nods. Glances back again at Calvin again, and Calvin seems to make up his mind and hurries across the waiting room to them to stand close to Tam.

"You're Calvin? Your brother is conscious now, and you can see him for a few minutes."

Calvin makes a small anxious sound. "Can Tam come with me?"

The nurse looks from Calvin to Tam, finally nods. "For a few minutes. With masks."

Tam knows she's been in James's hospital bedroom, but she remembers nothing about it. Nothing but the flat white-draped form on the raised bed. Unmoving. But no. A flicker of the eyes opening as Calvin takes a hesitant step forward, and Tam holds her breath.

"He won't be able to speak," murmurs the nurse behind her shoulder.

No. But those hazel heavy-lashed eyes above the bandaged mouth and throat are James's eyes, and they are searching, searching past his brother to find Tam. Asking—

"Step closer," suggests the nurse. "He can't turn his head."

James's eyes rise to hers as, slow step by slow step, Tam approaches his bedside. She feels light-headed with their intensity, with the fragility of their mortal body. Such a near thing. Fractions of inches from fatality. Beside her, Calvin whimpers.

"My fault. My fault!"

"No," breathes Tam, but Calvin is crying. "I'm sorry, James! I'm sorry!"

Then the nurse is at Calvin's side, leading him back and motioning to Tam with his chin. She nods, but she looks back at James. Touches his warm shoulder, which seems safe to do.

"We'll come back as soon as we can," she promises, and the hazel eyes blink twice.

Once back in the bland waiting room, Tam experiences a brief out-of-body sensation, that she herself is somewhere strange and unrevealing. Then, as the room slowly comes back into focus, Barb on the opposite couch looking up from her phone, Myah giggling into hers, Tam is gripped by a cold-burning anger: anger that James, *James*, has been transformed into that long powerless form under a white sheet. Anger that she is left desolate, that Calvin is left desolate, that Rob—*where is Rob?*—has been deprived of a father he loved, and all by a chattering madman who has insinuated himself into the body of a boy who once was beautiful, about whom the worst that could be said was that he was a spoiled brat.

She blinks. Calvin is looking into her face, his eyes widening, his mouth falling slightly open. He's afraid, she realizes. Afraid of what he sees in her face.

You get bucked off, you get right back on.

Yes. But there's also something else that must be done.

30

Transportation is Tam's first problem. Her Focus is miles away, parked by the cabin fence. Rob's Tahoe also is parked by the cabin fence, where he left it for his first horseback ride with her and then was driven away to Fort Maginnis.

But a plan is taking a vague and wavering form in her mind.

Incubus, that's the word she wants. She must hunt down the incubus, and she has to have a way to get to him.

As it turns out, the next morning Larry leaves the house early with coffee in a go-cup and a grim expression. Barb has a busy morning planned—"catching up the book-keeping, odds and ends, things that stack up"—but suggests there's no reason why Myah can't take the Lincoln and drive Tam wherever she needs to go.

And yes, Myah is delighted to be trusted with the Lincoln, especially when Calvin hustles to go along. Tam shakes her head—she doesn't think the kids have spoken a dozen words to each other, but they seem to have an understanding. Wonders if it will last when Calvin starts high school in Fort Maginnis next month.

If James recovers. If not—her throat constricts—who might take charge of Calvin? The grandparents who don't want to see him? Will he even attend school in Fort Maginnis?

Myah looks puzzled when Tam asks her to drive to the county jail, but she doesn't demur, and soon she's pulling up at the curb by the basement entrance. "Want me to wait?" she asks, and Tam nods.

The deputy at the window recognizes Tam. "You looking for the sheriff? He's not here, don't think he's in his office, don't know when to expect him back. Oh, it's Rob Heckman you want to see? I think he's down here."

A call over his shoulder is answered, and presently Rob appears at the swinging doors into the waiting area. Looks his question when he sees Tam.

"No news," she blurts. "And I can't just sit by. Will you help me?"

Rob measures her with his eyes. Seems to be doing calculations in his head. "If I can," he says. "I'm done here for now."

"Have you been working here long enough to get a Montana driver's license?"

Rob's face lights up as he grins. "I've had one since we came back to Montana. You might have noticed, I did all the driving for Dad. He had a fit about the license, but I figured I'd better be legal."

Funds. Tam's cash and her credit cards are, of course, in her wallet at her cabin. Will the bank allow her to withdraw funds without identification? But Rob is leading her out of the jail and up the flight of concrete stairs to street level. Looks appraisingly at the gray Lincoln, where Calvin, Tam observes, has climbed into the front passenger seat beside Myah.

"Will you drive us to the car rental place at the airport, Myah?"

Her curiosity is written all over Myah's face, but she pulls out into the street and drives the few blocks to the turnoff that leads to the airport on the plateau above Fort Maginnis. Finds the small car rental building with its Hertz and Avis signs in the window.

"I don't think you need to wait for us, Myah."

Tam wonders but doesn't ask if Myah and Calvin plan to go straight back to the Seidel home. Wonders again if the attraction will survive their going back to high school, where Myah, after all, will be a couple of grades ahead of Calvin. Shaking off her thoughts, she enters through the door Rob holds for her and approaches the counter, where a young man looks up from the magazine he is reading.

"Help you with something?"

"You don't think we'll need anything for off-road, say? No? How about a compact car?" Rob asks, and in a few moments he has displayed his driver's license and handed over a credit card for processing.

The agent speaks into the phone, nods. "All set. Zack'll have your car out at the curb in a few minutes. Enjoy."

The morning is still early, but the August sun already beats down on the concrete as Tam and Rob wait.

"Are you thinking—" Rob begins, but just then their car pulls up, a small black Kia, and he is collecting the keys from the driver and opening the front passenger door for Tam.

They ride in silence back down the grade to Main Street, where, after a few blocks, Rob pulls into a parking lot. Next to a sporting goods store, Tam sees.

"You said he had a rifle."

"Yes, but—" Tam hesitates. She hasn't fired a gun since she was Myah's age. "With a gun I'd be more danger to myself than anybody else. I'm not sure I even know how, after so long."

"I know how."

Rob grins at her, and Tam is struck by his new assuredness. From being on his own? Earning his own way? He must be doing pretty well as a night janitor to qualify for a credit card, for God's sake. But she remembers a remark of Larry's—"The kid actually understands that goddamned computer of mine"—and she wonders if Rob has been getting more hours at the jail.

Rob, who is already is out of the car and headed into the sporting goods store.

Tam puts down a window and leans on her elbow to watch sparrows pecking away on the paved alley. Wonders if somebody scatters seed for them. Wonders if she really knows what she is about to do.

But yes. She does. And here is Rob, returning already, carrying a long gun in a scabbard in one hand and a bulky paper sack in the other. Opens the driver's door of the Kia and leans over the seat to set down his purchases in the back.

"Anything else we need to do?"

"We might want to get some groceries."

As they drive along the burros' pasture, Tam notes sadly that the shaggy little critters are absent. Larry and his deputies were warning the neighbors, she remembers, about a shooter on the loose, and maybe the burros have been stabled for their own safety. Shakes away her image of Allen drawing a bead on a little burro.

Rob's eyes are steady on the road, his hands on the wheel are relaxed, and Tam realizes what she's known but never quite admitted—he's a grown man, after all. Knows how to drive. Knows a lot that she doesn't.

The first thing Tam notices as they reach the crest of the hill under the shadow of the lone pine and see the barn and sheds and corral stretching before them is the thin column of smoke curling from the cabin's chimney. Rob, seeing what she sees, hits the brakes, and they sit for a moment in silence, considering, while Tam senses the new tension in Rob's arms and shoulders.

"You didn't lock up, of course, when we left for our ride?"

Their ride. Rob's first horseback ride. How long ago it seems.

"The cars haven't been moved," Rob observes, and Tam sees that he's right. Her Focus, nose up to the yard fence, and the black Tahoe beside it. And, farther down the slope, the three horses—the Hellbitch, Buddy, and the filly Melanie, undisturbed and dozing in the shade of the box elder tree.

But then—movement. A small red-speckled dog, rising on his hind legs to look through the gate at the visitors.

"Zenith!"

Rob, visibly releasing his tension, lets off the brake and eases the compact down the slope and up to the cabin fence. And yes, the cabin's door has opened a crack, then opened wide as Zenith addresses Spotty's response to the visitors and steps out into the afternoon sunlight.

"Wondered when you'd show up."

Rob half-answers. "Have you seen him?"

"Glimpsed him a couple a times. He gives me plenty of space. But hell, come on in, I've got coffee on the stove."

Tam stifles her irritation at being invited, once again, into her own cabin. She and Rob load themselves with his new rifle and the groceries they had bought in Fort Maginnis and follow Zenith into the cabin. The smells are welcoming—fresh coffee and whatever Zenith has cooked for his breakfast—bacon and eggs, Tam thinks. Meanwhile, Zenith is setting down Tam's own mugs and pouring coffee all around.

"Figured it was easier to feed and groom those horses at your place, so I rode the brown gelding and led that black hellion," he explains, as though Tam had asked. "The filly sure was glad to see us."

Spotty has come to sit by Tam. "And you had to walk, I suppose," Tam tells him, and he lays his head against her knee and rolls his eyes at her. Somewhere she's read that humans are the only animals that show compassion, but surely Spotty—*Stop it, Tam! Don't let your mind wander!*

"Is he alone?" she asks, and neither Rob nor Zenith asks whom she means.

Zenith harrumphs and sets his coffee mug on the floor beside his futon, which, Tam sees, he's been using as a bed. "Haven't seen *her*. But they got that old rust bucket of a car hid out in the brush near James's buildings, so I s'pose that's how he got out here. They're holed up in James's house."

He shakes his head, looks squarely at Tam. "They can't hide out long, even if they brought provisions with them. Sheriff Seidel's going to send in a dog and handler and plenty of deputies, and they'll find them and surround them. Next thing Heckman will cut loose with that .22 rifle he's been brandishing, and the deputies will return fire. There's an expression they've got for what will happen. Suicide by cop."

Rob's face is stricken. "Which is why I have to find him first."

Zenith winces. "Dunno if you can do that. But s'pose you do. What are you planning to do with him?"

"I haven't thought that far ahead. Save his life. Try to get him dried out—his hospital stay must have drained out some of the junk. Then try to take care of him, I guess. He's my dad."

Zenith sits for a moment without speaking, looking into remote spaces. Then turns to Tam. "And you? What are you planning?"

Confront the incubus. She knows she should have talked more explicitly with Rob. "I'm going to talk to Allen."

Yes, stop referring to him as *him*. Or to Suze as *her*, as though she never had been the woman who mothered the motherless Tam.

Rob and Zenith are staring at her.

"I think I know what to say to Allen," she says. "I think I know how to say it."

Zenith opens his mouth once or twice and closes it.

"He'll hurt you," says Rob in a voice Tam hardly recognizes. "He hates you. You're the *last* one—"

With his words comes the splintering of glass above his head, followed by the reverberations of the .22 rifle.

Silence. Everyone crouching. Spotty cowering by Tam's knee, Zenith and Rob exchanging glances, Rob rising to his feet but keeping his head low—

"No!" he commands when Tam also rises, but she turns her back and walks to the cabin door. Steps out into intense sunshine and odor of pines.

Sees the apparition with the .22 rifle emerging from the boulders around the spring thirty yards away, a silhouette against blue sky. Tells herself it's time to play her part. Begins to sob loudly.

"Oh, Allen! Poor, poor Allen! Everyone's treated you so badly! *I've* treated you so badly! I'm so ashamed of how I've treated you!"

Tam is crying real tears now, crying for what might have been, for what was destroyed. "Oh, Allen, can you ever forgive me? When I'll never forgive myself for all I've done to you?"

She falls to her knees, sobbing, as the apparition draws closer, closer, as if hypnotized by the intensity of her distress.

"Tam?" A creaky old voice. "You admit it now? How you tricked me? You—"

"Yes! Yes! I tricked you, I almost snared you, I almost forced you to marry me, and I'm so ashamed. And that awful man who won't let you have your own ranch back—" Even in the service of her plan, Tam hesitates over the *awful man* who lies in critical condition after being shot in the throat—but she recovers and continues. "Poor, poor Allen! I've treated you so badly! Can you ever forgive me?"

He's approaching her, rifle lowered, his face a study of glee—"You finally admit it!"—and he's actually reaching a hand to help her to her feet when another apparition bursts out of the timber above the road, a woman in a flapping skirt who pauses only to toss something over her shoulder as she runs toward Tam and Allen, screaming, "No! Allen! Remember, I warned you about her—"

Suze snatches the rifle from Allen. Turns it on Tam.

"You! You nasty girl! Turned out just like your mother, didn't you! Tried to get my poor Allen in trouble, but then you had to leave town in shame! Well, I'm getting rid of you, just like I got rid of *her*. Just like I got rid of *him*. You thought you were snaring him in, didn't you, nasty girl! But I took care of him just like I'm taking care of you!"

"Bunce?" says Tam, catching a single thread.

"Bunce!" howls Suze and raises her rifle but sits down, instead, with a surprised look on her face. And Tam, realizing that a shot has been fired but that it came from the cabin, wrests the rifle from Suze's grip just as the hillside above the track bursts into dancing, leaping flames.

31

"You still haven't told me why you really came back."

"Maybe because I don't know."

In the familiar surroundings of the Home Plate, its counters stacked with pyramids of glasses and heavy white china cups and saucers, its tables covered with the last red-checked oilcloth in the world, Tam feels more herself than she has for several days. Maybe the odor of deep-frying, the banal sight of ketchup and mustard containers, help to dispel the dancing flames that have burned constantly at the backs of her eyes.

"Helluva thing you did out there, Tam. You talked him down—wouldn't have thought it possible. And the strange part is, I talked to him a little when Rob brought him in, and he answered me, more or less lucidly. Told me he felt all right. Wanted to stay with Rob. But I figured he was better off back in the hospital, getting checked out, and Rob stayed with him for now. Eventually, he'll be charged with attempted murder, Tam. And he'll serve time."

Tam stares at the red-checked oil cloth. Finally looks up at Larry's plain freckled face, his eyes that search hers.

"Not all bad, Tam. He'll be dried all the way out. He'll get treatment. And the boy won't be saddled with his care." Larry pauses. Draws a deep breath. "Rob's a good kid, Tam. Hope I can find a way to hire him full-time in the office. Let him get that damned computer system straightened out."

He shakes his head again, sips coffee. "Do you really think Heckman was planning on suicide by cop?"

"I was afraid it was suicide by son that Allen had in mind."

What she also fears is her bone-deep exhaustion, born of fighting wildfire. Herself, Zenith, Rob, armed with shovels and hoses and sacks, beating out sparks, watering the roofs of barn and sheds, running back and forth across blackened ground. Even Allen had flapped ineffectually with a sack, while Suze, hog-tied by Rob with rope Tam had bought for a clothesline, the bullet wound in her shoulder also packed and bandaged by Rob, shrieked her hatred from the steps of the cabin.

Run. Flap. Beat out another patch of flames. Never-ending *run, flap, beat out another patch of flame before it can reach the timber.*

Larry gazes into his empty cup, picks it up, sets it down again. "Suze, now, we locked her up after the doctor dug out the bullet and dressed her wound. If *that* wasn't a helluva show-up."

"Has she confessed to you?"

"Huh. To me and anybody else who'd listen. What she did to Bunce and your mother. Bragged about it. God knows what the county attorney will recommend. Once the lawyers get involved, she's likely to end up in the nuthouse in Warm Springs. And Em—I sent the social workers to check on her—I just don't know what they'll do with her. Put her in the state care facility, most likely."

He reaches across the table and touches Tam's hand. "We'll be digging for bones, Tam."

Tam nods.

"Warceski going to be all right?"

"He was able to sit up in bed last night when I took Calvin to see him. He can't speak. Dr. Mohr thinks he may never speak again, but he's hopeful he can restore his esophagus enough to get rid of the intravenous tube."

"God. A young man like that—who the hell knows."

"He has a gadget like an Etch-a-Sketch that he can write on. He wrote Calvin that he loved him."

She doesn't add what else he had written. *Tam, will you be Calvin's guardian until I can stand on my feet again?*

"How did his place fare?" she asks.

"He had a pretty good firebreak slashed and burned. The helicopters and the volunteers got there in time to save the house, but he lost the barns and corrals."

"It'll be the computers he'll want to know about."

Tam sets down her empty cup, stands to leave. Reaches out and touches Larry's arm. "You've been a good friend, Larry. You and Barb both."

Larry seizes her hand and holds it for a moment. "You taking Calvin up to see his brother again this evening?"

Calvin clearly has something on his mind as Tam drives them toward the hospital in the late August sunlight. She doesn't prompt him; she has enough to think about herself. She knows Calvin feels torn between staying with her in the cabin and continuing their rides—catching the school bus to high school—or boarding with the Seidels, who have offered to keep him, and walking to school with Myah.

"Myah was showing me her Facebook page," Calvin says at last.

"Yes? Interesting?"

"Kind of."

A long pause. "We browsed around some." Then, determinedly casual, he adds, "We found some pictures of Vay."

"Really?"

"Yeah. Showed her learning to surf with a bunch of other kids. Looked like she was having fun."

Thank you, whatever force of nature is out there to thank. Tam knows the results of James's and Calvin's DNA tests and has received her own letter from Ed Evenson.

Calvin sighs. "Looked like she was pretty cozy with this one dude."

"Do you think she's lost interest in horses?"

"Pretty much," he says.

A long silence. As Tam turns into the visitor's parking lot at the hospital and pulls into a slot, she's remembering a scene she observed through a window at Larry's house yesterday, overlooking his backyard, where he had set up a trampoline. How Tam had watched Myah bouncing, higher, higher, on the trampoline, until she suddenly turned a midair somersault and landed on her feet to smile at Calvin. And Tam had watched Calvin's face, how he had fixed on the girl's lovely athleticism, her strength, and her smile. Next minute the two kids were laughing together, something shared that Tam could not hear through glass but vibrant nonetheless, and she had been struck by the contrast between this laughing Myah and the sedate, contained Myah who had driven Tam and Rob to the Avis rental.

The sun's rays have colored the hospital steps with a rose hue that Tam tries not to associate with flames. Tries for a line of poetry—*While barred clouds bloom the soft-dying day*—

In his letter Ed Evenson had offered her first bid on the black thoroughbred mare, quoting a price as high as the stars. Knowing how few prospective buyers are likely to interest themselves in a spoiled mare that only can be ridden by an expert horseman or woman—as Hube always said, you can feed a good horse as easily as you can feed a bad horse—Tam plans to return a counteroffer, considerably lower. She suspects Ed is raising all the cash he can to face his upcoming charges.

And then what. Life in the cabin. Days of riding the Hellbitch. Afternoons and evenings working on her manuscript about horses.

The young male nurse walks with Tam and Calvin to the door of James's hospital room. "He's got another visitor in there now," he warns.

Tam and Calvin look at each other, puzzled. "Zenith?" Calvin guesses.

"No, no—it's a lady. Older. Never seen her before."

The nurse opens the door. The head of James's bed has been elevated to allow him to sit up with his legs stretched out in front of him under the sheet. The dressings for his throat wound have been lowered to expose his mouth, which is tightened with what looks like rage, and his eyes, now searching out Tam and Calvin, are belligerent. Tam, looking for the source of his anger, sees a straight-backed woman with silver hair seated in the visitor's armchair at the foot of James's bed.

Chiseled face, hawk's nose. Gray linen pantsuit. Tam assesses the silver hair, which is simply but expensively coiffed. Is this woman the cause of James's anger?

The nurse looks from James to the silver-haired woman and back to Tam and Calvin again, clearly sensing the tension. "I'll bring some chairs," he says nervously and ducks out the door.

"You won't be staying long enough to need a chair," the silver-haired woman tells Tam, and James seems to rise from his pillows, struggling.

"My name is Leah Warceski," she continues. "And you must be the romance writer. Perhaps my son has mentioned me to you. I've come to take him and his"—she glances at Calvin—"his *half-brother* back to Pasadena with me, where James can recuperate under competent medical supervision and the boy can attend school."

James has reached for not the Etch-a-Sketch gadget but a miniature laptop computer. Types a few characters and hands the laptop to Tam.

Get her out of here.

The nurse chooses this moment to return, carrying two folding chairs. He pauses, his red hair blazing in the sun that filters through the blinds.

"Ma'am?" he says.

"I've ordered a medevac ambulance that will be landing here this evening to take my son home with me. Tonight he'll be checking out of this"—she glances around the room—"hospital."

James's face twists, his lips move all the more explosively in their silence. Takes the little laptop from Tam and thrusts it at the nurse, who reads the line of characters and looks from James to his mother. Before he can speak, James snatches back the laptop and types furiously. Hands it back. The nurse reads, looks up at Mrs. Warceski.

"Ma'am? I'm afraid you're upsetting my patient. You're going to have to leave."

"I'm his mother! I'm taking him—"

"Ma'am, please don't make me call the orderlies. If you'll go now, you can come back tomorrow when you're not so wrought up."

The nurse has managed to lean his folding chairs against a wall, and now he stands, an unlikely stalwart in his green scrubs and flaming hair, holding James's laptop like a barricade between himself and Mrs. Warceski. A long minute passes.

"Fine!" Mrs. Warceski hisses. She gathers up her handbag, stands, and smooths her pantsuit. "But I'll be back! Even if I have to procure a court order—" She lets that threat fade as she tramps past Tam.

The door slams behind her. In the silence Tam is aware of Calvin cowering in a corner.

Mothers and sons, she thinks, and realizes she has spoken out loud.

"I dunno, Miz Bowen," says the nurse. "I've seen it a bunch of times. Somebody gets hurt, and their folks are so scared, they can't stand it, so they get mad. Blow their stacks over the darndest things."

James is reaching for the laptop. Types, hands it to Tam.

Heckman brought me this from my house. Knew what I'd need.

Take care of Calvin.

When Tam hands it back to him, nodding, he grasps her fingers and holds them. Blinks twice at her.

On their way out of the hospital, Tam and Calvin find a woman huddled and crying on the no-longer-rosy steps. Silver hair, gray linen pantsuit. Calvin and Tam exchange glances—*not good*. Tam sits down beside the sobbing woman, Calvin on her other side, their hands clasped behind her back, almost, not quite, embracing her. They sit in the gradually cooling evening until the woman's sobs subside, and she labors to her feet. Stands for a moment, recovering her balance. Mutters something that could have been *Thanks* and hobbles away to a waiting car.

Mothers, thinks Tam, remembering Heather Macclyn's outburst—*I don't know how . . .*

"Sheesh," says Calvin.

32

Tam sits on the cabin steps with the Fort Maginnis newspaper she bought when she made her grocery run, but she's having trouble focusing on the print, which seems to dance like the flames that danced across the opposite hillside. Or like the tumble of events during the last month that replace one another like the bits of color that fall into differing patterns with every turn of a kaleidoscope.

Rob's voice on the telephone: "Sheriff Seidel has locked up Dad. And I think Dad understands what he's in for—that he can't shoot somebody and walk away. He's—he's my dad, and as long as he's in the county jail, I can visit him every day. Don't know whether—when—the county attorney will charge him, and then I suppose they'll move him down to the state pen in Deer Lodge." Long pause. "No way he—I—could post bail. And—bail might not be the best thing for him. I can't"—holding back a sob now—"trust him not to go back on the shit. And I—want to see you."

Calvin's pleading voice on the phone: "High school starts on Monday, and I haven't ridden Melanie all week. Won't you please take me back to the cabin so we can ride Melanie and the Hellbitch? Please? They're really going to need it. And can we take Myah with us? She's never ridden a horse, but we could put her on Buddy."

Tam's own visit to the hospital yesterday afternoon. Meeting James in the corridor outside his hospital room, leaning on the arm of the red-haired nurse, but walking, walking on his own with the dressing on his throat reduced to a patch. James's face lighting at the sight of Tam.

"We're going to discharge him this evening," says the nurse, "provided he's got somewhere to stay and someone to look out for him. He'll need to stay on liquids and come in for a follow-up in a week."

James, tapping on his miniature laptop: *Will you take me home, Tam?*

Does life hold any order?

Tam scowls, wills the newsprint to stay in focus. Skims through the headlines for what she already knows, how an act of arson in the Sun Creek country ignited the beetle-dead pines at the top of the gulch and roared down the ridge trail. The Simmons ranch buildings destroyed, other ranch buildings destroyed, the pastureland above the ridge trail burned off.

Another paragraph lists the casualties. Dead livestock. Three of the Rocky Boy hotshot fire crew, which had flown down to assist in the ground operations, hospitalized for smoke inhalation.

Feeling as though she's reading of old disasters that have nothing to do with her, even with the blackened hillside opposite her, Tam skips on to local news. Street closing in Fort Maginnis for paving. City council to consider curbside recycling.

The tiny ad on the third page: *The Working Poor, down from Versailles, Montana, live for three nights only at the Bar Nineteen.*

The Bar Nineteen is a low brick building set back from the highway on the west side of Fort Maginnis, its neon *19* sign barely visible, even from the parking lot. Locals know where to find the joint.

James, who has fought Tam for the keys to his truck and won, pulls into the parking lot and angles into a vacant slot several rows back from the entry of the building.

"Looks like they've got a good turnout tonight," grunts Zenith from the rear seat, as James cuts his lights and ignition and throws Tam a menacing look she correctly interprets as a command that she wait, *wait* until he can get around the truck and help her down from the high seat, before she jumps down the two or three feet by herself.

The three of them, James, Tam, and Zenith, feel their way across broken pavement toward the dim neon of the bar's sign and a door that opens on noise and heat and a crowd around the lighted backbar, with its mirror and tiers of bottles. Empty bandstand, something playing on a jukebox that Tam doesn't recognize. Tam feels a shiver. She's never been inside the Bar Nineteen, and this is forbidden territory, rigorously carded to keep out underage drinkers. She smiles to remember Calvin, who had pleaded to come along.

Tam and James are clad in ordinary ranch wear—Levi's and long-sleeved shirts, moccasins in Tam's case and boots in James's. But Zenith, despite his grumbling, has taken pains. He's groomed his dandelion curls and beard into submission, and he's dug from a closet what must be relics from his days as an oil field geologist, a dark plaid western-cut jacket and black slacks. As he elbows his way to the backbar, for just a moment Tam sees a lean and handsome white-haired stranger. Then Zenith is back with bourbon and ice for himself and Tam and a Coke for James, pointing with his chin—"Maybe over there?"—toward a vacant high table with stools across from the bandstand, and James and Tam look a question at each other but follow him to take their seats.

A sudden hush as the canned music from the jukebox is cut and the members of the band push through the crowd to step up to the bandstand and take their places behind their instruments. Four guys in black linen shirts and black jeans and one woman with long dark hair, wearing a dark-red shirt with black jeans.

From a microphone somewhere: *Ladies and gentlemen, the Working Poor!*

The lead vocalist—to Tam's surprise, he's a biracial man, a rare sight in Montana—steps to the front of the stand to introduce the band members.

"We got Stu Connor here on bass"—a pause for applause and whistles—"Bill Margaris on the drums"—more applause—"Cryin' Brian Davies on the steel"—whistling, stamping—"and Ruby Gervais on the keyboard." Rapturous applause. "And I'm Isaiah Pence!"

Suddenly the barroom erupts with whistles and stamp dancing to a thunderous "Indian Outlaw." Tam wants to plug her ears, at least turn the volume down. In the meantime she studies the band members, who clearly have been performing together for some time, picking up on each other's riffs and grinning over the lyrics that the baritone vocalist—Pence—sends soaring over the instrumental background.

James nudges her, points at her empty glass, and Tam nods, watches as James picks up their glasses and threads his way around the dancing crowd to the bar. James, back on his feet and almost whole.

Then she happens to notice Zenith's face. His eyes on the dark-haired keyboardist, his face working.

The set continues; the energy level rises around Tam and James and Zenith. And then the lead vocalist, Pence, is calling the keyboardist—Ruby—to the front of the bandstand. They stand side by side, his dark fingers interlaced with her light fingers, and begin a cover of the old Gram Parsons and Emmylou Harris duet "Love Hurts." Tam glances at Zenith and hastily looks away, feeling like an intruder when she sees his tears welling.

The set is closing, instruments being laid aside as the band takes its break. The tall brown-haired drummer lays down his sticks, stands, and stretches, then catches up with Ruby and throws an arm around her as she laughs up at him.

James leans over to Zenith, nudging him. Zenith glares at James. "What? I'm not walkin' over there!"

James, of course, can say nothing, but he holds Zenith in his gaze, shaking his head, until Zenith curses under his breath and slides off his stool just as the band members begin to walk past the table where Tam and James are sitting. They watch as Zenith steps in front of Ruby and the drummer. Hear him speak.

"My name is Mark Gervais."

The young woman looks up at him, the drummer's arm tightens around her shoulders, and suddenly Isaiah Pence is with them. "Ruby?" he says.

"I—" she starts, hesitates, as Zenith clears his throat.

"You can ask me anything you like," he says, "but I've just got one question for you. Does Rosalie still sing?"

The three of them, Ruby, Isaiah Pence, and the drummer stare at him. Pence is the first to find words. "She won't sing with us in the band, but Ruby and I have coaxed her to sing a little when we're alone with her."

A pause. A struggle on Ruby's face—incredulity? She lifts her chin. "I've got quite a few questions for you, Mr. Mark Gervais," she snaps, and she draws Zenith along with Pence and the drummer toward what Tam guesses is their break room.

She feels the warmth of James's arm around her shoulders and turns to him. "Is good going to come of this?"

James smiles, shrugs. Tam reads what might be his words. *Which "this"? Them or us?*

She settles into his embrace. "We'll ride in the morning?"

James nods. Makes a breathy sound in his throat that might be her name.